HUNTING
the
SHADOWS

HUNTING
the
SHADOWS

the selected stories
of
TANITH LEE

VOLUME TWO

**WILDSIDE
PRESS**

Hunting the Shadows

PUBLICATION HISTORY

"Profile: Tanith Lee" first appeared in
Weird Tales, Summer 1988.
"The Woman in Scarlet" first appeared in
Realms of Fantasy, April 2000.
"Zelle's Thursday" first appeared in *Asimov's*, October 1989.
"Unlocking the Golden Cage" first appeared in
Weird Tales, Spring 1999.
"The Eye in the Heart" first appeared in *F&SF*, March 2000.
"Vermilia" first appeared in *Dreams of Decadence*, Fall 1999.
"Flower Water" first appeared in *Weird Tales*, Summer 1998.
"Doll Skulls" first appeared in
Realms of Fantasy, February 1996.
"Queens in Crimson" is original to this collection.
"All the Birds of Hell" first appeared in *F&SF*,
October/November 1998.
"The Persecution Machine" first appeared in
Weird Tales, Spring 1994.
"Antonius Bequeathed" first appeared in
Weird Tales, Spring 1993.
"One for Sorrow" first appeared in *Weird Tales*, Spring 1994.

Wildside Press LLC
www.wildsidepress.com

CONTENTS

PROFILE: TANITH LEE

by Donald A. Wollheim

IT WAS the Dutch publisher, Meulenhoff, who first termed Tanith Lee "Princess Royal of Fantasy." The *Village Voice* (New York) promptly took up the title with a rave review of the work. And DAW Books has continued to so term her ever since. Nobody has challenged the title, because nobody dare claim that it was not deserved.

From the day that her novel *The Birthgrave* was first published (by DAW Books in the U.S.A.), Tanith Lee has been a blazing gem in the crown of fantasy literature. She has written many novels, and varied they have been, but all have been outstanding instances of brilliant coloration, poetic conceptions, and sheer imaginative brilliance. She has written many short stories and has been sought after eagerly by the major magazines of the science fiction and fantasy fields, and yet she has appeared in semi-professional magazines and even fanzines. She has been Guest of Honor at conventions in the U.S.A., Great Britain, The Netherlands, Sweden, and elsewhere. And of course she has won awards.

But who is this whom Arkham House termed the Scheherazade of Fantasy? Born and raised in London, she has been writing tales since the age of nine, and went through the usual assortment of unrewarding jobs until she broke through into the publishing world. She did two or three children's novels before her discovery by the American SF/fantasy field. Since then, she has been writing for her living with success after success: over thirty novels, and innumerable translations and reprints, in the last fifteen years. Her stories appear all over the world. She has written episodes of serials for the B.B.C. and has had poetic dramas read over the British radio. Fantasy is her realm and she wears its crown as born to it.

As perhaps she was. When her mother was fifteen, she read the name *Tanith* in a book of mythology and decided that that would be the name of her daughter if she were to have one. And it did become her girl-child's name. Tanith, the Carthaginian equivalent of Ishtar, of Venus, of Aphrodite, turned out to be most fitting. There is no Tanith but Tanith . . . slightly sinister, dreamer of darkness and light, explorer of the supernatural and of the lore of ancients, who can tear aside the veil of the future and the stars, while insisting on her belief in reincarnation and its unending ties to the past, this is the stuff from which great writing flows — and continues to flow. No two stories are alike. Her world of the Flat Earth is not that of the Goddess of the Volcano nor that of the Electric Forest nor yet that of the French Revolution, but she knows them all in living color.

For me as her primary editor, the arrival of a manuscript from Tanith Lee is always an event, for who knows what wonders it will contain? Sometimes months will go by while she works on a long tale of time past or time future. And sometimes short stories will come one after another as she works that strain of her imagination which bounds from one marvel to another. . . .

Now she has moved from the noisy city to the more rustic settings of Kent. Here we can expect new challenges and writings greater than before. "Princess Royal" . . . perhaps better the Empress of Dreams. I am reminded of Clark Ashton Smith's magnificent poem that begins (with one word changed):

> *Bow down: I am the empress of dreams;*
> *I crown me with the million-colored suns*
> *Of secret worlds incredible, and take*
> *Their trailing skies for vestments. . . .*

—"Profile: Tanith Lee," *Weird Tales*, Summer 1988

THE WOMAN IN SCARLET

IT WAS always one way when he met them, on the long roads, high lands, low lands, rich or not, at the little villages, in the towns, too, and in the slim white cities, even there, or under the green roofs of forests, or on a seashore washed by the sea empty of most things but air and light. *"Look,"* he noted them whisper, the men, the women, the children, the slaves. "Do you see him? He is a *Sword's Man.*" Sometimes they would follow him a short distance. If not, they stared till he was out of sight. Occasionally, not that often, they might approach, more likely send a servant after him. Otherwise, the approach came from strangers still unseen, who had heard tell of him, or sensed his arrival, like a season. The men generally wanted straightforward help, rescue, or to train some rabble of an army, or teach their sons to fight. The women usually required him to murder somebody. Then again, men and women both, now and then wanted him for other things. To show him off, display him, to bed him or own him, if only for a night. He said No more times than he said Yes, to all the requests. But for the beds it was always No. They should remember, and they did, but hoped he might forget: He was wedded to his Sword. All his kind were. Married to her, and her possession, never theirs.

"COOR KRAHN, must you be going?"
"I must."

"Can't I tempt you to remain a handful more days? There's the horse I spoke of . . . why don't you come and see if you like it?"

"I walk where I go, Lord Juy. It keeps me fitter."

"Oh that. You're fit as three men. Stay for the dinner tonight. It's my daughter's birth-feast."

"My work's done here, Lord Juy. My thanks, but I'll be on the road by noon."

"She's restless," said the rich aristocrat, half contemptuous, and half jealous, frowning, admiring, uneasy, "is she?"

"Maybe."

"Tell me her name again."

Coor Krahn did not like to say his Sword's name to others, but also he did like to. He stayed in two minds on this. "Sas-peth," Coor Krahn said, unsmiling, his black eyes burning up, so Lord Juy slightly recoiled. "Sas-peth Satch."

"And that other name she has—no, don't say that one. I recall that one. And why she has it. It's a good name, Coor Krahn. And you are a mighty Sword's Man. Now, because of your skills, my lands stretch to the Black River. I'm grateful. The slave will bring your fee. It's as we agreed."

"I never doubted that," said Coor Krahn. He bowed and turned his back upon Lord Juy. (They both understood he had referred not to a lord's honor but to a Sword's Man's power and rights.)

A few minutes later a slave came, and presented the wallet of gold, crawling on his knees.

The Sun was high over the scaled towers of Juy's mansion as Coor Krahn turned on to the road out of the valley.

The wallet was stowed in the leather pack across his back. No sane man in half a world would ever dare to try to steal it. Nor any of the ornaments a Sword's Man wore, nor any piece of his armor or arms.

At Coor Krahn's side, she hung from the belt of red leather in her scarlet silk scabbard. Although young still, he had walked so long, so many years, with that feel of her beside him, that to walk without her would have seemed like lameness. And in the same way, to sleep without her lying along his body and under his hand, like death.

"Sas-peth," he murmured once, as he walked up from the glowing valley, "Sas-peth Satch." But now he smiled, to himself, or to her. He often spoke a little to her, though he never spoke very much to other men, and to women, less.

TONIGHT he dreamed of her.

In the dreams he saw her in her spirit shape, which naturally was female. But also, in dreams, she put on flesh and blood. They were walking in a night garden, high on a roof above a city, perhaps Curhm-by-Ocean, or Is-lil in the north. Slender and dark, the sculptured trees rose from stone pots, and a stone lion, polished smooth as water, held the round orange Moon between his ears.

Coor Krahn could smell a perfume, like a spice, which in her woman shape the Sword had put on. Her hand rested lightly on his arm. Her face too was powdered pale, as the faces of aristocratic women always were. (Although in other dreams, when she strode or rode with him into battle, she was tawny as any peasant boy.) Her long hair looked smooth as the lion, as night water. She wore her color, as she always did, deep red, bordered with flame red. Her eyes were black as his own.

"Why are you up here, Lady Sas-peth?" he asked her courteously. He was unfailingly formal, when first addressing her, even when, as in some dreams they did, they lay down together.

"There is the sea," she said, pointing her narrow finger away across the houses and the temples, to a curving line of fine white fire, which described waves breaking on the city stones. This was Curhm then, yet it had a look more of Gazul, which rose by a desert.

"Do you wish to go to the sea, Sas-peth?"

"No. Away from the coast."

"Tell me then, where shall we go?"

Then she turned her narrow, perfect face and gazed at him. Her gaze was not like that of any woman he had ever met, high-born or lowly. Nor, for that matter, like the gaze of any man.

"At this time, I grow tired of our wandering about, Coor Krahn. Let us rest soon."

In the dream he was startled. But she sometimes made him start. During the first dream in which she had bared her breasts and kissed him and drawn him down, he had been amazed, so amazed that it amounted to fear, until, presently, everything was lost in her.

"Then—then, lady, we'll rest a while. Where would you wish our rest to be?"

"Some small place," she said, idly now, more womanly. She glanced away, and smiled secretively, as sometimes she did before they coupled. But she drew her hand from his arm, and the long tail of her scarlet sleeve slipped over his wrist, cool as a snake. "The next small place, perhaps."

"It will be some upland village—" he said, almost protesting.

She did not reprimand him.

Instead, she drifted off, crossing over the face of the Moon, moving away through the garden, until she vanished behind the trees.

He woke, disturbed slightly, and lay thinking of the

memory of her, her shadow-silhouette against the face of the Moon.

But under his hand, she lay silent now, and steel hard, out of her scabbard.

"Whatever you wish, Sas-peth Satch. As always. I am your warrior, master of all but you. Your slave, Sas-peth."

HE HAD slept that night under the pines and sobe trees of a little wood, and in the morning, when he walked out of the wood, he could see nothing below but the track and the sloped shoulders of the hills. At once he felt relieved, and wondered at himself. In the past, now and then, she had come to him asleep and told him they must do certain things, take a certain direction or avoid another. So far as he knew, no loss had ever resulted from his obedience. Why should it? A Sword could only bring her warrior good; fame, wealth and kudos, through lawful battle, which was the reason for his life.

He walked on, along the hills, she at his side.

COOR KRAHN had been born in a poor town, whose name meant Pigs City. Undoubtedly pigs were kept there, and provided the mainstay of the town's economy. Coor Krahn grew up in a thatched house-hut, one of three belonging to the town's overseer, and overlooking five courtyards, each full, like all the town courtyards, and the town streets, of pink and gray pigs.

When Coor was nine, some Sword's Men entered the town. The overseer had himself called them, because Pigs City was experiencing conflict with a neighboring brigand across the river. (There had been trouble for months, and one night part of the town burned — Coor remembered well the cries and shrieks, the streaming metallic flames, and the odor of roast pork — that in later years he realized was not all attributable to unlucky pigs.)

Waiting on his father the overseer's table, with several other older sons, Coor was dazzled and astonished by the four warriors, the Sword's Men. They blazed in the greasy torchlight in their mail and ribbed plates of armor. These carapaces had been decorated with chasings and bosses of gold and silver so intricate they seemed embroidered there, while jewels blinked and gleamed like coals, or witch's eyes of glacial ice. The men were tanned to bronze, their hair long, braided or worn tied high, as the tails of the horses they had brought. One had a scar across his cheek that pulled his face that side always into a grin. It was a wonderful scar, and he was rightly proud of it, sometimes fondling it, and he had given it a name: The Moon's Tooth, which Coor never forgot, though afterward he forgot the names of all four men.

Their Swords also had names, and these names Coor forgot as well, but for perhaps another reason—they daunted him so. Slanting from the belts of their men, as the warriors sat at the overseer's dinner, each Sword leaned in her scabbard of silk over leather over steel over velvet, and force swirled from them. The Swords were four queens, four enchantresses, and this was made most plain. A cup of hot wine was set before each Sword, which drink her Sword's Man never touched, also a platter with a little of the best meat, and a flower laid on it, as if for a great lady.

Within a single day, the Sword's Men had settled the brigand across the river. His head, and those of his two lieutenants, were fixed on poles by the wooden town gate, for everyone to delight in. The heads had not even quite rotted down to the skulls when Coor ran away from Pigs

City and followed the road the Sword's Men had taken, eastward, to Curhm.

He had seen the warriors paid in silver and gold coins, all the town could spare. It was not that which made him run after them. He knew they, and their kind, maintained the fabric of law and justice across the sphere of lands too great for him, then, ever to imagine. It was not that either. Coor was strong and healthy and bored almost to a stone with pigs, and of course the men, their magnificence, had impressed everyone. Nor was it that. It was the swirl of half-seen lightning, the presence, the essence of the four Swords, and of one in particular. He learned after this was not quite unheard of. The Sword had "flirted" with him, as an empress might, leading him on just a short way, to bring him to awareness of his fate. She had been sheathed in jade silk. Not recollecting her outer name, he had yet some idea she was also called for something green, but that inner name her Sword's Man had never revealed. Any more than Coor, when once he had become a Sword's Man at the Sword-School of Curhm, would much reveal the inner name of Sas-peth Satch. For the inner name was given mostly at the first meeting, awake or in dream, after the man was wed to her. Only those you allowed to hire you, or were close to you in other ways, had a right to hear it. And then, generally, they—like Lord Juy—were too afraid to speak it aloud.

THE SWORD-SCHOOL was harsh. It needed to be, to slough off quickly those who had mistaken their destiny. Some few died in their first months. Not many. Most simply failed and went home, or to other vocations. Sad, bitter even, but resigned. Only now and then one who failed killed himself. There was one of those during Coor's second year. This boy, called Fengar, threw himself from the top of the Sun Wind Temple, and died on the pavement below, an offering to the wind goddess.

Coor had known, or believed he had known, he too would rather die than fail.

But he did not fail, he did extremely well. He rose straight, like a star, as if all of him, body, mind, and spirit, had already been honing itself, unsuspected, for this work.

At first his teachers were stern with him, zealous in case he should turn out only to be a star which burned up and fell. But after five years at the School, they were stern in another way, harsher if anything, to hammer him flawless.

From a yokel of the low lands, just able to scratch his name, he became educated and fined. He learned not only the arts of the warrior, but some of the knack of a scholar, able to read and to write, and of a courtier, who can speak and behave gracefully, unless provoked. No Sword's Man ever had a wish to insult through ignorance, for any unwise enough to anger him he would be able to destroy. But these were material things.

In his 17th year, the mystery began to be taught him.

This was the mystery of the Sword, the core of the ethos of a Sword's Man. Until reckoned ready, the apprentice owned no sword of any type. The blades he fought with and learned by were common property. But now the night approached when the School would give to Coor his own individual weapon. Not a sword, but a Sword. An artifact which had been forged for him alone, occultly, hidden from all but its makers. In other hands, it was not yet female, only he would wake it to its feminine life, and to its power.

At phases of the Moon, junctures of the zodiac, the concealed artisans of Curhm-by-Ocean created a Sword for Coor, as they, or their forebears, had done, through a thousand years, for every Sword's Man of that School.

First came the ceremony that made Coor a warrior. Before it he was starved a month of food and sleep, and drawn by draughts of midnight herbs and tart, transparent smokes, into some other state, half from his body, which in turn seemed eccentric, wilder, and curiously less finite than he had ever known it. In this strange condition, he viewed eternity, the unimportance of everything else, and its contrasting utter necessity, for trivia held the seeds of different, higher matters, to be discovered only after death.

Thirty-one endless days and limitless nights Coor lived in this mode. On the evening of the 32nd day, as stars dewed the twilight over Curhm, they led him to his wedding.

A Sword's Man stayed celibate. That is, he was faithful only to his Sword. Although female, it was his phallus. Yet it — she — and only she — might make love to him. And her only might he ever take. She would lie at his side, in his arms, every night. And in dreams, if by his courage and his genius in combat he made her care for him, then she would give him pleasures no human woman ever could.

Coor, now named Coor Krahn, stood naked in the unlit dark of that huge granite chamber, and when they brought her to him, his steel mistress, without a scabbard, naked too, his sex rose hard, and he shook as if meeting at last his one true love.

He made his vows. In the luminous darkness, he thought he heard the Sword faintly singing at each resonance of his voice.

Then as he gazed at her, a hooded man was there, and as always he did, with exaggerated gentleness, lifting Coor

Krahn's left forearm, made a long thin cut in it with a virgin razor.

The blood ran out and dripped away and away, ruby beads, and finally they brought her his Sword, to drink his blood, and as she drank, he kissed her, her silken skin of steel, for the first time.

When he did so, his erection faded and sank down. But he was appeased; as if he had reached a climax, and that energy was spent. While from the lessening of his flesh, vast vitality seemed to burst back through him. And in that moment, he knew the Sword's inner name.

After the marriage, they took him to a couch, where he was to lie down and hold her, and sleep, and have the beginning dream.

The wine was drugged, and he slept instantly.

He found himself on a mountaintop, among the white, cold snow, under a sky glittering light, without color. But the Sword stood before him, and she was a woman, and clothed in red, and so he knew he had been right in the name. Touching his body lightly with pearl fingers just above the heart, the Sword spoke to him in her woman's voice, while her beauty scorched him like the fiery sky.

"I am to be called Sas-peth Satch. Say my name."

"Sas-peth . . . Sas-peth Satch, my lady."

"My inner name you may also speak, since I informed you at our kiss, and you heard me."

Then he said that name, and she nodded, and the dream was gone. After this he slept for a hundred hours.

Waking he remembered as they always did, and both the names. Sas-peth Satch was The Woman In Scarlet.

WHEN it appeared, five days after she told him of it in the garden dream, the "small place" turned out to be attractive enough.

The hill itself was terraced for agriculture, and brilliant as if carved from emerald. There were fields, and yards of vines. A river, crystalline and thin in spots as a rope, threaded all through, and sallow willows hung over it, and then an orchard of ash-plums, and hyacinth trees.

The town was prosperous. Having reached the wide main street, which had been paved, he looked through to a second hill, and there was a lord's mansion on it, with dragon-tinted roofs. Had the Sword brought him here for war? It seemed unlikely. Even the people on the street (who stared after him in the usual way) looked otherwise carefree.

Coor Krahn went to the inn. The slave by the door was well fed and went down on his knees, smiling, to welcome a guest.

The inn master saw to the care of a Sword's Man personally. It was his pert wife, eyeing Coor Krahn in a fashion he knew quite well, who said to him, "And why can you be here, a great Sword's Man, in *our* peaceful little pond?"

"I'm on my way somewhere," he answered. When she tried to improve on this, he did not reply, and sat as if thinking, until she left him alone.

The day passed with sunlight and the mooing of cows in the water-meadows. As evening stole through, Coor Krahn heard the inn filling up below, and kept to his chamber. They would be discussing him sufficiently as it was.

Lanterns lit in the courtyard. Moths danced. Cool breezes blew the veils of night, and a firefly winked on and off by the well.

He was restless. He did not know why he was here. Did she mean him to stay here for sure; as she had said to *rest* here, and as the inn slut had said, in this peaceful little pond? He was young, not yet thirty. Sufficient time for restful dawdling in a decade or so.

"Why have you sent me here, Sas-peth?" he asked her softly, as she went up and down with him across the room. "Why must I loiter? Do *you* aspire to loiter — to rest — *you*? Or were you only playing a game with me?"

He thought, if he slept, he might dream of her and then she would tell him why, or what she really wanted. Or even that she had been testing him, his loyalty to her that she had never, in any case, doubted. And that tomorrow they would go on, away from here.

But when he fell asleep it was late. The youthful Moon had sailed over, and the town was silent as a grave. And he only dreamed, incredibly, as he seldom did, that he was once more living in Pigs City. The change was, in this dream, he was a man full grown, yet not a warrior. He was the overseer, since his father and the other sons were all dead. He was sitting in a courtyard, with pigs everywhere, seeing to a judgment of some errant wife. She looked, of course, exactly like the pert wife of the inn master, who had tried to interest him earlier.

When he woke, dawn was ahead of him, the sky beyond the window like a peach. He caressed the steel skin under his hand, his wedded wife, the Sword.

"Perhaps, lady, I need some sign from you. Pardon my asking it of you. But I'm foxed. I don't understand. Perhaps give me some sign today, why it is you truly want to remain in this *small place*. Have I mistaken it? Was it some other town you had in mind? Guide me, Sas-peth Satch. Or maybe I'll have to go on anyway, a little distance, to make sure I didn't mistake your meaning."

When he said this, a shudder went over him. The dawn was cold, despite its flush, and he had thrown off the blanket. But it was not because of that. He felt his words had been dismissive, a threat that he would have his own way in spite of what the Sword wished. And that could never, must never be.

"Whatever you want, lady," he said.

As he got up, his limbs seemed stiff. For a second he caught sight of the ghost of some man's old age. But Coor Krahn was young, and in a moment was as he had been. He put himself, his character, on again, like his clothes.

But buckling on the belt of the Sword, for the first time in his life, it slipped through his fingers. He caught the scabbard before it met the ground. The Sword had not been in the scabbard, or the omen would have perturbed him more.

At NOON, an elaborately dressed servant was waiting for him downstairs.

"From my master, I bring you greetings, Sword's Man. And this modest trinket."

Coor Krahn accepted the modest trinket — a broad silver arm-band set with several clear gems—such tokens were frequent enough. He thought, Now I shall discover why I was brought here. He said, "What's the name of your master?"

"The Lord Tyo Lionay."

Coor nodded graciously. Of course, he had never heard of him.

Lord TYO'S house was very fair, not large, but exquisite in all apparent detail. Beyond, elaborate gardens ran down the hill, and next there was Lord Tyo's game park, full of spotted antelope, blond foxes, and rare tigers whose eyes were blue.

The aristocrat met Coor Krahn in a marble yard. It

had a marble cistern of water, where great gold and black carp swam, or put up bold heads to look at them—at which Tyo laughed, and fed them dainties, and stroked them, too. A nightingale sang by day, in a mulberry tree of purple fruit.

"How may I assist you, Lord Tyo?"

Tyo only smiled, and the servant refilled their cups.

"I need nothing, Sword's Man. I have no enemies. Nor any war-goals: I possess already almost everything I want."

Coor did not frown, though he suspected now duplicity. Tyo was handsome, perhaps a year or so younger than himself. Tyo's manner was frank and charming.

"Then, my lord, you're too generous. If you require no service from me, I'm uneasy at accepting your gift."

"Please keep the armlet. I collect such things—it's my pleasure to gift them. Your service to me you perform in allowing me to meet with you. I'd heard much of you, Coor Krahn, your valor and ability."

"You're again too generous, Lord Tyo."

"Then permit my excess. Dine with me—stay in this house, and lie soft for once. There are many diversions here. I also collect curious creatures . . . and there are lovely women, if you incline to them."

Coor Krahn did frown. He said, "I am a Sword's Man. When you heard of me, had you never heard that?"

"And married to the blade? Naturally. But surely that isn't always so . . . "

Coor Krahn felt a low dull anger. (In his mind he remembered the falling empty scabbard.) Did this lordling dare insult him? "With myself, Lord Tyo, always it is so."

"Forgive me ignorance, then. I'm sorry to have offended you, my noble guest. But, stay and dine."

"I'm bound elsewhere."

As Coor said this, the Sword lay heavy at his thigh. He was very conscious of her. No, he was not bound elsewhere, for she had bound him here. But why—for this? To bear with this rich fool and his rich fool's whims?

"Must you hurry on your road? Is it an urgent mission?"

Now Coor did not answer, scorning a lie.

And his silence, Lord Tyo Lionay took, it seemed willfully, for agreement.

H E DREAMED of the Sword that night, when he slept on the silken bed, at Tyo's mansion. A girl had come to bathe him, a lovely girl indeed, with skin like cream and hair like night rain. But he sent her out. After this, and the heavy food and wine, sleep and the dream came swiftly.

Sas-peth Satch lay by him on the bed in Tyo's house. She was naked as a moon, and at once put her hands upon him, watching him as his excitement mounted, playing his body like her instrument until orgasm released him with its death.

"You see that I reward you," said Sas-peth then.

"Yes, my lady. I'm rewarded beyond all treasures."

"Then you will cease your argument with me."

"I'd never argue against you, Sas-peth."

"But you have."

"How have I?"

"You resist my will that you remain here."

"Ah, lady," he sighed. *"Here?"*

"Here."

"In this house?"

She said nothing.

"If you demand it, I shall. But won't you tell me — ?"

She rose, and stood, garbed suddenly again, in the

facile way of dreams (and magic) in her scarlet garments. She turned her face aside from him. For a second she seemed to him nearly evasive. "Do you question me still?"

"Not your *right* to command me, lady, only the reason. A warrior isn't made for much of such a life. Perhaps with me — not even for a single day. To *lie soft,* and eat and drink over and again, and talk and talk — to tell stories of his acts that sound like boasting, to listen constantly to some lord's worthless chat — *he* jabbers like some farm-girl — "

Between one word and the next, she was gone. Like the firefly by the well, her glow winked out, and he lay alone in the dream, and waking, under his hand her steel was that of an icicle, so his palm seemed stuck to her and scalded by her coldness.

"How have I angered you, Sas-peth, Sas-peth Satch?"

He knew. He had resisted. She was his empress; he must obey.

Coor Krahn turned over sullenly to his left side, letting go of her as sometimes — rarely — had happened in sleep. He lay with his back to her, and in the marble court below the nightingale sang on, like a clockwork engine, itching inside his brain.

"MAY I SEE IT? — pardon my clumsiness — may I see *her*? I mean, the Sword?

It was the second day here. Coor looked at Lord Tyo, who stood there, mannerly, groomed and good looking, ingenuous perhaps, or merely stupid.

"A warrior doesn't give over his Sword to any man but his brothers, his master, or his smith."

"I meant, evidently, that you should hold her, but perhaps I might look. Her power's very glamorous. It attracts me."

"Let me enlighten you, my lord. What you ask is like wanting a squint at my prick." Coor Krahn had intended uncouthness. But Tyo only put back his head and laughed. Coor Krahn said ironly, "She is only drawn out for me, in privacy. Unless I draw her to kill. If another man sees her, as you ask to do, she must taste his blood."

Tyo gazed straight in his eyes. Tyo's eyes were steady and pure.

"If that's the price, I would pay it. I take it you mean a sip, not my life's blood. I've heard of this custom, I believe. Yes, why not."

The provision of the blood—a sip, as the wretch had said—had been made of necessity. There could come certain occasions when, as Coor had mooted, a Sword must be drawn outside the need of war. For repair, or before a peer. Then the Sword's Man himself did not give her his own blood. Some fitting other was selected, by the warrior, his School or the smith, one who reckoned himself honored to be used, and would wear the scar of her bite with colossal pride.

"Again, I've offended you, my dear," said Tyo familiarly, and Coor wished to slap him like some silly slattern fumbling him at an inn.

"You make light of what is profound," said Coor Krahn.

"Not I. I'm caught in the web of her fascination. Soon you'll be gone. I must take up again my restricted life. Do you really grudge me this? Oh then, I'll say no more."

A board game was brought. They ate ash-plums, and played it, as if it mattered.

IN COOR KRAHN a fury was rising like a storm. It began in him on the second day at the mansion, by which time anyway he was already sick of the place and everything it held. The decorative food curdled in his belly, the nightingale hurt in his ears. The tamed beasts that strolled about the marble corridors, and lay sunning themselves in Tyo's park—where his lordship did not even hunt them—seemed to be other versions of Coor Krahn, also trapped and tamed, his teeth grown sticky from candies. Ten days and nights went like this. All alike. Music was played them, girls rippled in lascivious dances, board games were set for table-wars, intellectual verses read out. The lord and Coor rode and dined, and talked, and talked, and separated only to sleep. Tyo was affectionate and nearly deferential, so that Coor came to believe this lord found him most amusing. Not one dream came to Coor, not one dream of her, to tell him what he should do. Except, alone with her one night, he said, "Let me go from here, my lady. Or I must go from here—without your letting me." And in the dark spaces of sleep after this, he thought he caught a glimpse of her, faint as a candle flame, miles ahead and carried away from him. And he followed in vain.

PERHAPS the 11th night arrived, or the 12th; 12 — the number it was sometimes believed was unlucky. He had that day ridden all over the park (as if searching for escape) and the tigers had watched with lolling tongues. In sleep he saw Sas-peth walking under the Sun with a tiger, which had red eyes, not blue. And he followed, but now not in vain, although he did not instantly catch up to her.

If it was the fool's park they were in he was not sure. But it was a park, cultivated, the trees grown for effect, pruned to ardent shapes that obscured no possible vista.

He came on Sas-peth Satch again suddenly. She waited under a cedar, and the tiger was gone. She looked away and away, and when Coor spoke to her, she did not reply, or turn to him. And then he realized that another was there with her, someone that he, Coor Krahn, could not see, so that at first he took the vague figure only for a shadow — although Sas-peth, in dreams, cast no shadow at all.

"Here I am," she said, "do you see?" But not to Coor Krahn.

The shadow-figure became a little less vague. It held out its arm, and Sas-peth put her hand on this arm.

Who is this that she touches?

Then there was nothing there, and she looked back at Coor Krahn, and her face was expressionless as she said to him, "I have not called you to me, Coor Krahn. What do you want? Must I forbid you, like a child, to follow me at such times?"

She had been communing with some spirit of her own kind, he reasoned. He felt shamed, and begged her forgiveness. But she merely looked away once more, and then he woke, and the fury stirred blindly inside him, like thunder under a hill.

STILL, time passed. It hurt him, each wasted hour an injury. But why was the hurt so much? It was a pleasing place, this small place. No, it was a hell for him. Sleeping or waking, here he was, with this pampered lord fool, like the lord fool's slave. And the fool wanted a look at the naked Sword, and would pay in fool's blood —

THEY WERE in the marble courtyard when the fury burst, staining the air, and the aura of Coor Krahn's soul, with a black shot by fire.

But Lord Tyo did not seem to notice. Urbanely he toyed with an ivory gamepiece, smiling on.

"*Then*, my lord, if you *say* no more, *I* say as you did, *why not?*"

Stunned, bewildered, Tyo blinked at him.

And Coor Krahn put his right hand over on to the hilt of his Sword.

When he touched her she was like some electric thing. Sparks flew up inside his arm, but he wrenched her from the scabbard with a noise like a rusty scream, and in the air she blazed and rang, slicing the light of day like gauze. The whole landscape seemed to gasp and petrify in awe. The Sun, wounded, trickled sparkling on her blade's edge. And Tyo stared up at her, where the Sword's Man had lifted her high into the sky. Tyo was white, he was trembling. He said softly, "So beautiful she is. Better than any jewel. Better than anything, even a woman dressed in lilies."

"Yes, so she is. Better than anything." The rage now had remade Coor Krahn. He was remote and in control of himself. It was like a battle-anger, and yet, not quite. "She's thirsty, too. Are you ready?"

"Yes."

"So brief a word. Only one? I thought you'd talk more. Bare your arm for her, then."

Tyo rent his sleeve. Expensive sequins spun off like tears, or like the blood to come.

Coor Krahn slit the aristocrat's skin with great delicacy, being careful not to cut too deep, as he longed to do, careful not to shear off his foul and hated head.

Tyo made no sound. The blood welled up, and Saspeth Satch drew herself along, by means of Coor Krahn's grip, all the flat of her shining blade, until she was scarlet from hilt to tip.

And in that moment, as once before, long ago, Coor Krahn knew her secret.

He snatched her off, and in that same movement, she dropped from his hand, his fingers nerveless. She fell away from him. She fell at the feet of Tyo Lionay.

Tyo whispered, "What — what is it? Pick her up, man. She's not some stick—she's a Sword."

"Pick her up? No, let her lie there."

"What — what are you thinking of, Sword's Man? Have you gone mad?"

"Yes. It could drive me there."

"Take her up."

"You take her." Tyo gaped at him, his color oddly coming back from shock, though he swayed like an uprooted tree. "You take her, Tyo Lionay. It's you she's chosen."

"This is madness."

"I told you, perhaps it is. But now I see. Why she sent me here. She *smelled* you, like the fruit trees. I should have seen through her, she showed me often enough, in her own woman's way."

"Coor Krahn — "

"Don't speak my name to me, you thing of shit. Take her and keep her. Here's the scabbard too." It went down by her, on the marble, with a crack. "Keep her with your other collected stuffs. Take her to bed at night. See what you dream."

And turning, he left Lord Tyo, still somehow standing, among the scattered Sun on gold and red, and above the faithless Sword that had named herself The Woman In Scarlet, since she must always be sheathed in blood.

ONLY WHEN he reached the city of Gazul did he stop for as long as a day and a couple of nights. And then he left Gazul and went on, into the desert beyond.

Events had happened before that, during three

months of travelling. He had been called for by a pair of lords, to fight for them. He said No. But then a peasant village had entreated him to rid them of a local tyrant, showing him the bodies of four young men whipped to death. So there Coor had paused for an afternoon. He had had to ask them for a sword. It was a rough old thing, some tarnished heirloom of the village overseer's, but it did his work well enough. He saw then, with a deep bitterness, that it was his own skill in combat, as much as any weapon, which gained results.

Afterward, they begged him to keep the sword. They said they would be vainglorious, telling others they had given the sword to a Sword's Man whose own blade was currently under repair. (They were so restricted in their knowledge, they had not faltered at his lack of his Sword, and concocted this explanation from spontaneous ingenuity.)

He accepted the old sword, and refused other payment. He left the slain tyrant for them to tear in ritual pieces and bury in twenty different unmarked graves. (The man had been a monster.) Inasmuch as he could feel anything, save his bitterness and insane agony, Coor was not sorry to have helped the village.

The ugly old sword was quite good, quite reliable. At another place, after another fight, he had it new-surfaced and strengthened, and made a little heavier, to suit him. Here at the smith's, no one offered comment. Only the smith's boy asked anxiously if he should find a worthy man, so the drawn sword could taste blood. Coor Krahn did not answer. It was the smith who shut the boy's mouth with a glare. Even fancied up, it was sufficiently obvious this sword was not any sort of Sword.

Coor Krahn did not speculate on how others regarded the facts. Probably they invented halfway logical tales, as the village had. The Sword's Man's true Sword was being mended or specially garnished. Instead of impatiently awaiting her, he had journeyed on, and would then go back to collect her. Or maybe some of them realized he had lost his Sword, supposed she was broken, or taken from him, perhaps even dishonorably. But where they required his talents, and he gave them, no one expressed an opinion.

He slept under trees, under hills, in caves, at the wayside. He would not go in to sleep in any house, hovel, or palace.

There was, in the third month, a woman in a town a few miles from Gazul. She was a paid girl of the streets, but clean and pretty and young. When she spoke to him he went with her through the back alleys to her tiny dwelling. He had lain with only one, and that in dreams. This girl was limber and cunning, and scented with jasmine, but although he could rise up and enter her gate, though he could ride her well enough that she sobbed and melted like warm honey, there was no resolution for him. He could not reach it. And at last he pretended, as she herself might normally have done.

She would not presently accept payment, not, she said, because he was a warrior, but because of the pleasure he had given her. She vowed too, on a mighty god, she would tell no one he had lain down with her. "Tell any you like," he said. "Tell them, Coor Krahn had you." And then she shrank from his face.

There were never any dreams save the dreams any man might have, save once. Then he did dream, he thought, that far off he saw her — saw *her* — Sas-peth. She was standing up in water, like the sea, the waves shattering round her in white mirrors. But she was a woman only to her hips, and from there she was only a Sword, her female center locked in steel, impenetrable. And her face was averted from him, and anyway at a distance.

Gazul was closing the gates when he reached them. It was night, but a city night, thick-starred with lit windows and gaudy paper lanterns. He stayed that night, and the following day and night. He entered nowhere, not even an inn. He wandered the streets, the marketplace, and was stared at, and he heard the mutter: *Look! A Sword's Man.* But then he heard them saying, But whose sword is that? Never his. That old battered black cleaver. What can that be about? Of course this was a city. They were sophisticated and had no manners. Next morning, when the gates were opened, he walked away.

Look! Look! He thought he heard them cheeping. *There he goes into the waste land. What is he at? Why? Why?*

Oh, I could tell you, he thought.

And then, when he looked back, and Gazul was only a smudge of Sun on the horizon, and the barren Earth, powdered with dust, unrolled before him like existence, he wept. The tears were hard as bits of marble to shed. They tore his eyes and lay salty on his face like blood.

He sat under a lean, crippled tree and crumbled the dry dirt in his fingers.

Coor Krahn recalled the first Sword he ever saw, the Sword in the jade scabbard, when he was nine, at Pigs City. He had learned then that such a blade was always capable of seducing another, man or boy, of leading him on. But she did not then give herself to him. She stayed faithful to her husband. Only his Sword, only Sas-peth Satch, The Woman In Scarlet, had betrayed her bonded warrior.

He thought he might as well sit there, in the dust, under the tree, until he died. He drew the black sword, which was sexless, not even male, and laid it down. Coor told the sword he was sorry, and thanked it for its service.

He would bury the sword, it deserved that much. But first Coor Krahn would use it to cut his veins.

However, he had not slept for two nights and two days. He fell asleep before he could pick up the black sword again.

She came to him in the night.

THE DESERT, in the dream, was gilded by faint fires. A round Moon of red amber was nailed in the sky above.

Sas-peth had been brought here apparently in a roofed litter, tasseled and draped with silk, by slaves, and these all waited for her some way off. She wore her scarlet, and many jewels. Her hair was elaborately dressed.

"Coor Krahn," she said, "say my name to me."

He looked at her. He paused, and then said, "Your name is *The Bitch*."

Her face did not alter. He had never seen her angry, only stern for battle. While during love, she had been amorous, sly, coaxing. Never passionate, or tender.

"Why are you here?" he said.

"What do you believe the reason might be?"

"To show me he adorns you with silk and jewelry. Does he wear you to war, too, that little boy, Tyo?"

'There are no wars in Tyo's place."

"Rest there, then. Rest and rust."

"Shall I come back to you?" she asked, surprising him, jolting his heart to the core. "What would you do?"

"How can you come back, unless I go and fetch you, Sas-peth? Do you want me to fetch you? Want, then."

"You will do without me? How?"

He said nothing.

"And now," she said. "Imagine I were to say, I am here to show I am ready to be with you again."

"I would say, Sas-peth, that I won't have you."

"Even in your dreams? Even as a woman? Even in love?"

It was an awful thing to know, as Coor knew it, that to take to her again would be worse even than when he had been robbed of her.

Coor Krahn, in the dream, shut his eyes and commanded himself: *"Wake* now."

But when he opened his eyes, he was still in the dream with her. And now she stood naked, pale as ivory, her hair combed down and down.

"No, Sas-peth," he said, "it was Tyo you wished to have. Fill his dreams, not mine. Let him wear away his spirit on your edge. In all the lands, I never heard a story of one such as you. Did I shame you in combat? Did I fail you? Did I abuse the poor, insult the helpless? Was I a drunkard, a cheat, a coward — was I a weakling or an idiot? Or *unchaste?* Go out of my dream, you whore."

She turned away. It seemed to him then, in all his dreams of her, she had so often, just like this, turned from him, hiding, masking herself in his trust or his lust. Worse than that, in his respect for her.

"What life will you have," she said, "without me?"

"What life indeed."

"It was a passing desire," she said, head turned, strands of her fine hair blowing like smoke against the Moon. "A momentary, weightless thing, to be with that other one, to live another way. But only for a while, a little minute. And perhaps, I tested you." (He knew she lied.)

Bluntly he said, "What could he give you?"

"Nothing," she said softly, the woman Sas-peth.

"And that," said Coor Krahn, "is all now you will get from me."

Then she turned back, and she was beside him, lying against him on the dust, her arms wound round him and her lips on his. "I have been everything to you," she said. "I am your life."

"So you are. I see it now, Sas-peth. I'd thought I would have to die, and I was wrong in that."

He held her fast with his left arm, and with his right hand, drew up the old black genderless sword, which had come into the dream with him, as it seemed for this purpose. Coor Krahn drove the sword into her, up through her belly into her heart.

Her head curved back, and she looked at him, his Sword. She looked at him a long while, not speaking, until her eyelids fell like two white petals.

Raising his face from hers, Coor Krahn saw a lion standing on the desert, the red Moon between its ears. Eventually it vanished, but Sas-peth Satch did not. She lay heavy as lead in his arm until he let her go, and woke at last.

With sunrise, he buried the black sword, as he had promised.

IN THE SWORD-SCHOOL of Curhm-by-Ocean, he was questioned all the days of three more months, terrible questions on and on, over and over. They examined his dreams too (in none of which did she appear). They drugged him and beat him and starved him and made him drunk. And in the end, when they were sure he had not lied, they made him well again, scoured out like a shell. That day he was brought a new Sword that had been made randomly for him, or for one in his predicament. It was one of only twelve hoarded at any given time, in a secret store against such a need as his own. Coor Krahn was told, and it was the elderly master who told him, so he should grasp it could not be false, that though it had not often come about, the thing which had happened with him, yet, along the years, still it was clandestinely known. He was not the only one to die this death.

The new Sword was male. It had no name, was his to name. It was a slave, not an empress, but a mighty slave, headstrong, gorgeous, and dangerous as that other slave who might rebel, fire.

Once Coor had come to know it, and wore it at his side, and walked with it, he met it in a dream. In the flesh it was himself, but younger, and a little less, and a little more crazy. It — he — laughed, the new Sword, clowning, amusing Coor. Coor Krahn called it, therefore, Coor's Brother.

Then the master took Coor Krahn half a mile down to a small room in the rock below the School's temple, and showed him a horrible thing, which was a line of narrow vitreous boxes. These were the graves of some twenty-five or twenty-six or -seven Swords, mostly broken in pieces. And the last of the metal corpses was Sas-peth Satch. But she was pierced tidily right through, not mutilated. She had kept her glamour. Even ruined, she was beautiful, peerless.

"He sent her here to us," the master said, "Lord Tyo Lionay. He found her lying so on his floor one morning. She'd cut him as she fell. He will always carry the scar. He knew enough to want her, and enough to know what had been done. He sent jewels with her, rubies and pearls. Removed, as you see. He begs your forgiveness."

"He will never have that," replied Coor Krahn, without interest. Then he said very low, "But is she dead? Yes. She's dead. I see she is. Sas-peth, better than rubies and pearls."

The sword shone, even without light. In memory he gazed again at the closing of her petal lids, her smooth hair poured in the dust. He murmured to himself, "Perhaps."

ZELLE'S THURSDAY

THURSDAY was rather difficult. In the morning the children attacked me again, which was a pity, they'd been quite reasonable since that incident in the spring.

The trouble began because of the myrmecophaga, which had climbed up into one of the giant walnut trees on the west lawn. In the wild state, this species doesn't climb, but genetic habilitation sometimes causes sub-aspects, often feline, to establish themselves. Having climbed up into or on to or out of various objects, the myrmecophaga then tends to jump. This, in a heavily-furred, long-clawed animal weighing over two hundred and ten pounds, cannot always be ignored.

I ran down across the lawn to the tree.

Angelo was still standing under it when I arrived.

"Angelo," I said, "please stand away."

"Why," asked Angelo, "are you calling me 'Angelo'? It's Mr. Vald-Conway to you."

"Of course, if you prefer. Please do stand away, Mr. Vald-Conway."

Angelo, who is currently twelve years and three months old, will one day be handsome, but the day has not yet come. He gazed up into the tree and casually said, "Oh, look, Higgins is up there."

"Yes, Mr. Vald-Conway. That's why I'm suggesting you should stand away."

At that moment Higgins (the myrmecophaga) lurched forward on his powerful furry wrists. Two branches broke, and showered us with green walnuts. I was poised to pull

Angelo from danger, but presently the spasms of move-ment ceased. Angelo said admiringly, "What a mess you're making, Higgins."

(Angelo is at the age of taking pleasure in the dam-aging of his father's property. In the case of property of his mother's, he is more ambivalent.) Angelo stared up at the hugely draped coal-black shape of Higgins.

"Isn't he a beauty."

"Yes," I agreed, "Mr. Vald-Conway. Higgins is a fine example of a myrmecophaga."

"You can stop calling me *Mr. Vald-Conway*. That's what you call my father. And why do you call Higgins that? He's an ant-eater."

"I shall try to remember."

"Are you smarting me?" Angelo asked suspiciously. He is extremely sensitive. "You just watch that."

"I meant, Angelo — (?) — that I'll try to remember you'd rather I referred to your pet by the common term."

"Well. . . . Just watch it anyhow."

Ursula, Mister and Madam's daughter, had mean-while appeared on the lawn. She is two years and five months older than Angelo, a tall slender girl, like her brother having the black hair and black eyes of Madam Conway. She had been on the games court and had a racket in her hand.

"There's Higgins in the tree," said Ursula, "and there's Jelly underneath."

"Don't call me Jelly," snarled Angelo.

"And the Thing," added Ursula. She sank down under the combined shade of the walnut tree and Higgins. "Thing, go up and get me some iced lemonade. I'm dry as an old desert."

Precisely then, Higgins jumped. It was an especially

spectacular launch, and may have been occasioned by a flea, as he was due for a vacuuming.

I saw at once that the climax of his trajectory would be Ursula. She too seemed to have deduced this, for she started a frantic roll to avoid him. I dashed forward, swept her up and deposited her on the grass three meters away. Higgins landed, and for a moment looked stunned and partly squashed. Then he glanced about at us in slight surprise, shook himself back into shape, and began to groom twigs and walnuts from his fur.

Angelo ran forward and clasped Higgins, who began idly to groom him also, then lost interest, having refound his own tail, always a time of inspiration.

"You tried to upset him — " Angelo cried at me, nearly tearful. "You wanted him to fall hard and get hurt."

"If you think that falling on your sister would have made for a softer landing, I doubt it."

Ursula screamed, "What do you mean, I'm bony or something? You rotten *Thing.*" She slapped me in the face. Though I saw the blow coming, it obviously couldn't harm me, and I judged, perhaps wrongly, she would be relieved by delivering it.

"I meant," I said, "that the animal might have crushed your ribs. Only something bone-*less* could act as a breakfall for such a large — "

"And *you* nearly dislocated my pelvis, dragging me like that. You pig! I could have got out of the way — "

"Not quickly en — "

"You just wanted to bruise me. *Look!* You're horrible. You're OBSCENE — "

And Ursula flew at me and began striking me with her racket, which all this while she had held on to.

Angelo with a wail tore over and joined in enthusiastically.

As they punched and whacked and kicked, Higgins curled up in a ball, wrapped his groomed plume of a tail around himself, and contentedly fell asleep.

I WAS VACUUMING Higgins that afternoon when Mr. de Vald came to me in deep distress.

"My God, Zelle. I don't know what to say."

"I'm still under guarantee, Mr. de Vald. There won't be any charge. Most of the damage was external and took only half an hour to put right. The internal damage is being repaired even now, as I work."

"Yes, Zelle. But it's not that. It's the horror of it, Zelle."

"Which horror, Mr. de Vald?"

"That they could do — that such a thing — children of *mine*."

"It's not entirely uncommon, Mr. de Vald, in the first year or so."

I had by now switched off the vacuum, and Higgins was recovering from the swoon of ecstasy into which he falls when once the vacuum catches up with him, since at first he always runs away from it. While I had watched them going round and round the pavilion on the east lawn, I removed the last of the debrasion mask from my cheek. Actually, the cosmetic renewal of my face, arms, and shoulders had taken longer than I'd said, for I'd tried to relieve Mr. de Vald's mind.

"You see, Zelle," said Patrice de Vald, sitting down beside me on the steps of the pavilion, "it's the trend to violence I abhor."

"Please don't worry, Mr. de Vald, that anything they do to me they might ever be inclined to do to a fellow human. It's quite a different syndrome."

"Syndrome. Christ, my kids are part of a syndrome."

He put his blond head in his lean hands.

(Higgins, annoyed at the vacuum-cleaner's sudden lack of attention, stuffed his long tube of black velvet face into the machine's similar slender black tube. It has occurred to me before that he thinks certain household appliances to be [failed, bald] myrmecophagae.)

"You see, Zelle. I want you to be happy here."

It's useless to explain that this terminology, or outlook, can't apply to me.

"Mr. de Vald, I'm perfectly happy. And in time, Angelo and Ursula will come to accept me, I'm sure."

"Well, Zelle, I just want you to know, the house never functioned so—elegantly. And my partner, Inita — she's sometimes reticent about these things . . . But she thinks that, too. It's so much better to have you in charge than a — just some faceless — " He broke off. He blushed. Trying to be tactful, he always came around to this point, exaggerating what he meant to avoid.

Higgins withdrew his face from the face of the vacuum-cleaner.

"Here, boy," said Mr. de Vald jollily.

Higgins gave him a look from his onyx eyes, and shambled off across the lawn towards the lake. In the wild, myrmecophagae have limited sight and hearing, but the habilitation reorganizes such functions. Higgins has twenty-twenty vision and can detect one synthetic ant falling into his platter at a distance of two hundred meters.

"Guess he didn't hear me," said Mr. de Vald. He looked at me, his own eyes anxious and wide. "All I can do about the brats is apologize. They've been punished. I've vetoed those light concerts in town they're both so keen to visit." It wasn't up to me to advise him, unless he asked for advice. But now be added meekly, "Do you think?"

"Mr. de Vald, as the property of yourself and your wife, of course you could say that any damage to me must be punishable. On the other hand, half the problem arises because your children can't quite accept, as yet, that I'm no different than — say — that vacuum-cleaner."

"Oh, Zelle."

"Technically," I said, "there's nothing to choose, except that I am entirely self-programming, autonomous, and, therefore, ultra efficient. That I look as I do is supposed to make me more compatible."

"Oh and, Zelle, it does. Why, our house parties— And the number of people who've said to me, who's that pretty new maid, how on earth can you afford a human servant, and so cute — just as though you were — I mean that they thought you were — weren't — " He broke off, red now to the ears. "You think I shouldn't punish Ursula and Angelo. Just explain it over to them. That you're . . . not — "

"That I'm just a machine, Mr. de Vald. That I'm not a threat. That if they would try to think of me more on the lines of an aesthetic, multi-purpose appliance, this fear they have of me would eventually fade."

"I guess you're right, Zelle."

My smiling circuit activated.

He dreamily patted my no-longer-broken shoulder and went slowly away across the lawn after Higgins, who never quite allowed him to catch up.

By the drinks hour, every bit of me was repaired, outside and in. I was on the terrace, supervising the trolleys and mixers, and the ice-maker. Mr. de Vald had driven over to the airport, and there was some tension, as Madam Conway, who had been away on her working schedule, was returning unexpectedly.

The children had reappeared on the east lawn, cooler at this time of day, and were sitting near the pavilion looking very subdued. Sometimes I detected — my hearing is as fine as Higgins' — Ursula's voice: "Mother said she'd bring me the new body cosmetic. She *did*. But will she remember? I wonder how many paintings she sold? If she got het up, she'll have forgotten the body cosmetic. I don't want to look like an old immature frump all the time." Angelo, who was being restrained, only spoke occasionally, in monosyllables, as for example "Red light. Looking forward. *Knows* I was." Higgins had fallen in the lake during the afternoon, and was being automatically dried in the boating-shed.

Presently the car appeared in the ravine, rounded the elms, and curved noiselessly up onto the auto-drive. Here it began to deposit Madam Conway's thirty-five pieces of luggage in the service lift.

Inita Conway came walking gracefully over the lawn with Mr. de Vald, raising one hand languidly at her children. Ursula evinced excitement and rushed towards her mother. Angelo rose in a sort of accommodating slouch designed to disguise concentrated emotion.

Inita Conway wore golden sandals, and her black hair in the fashionable spike known as the *unicorn*. Ursula exclaimed over and examined this with careful admiration. "'lo, mumma. Did you sell a lot of paintings? Why are you home so soon? I'm glad you're home so soon. Did you bring my body cosmetic?"

"Yes, Ursula, I brought your body cosmetic. Your tidy's carried it up to your room."

"Can-I-go-and — "

"Yes, Ursula."

Ursula bolted.

Angelo approached his mother and said, "Hi. Dad's vetoed the concerts."

"So I have heard. And I heard why."

Angelo lounged by the drinks table, which the organizer was now setting out. He kept putting his hands down where the organizer was trying to lay tumblers, so that it had to select somewhere else.

"You're home early, motherrr," slurred Angelo. "Whysat?"

"To catch your father out," said Madam Conway. She looked at me and said, "Zelle, I want you to come up to my suite after drinks. I have three original Sarba shirts and some things for Ursula. They need to be sorted before dinner."

Then turning to Patrice de Vald she snatched him into a passionate embrace that embarrassed Angelo and apparently embarrassed also Mr. de Vald. "Darling. Have you missed me?"

"I always — "

"Yes, but in the past, you were *lonely*."

Mr. de Vald looked terribly nervous. There was no reason that I knew why he should be, but sometimes the communications between these two partners are so complex, and have so many permutations, that I can't follow them. Their relationship seems to be a little like chess, but without the rules.

There was a dim uproar from the boating-shed.

Madam Conway disengaged herself from Mr. de Vald's uneasy arms. "I suppose that's that bloody anteater up to something."

She downed her drink, a triple gin-reine, and took a triple gin-colada. She beckoned me towards the house.

As we went along the terrace, she called back, "Oh, Patrice. Someone's coming to dinner. A young designer I met."

Having killed the automatic drier, Higgins burst from the shed and pounced along the lawn, his fringed coat now fluffed and shaking like a well-made soufflé.

"Bloody animal," said Madam Conway. "I'd have the

damn thing put down if it weren't for the Animal Rights regulations."

"Angelo would be distressed," I said. "He's very fond of his pet."

"Yes, we're very fond of our pets, Zelle. By the way, I didn't think you offered advice unless asked."

"I was not, Madam Conway, offering advice."

"You mean it was just a casual human comment?"

"An observation, Madam Conway."

"What else have you observed, Zelle?"

"In what area, Madam Conway?"

"Well, I realize you have to study us all minutely. In order to fulfill our wildest dreams correctly."

The house door opened and we stepped on the moving stair. (As we rose past the windows, I noticed Higgins was in the lake again.)

"For example," said Madam Conway, as we entered the elevator for her suite, "what have you found out about Patrice's wildest dreams? Anything I ought to know?"

"I'm sorry, Madam Conway. I don't understand."

"I'll bet."

We entered the suite. It is white at the moment, with touches of purple, blue, and gold. Inita Conway, with her slender coffee body and two meters of inky hair, dominated every room, even the bathroom, which was done in dragons.

"You see, Zelle, dear," said Inita Conway, "I happen to know what goes on in a house once your sort of humanoid robot is installed."

Her luggage had arrived, and I saw that the suite tidy had already begun to unpack and service the Sarba shirts. I had not therefore really been summoned for this task.

Instead it seemed I was being attacked again. And that

this was rather more serious than the assault instigated by the children.

'Well," said Madam Conway. "Go on, deny it."

"What do you wish me to deny, Madam Conway?"

"That you're taking my partner to bed."

"Exactly, Madam Conway, I deny it."

She smiled. Throwing off her clothes she marched into the shower. A dragon hissed foam upon her. She stood in the foam, a beautiful icon of flesh, and snapped, "Don't tell me you can't lie. I know you things can lie perfectly damn well. And *don't* tell me you're frigid. I know every one of you comes with sex built *in* — "

"Yes, Madam Conway, it's true that my model functions to orgasm. But this is only—"

"I can just *imagine*," she screamed, turning on another dragon, "what erotic pleasures have been rocking the house to its core. If the bloody automatic hadn't picked up my return flight number, I'd have got here when you weren't expecting me. Caught the two of you writhing with arched backs among the blasted Sarba sheets I bought that *bastard* last trip — " A third dragon rendered her unintelligible if not inaudible. She switched off all three suddenly, and coming out before the drier could take the jewels of water from her skin, she confronted me with one hand raised like a panther's paw. "You — you *trollop*. I know. Couldn't help it. He made you. Oh, I've heard *all* about it. Men get crazy to try you. The perfect woman. HAH!"

"I have to warn you," I said, "Madam Conway, that I've already had to facilitate quite extensive repairs to myself today, and although the guarantee *may* cover further willful damage during the same twenty-four hour unit, I'm not certain of that. If you wish, I can tap into the main bank and find out."

"Oh, go to hell, you moronic plastic whore."

"Do you mean you'd prefer me to leave your suite?"

"Yes. My God. You and that ant-eater. I'd put the pair of you — "

Although she told me, I did not grasp the syntax.

THE DINNER GUEST, Madam's designer, arrived late, in the middle of the argument over Ursula's body cosmetic. Mr. de Vald insisted that his daughter had used too much of the cosmetic and looked like a fifty-year-old. (In fact, Ursula looked about nineteen.) Madam Conway laughed bitterly and said that a woman needed every help she could get with all the competition around. Angelo was sulking because his mother hadn't brought him anything back from her trip; he had earlier requested her not to, on the grounds that being given presents was for girls and babies.

The fourth argument over the cosmetic was in fact a second installment of the second argument that had taken place since the start of the meal. The first and third arguments, though having differing pivots, actually concerned Inita Conway's guest, who had seemed to fail to call.

I was stirring the dessert (a flambeau, which Mr. de Vald likes me to see to by hand), when the guest after all was shown out onto the terrace. An utter silence resulted. Angelo glared, and Ursula gaped. Mr. de Vald spilled his wine and when the tidy came forward pushed it roughly away. Madam Conway did not look up. She merely smiled into her uneaten salad.

"Oh, Jack. I thought you'd never get here. Just in time to rescue us all from the familial slog."

Jack Tchekov was a most beautiful young man, who is sometimes featured in moving-picture zines. He has been described as having a dancer's body, a wrestler's shoulders, a pianist's hands, the legs of a marathon runner, the face of a young god, and the hair of a Renaissance prince. None of these descriptions seemed, to the off-hand observer, to be inaccurate.

As the guest seated himself (by Madam Conway, glittering his eyes like those of a cabalistic demon [or it may have been that the analogy of a falling angel was more to the point]), some stilted conversation began, introductions and so on. I continued to whip the flambeau and, at the crucial moment, pour it into the smoking spice-pan.

"My God, that smells wonderful, I was in time for the climax of the feast," said Jack Tchekov in the voice of a Shakespearean actor.

"Yes, timing is important, with that dish. But Zelle's timing, so I gather, is always flawless," said Madam Conway.

When the flambeau was fumed, the service took over. Mr. Tchekov was looking only at me.

"And this is the formidable Zelle."

"That is she," said Madam Conway.

"May I — " said Mr Tchekov and hesitated dramatically. "Might I go over and touch her?"

"For Christsakes," growled Patrice de Vald. "What do you think you're doing?"

But Mr. Tchekov had already come up to me with his walk like a tiger, and taken my hand with the firm gentleness always mooted as being that of the probable connoisseur. "No," he said, looking into my eyes with the power of ray-guns, "I don't believe it. You're just a girl, aren't you?"

"I'm a robotic humanoid, Mr. Tchekov, issue number z.e.l. one zero nine nine six."

"Take your hands off," shouted Mr. de Vald, coming up behind Mr. Tchekov angrily. "You may have been all over Inita, but you'll show some respect to my — to Zelle."

"Over Inita?" cried Mr. Tchekov. "Save me from the universal jealousy of the inadequate partner."

"Come on then," said Patrice de Vald.

"Come *on?*"

"You want to make something of it?"

"Don't be a Martian," said Mr. Tchekov.

"I said, make something!"

"Dad — " honked Angelo.

"Oh! Oh!" screamed Ursula, hoping Jack Tchekov would turn to see why, but he didn't.

"Oh go on, fight over her," said Inita. "I brought Jack," she added, "so that he could try Zelle out. You know, darling, the one thing she can do that you, of *course,* haven't *any* interest in."

Patrice de Vald looked at me in an agony.

"Zelle — I'll throw him straight out."

"Shit," said Ursula.

"Don't use that *word,*" said Inita. "My God, haven't I, for the past fifteen fucking years trained myself never to use words like that in front of her and then she goes and does it when we have people in."

Jack Tchekov leaned close to me.

"Let's walk by the lake, Zelle. Away from all this domestic unbliss."

Patrice de Vald took hold of Jack Tchekov's shoulder and Jack Tchekov gave a little shrug and Mr. de Vald fell among the flambeau dishes.

Inita screamed now.

"Take her away! Both of you! Get on with it — get out of my sight."

"She's given you her most gracious permission," said Jack Tchekov. "Will you, now?"

I could see that Mr. de Vald was only winded, although several of the plates, which are antiques, had smashed. I am not, of course, a defense model, and so can do very little in this sort of situation. I am not able, for example, to separate human combatants. There was no need to carry Mr. de Vald to the house or administer first aid.

Angelo was frightened and Ursula was crying openly.

I could only allow the insistent guest to steer me away along the lawn.

IN THE STARLIGHT by the lake, the fireflies, which, like the diurnal bees and butterflies, are permitted to get inside the insect sensors, hovered about the bushes. Jack Tchekov drew me into his arms and kissed me tenderly, amorously.

"No, you *are* a girl. Some bionics maybe. But this flesh, this skin—your hair and eyes — and this wonderful smell — what perfume is it you're wearing, Zelle?" (In fact it was not any perfume of mine, but Higgins. Having rolled in some honeysuckle he was now prowling the lakeside.) "And you can't tell me you don't feel something when I touch you, like this . . . ?"

Of course, I felt nothing at all, but my affection-display mechanism activated on cue. It had had no chance to do so in any of its modes, until now. I can report that it's most efficient. My arms coiled about Mr. Tchekov.

We sank beneath a giant pine. Soon after, my orgasm mechanism was activated. My body responded, although naturally, it felt nothing. (The stimuli operate on evidence gleaned from the partner, therefore at the ideal instant.) Mr. Tchekov was also as apparently ignorant about this as about the affection response, and might have been greatly satisfied. Unfortunately, Higgins chose that moment to surface from the lake, into which he had again insinuated himself. He is evidently due to become a strong swimmer.

His slender nose, a tube of jet on softer darkness, lifted some eleven meters from shore. He blew a crystalline water-spout that seemed to incorporate the stars.

"Go-od-wh-at *is it?*" ejaculated Mr. Tchekov.

As my response subsided, the heart mechanic slowed and I was able to breathe more normally, I replied with the reassurance, "Only the myrmecoph — the ant-eater."

"*Dangerous?*" Jack Tchekov did not seem to relish this combat as he had the fracas at the table of his host. "Awfully damn large."

"They're insectivorous," I said.

Intent on some quest known only to himself, Higgins swam powerfully and liquidly away, and left us.

"Inita says she plans to shoot that thing and say it committed suicide." Mr. Tchekov laughed, somewhat raggedly, tidying his clothes. My laugh mechanism was activated. I was more spontaneous than he. "Frankly, to the point," said Mr. Tchekov, standing up with a slight scowl that could have been a Byronic brooding post-coital depression, or only a cramp, "I can tell Inita your seal was completely intact. I was the first. Can't imagine why it should matter to her, that spineless Aztec of a partner she's got. But there you are. I'd better not mention to Pat what a little nymphomaniac he's got, under his roof."

All devices come properly sealed to new owners. Mr. Tchekov is evidently unaware too that such seals can be indefinitely renewed.

ALSO Inita Conway.

"I wronged you, Zelle."

"Not at all, Madam."

"And I wronged *Patrice*."

ALL OVER the house the lights are on, and it is now four hours into Friday morning. Ursula is playing music and crying because she has fallen in love with Jack Tchekov who never even looked at her, and is unlikely to return. Angelo is crying because he has seen his father knocked down and his mother hasn't brought him a present. Mr. de Vald and Madam Conway are crying and shouting at each other, but there is nothing unusual in that, nor in the words they employ, which refer to painting, separation, emotional vampirism, and sex. A note addressed to me and delivered by the service informs me in contrite tones that Mr. de Vald is aware of my rape, and the dreadful distress I must be suffering. He begs me to be honest with him, in the morning — presumably *later* in the morning — and not to blame Inita Conway, although she has behaved "unforgivably." I must marshal sympathetic explanations for Mr. de Vald, to help him see that I am not harmed, and also to prevent his making the mistake of which so far he has been innocent. But probably, as with my last employer, he will not be able to resist.

Then, seal or no seal, he will confess all to his partner. Just as my last employer did. Repairing the entire cranial region after the blast of a sports rifle at close range is a job only the central bank can attempt. A fine is levied from the offending owner. Madam's paintings are not selling as well as they did, and I think both she and Mr. de Vald would find payment for hasty actions inconvenient.

But, too, Madam may relent in her pursuit of vengeance. Earlier, she pursued Higgins to his ant-hill-shaped platter and poured out for him too many synthetic ants, stroking his wet fur and sobbing that he was the only clean decent thing in the house. Higgins ate all the food, and was consequently extensively ill on an antique carpet.

Altogether, Thursday was not a good day, and Friday doesn't seem set to be much better.

UNLOCKING THE GOLDEN CAGE

To BE POOR, not young, unlovely — and alone — is a composite fate inflicted on many by the Angel of Misery. And so it was upon Agnes Drale, who, thirty-three years of age, and in a faded gown and unfashionable bonnet, walked up the two miles of the drive, to her late Uncle's manor, carrying her bag, one evening in the early autumn of 18—.

Another might have had high hopes, but not Agnes. Although it seemed, by the terms of the curious will, she was now supposedly to want for nothing, she understood quite well that the house and grounds, the title, and the coffers of the fortune had passed to her eighteen-year-old cousin, Genevieve, who was already wealthy and notoriously fair. Agnes was to be this woman's supplicant. And although, as the will stated, Agnes was to live in the great house, and have everything she required, it was to come to her by means of asking.

Throughout her life Agnes had learned, utterly, that asking was ruinous, and mostly unwise. In church, at the age of ten, and on her knees by her narrow bed for three years more, she had asked God daily, nightly, to improve her looks. But God preferred to keep her as she was, thin and sallow; indeed He liked this so well, He added artistically to her appearance by bending her back and blearing her eyes, in the service of ungrateful and sometimes vicious children, so that now she had a sort of hump, and wore spectacles.

Other than God, the human race provided evidence of the inadvisability of asking: Those who did not wish to employ her or, having done so, pay her; those who did not care to take a cup of tea with her in her room, preferring other friends more galvanic; those, like her father who, when she was twelve, refused her desperate plea not to die and leave her.

Agnes had never met her Uncle; but he seemed to her, rather than a benefactor, a cruel and perverse man, wishing to play some game even from the grave — for things were said of him, of his journeys in the East, and his private pleasures, which included alcohol and perhaps other stimulants more foreign.

Genevieve, of course, he had once visited, when she was a glimmering, ormolu child of fourteen. Agnes he had never bothered with. The tone of his testament, conveyed to her by the lawyer, was of impatient remorse. As she did most others, Agnes had apparently annoyed him with her lack of means, and must be tidied up, like spilt milk, before he could depart the world.

Having just been ousted from her work as governess in a drab, unclean, and misogynist household, Agnes had already packed her bag. She next came across the length of England, through the first flame of September in a cheap, close, and bouncing public carriage. And so now walked up this drive, through this glorious park which, presently, was faintly tinged itself with the shades of butter, copper kettles, honey, rust, amber, and ruby wine.

When she reached the house portico, arranged with the Greek columns that showed one of the flighty turns of the building, Agnes activated the bell and stood in its clanging, to wait. Governess, servant, dependent, drooping under her hump at the great front door, she expected insults, and having to explain herself. But despite her droop, she was ready. For suffering and ill-treatment had done to Agnes Drale that which they usually do — soured and twisted her, made her bitter as the aloe, and hard, under the layers of her physical weakness, as a cold and ancient stone.

THE COUSINS, Genevieve and Agnes, did not meet until the evening, the hour of dining, in the Old Hall of the manor.

The Old Hall was not, in actuality, very ancient, but had been arranged in the Gothic way, with a vast fireplace, black beams, and shields and swords to mingle with the portraits on the walls. An angled passage led from the Hall directly to the chapel, done in the same mode, that had, so the lawyer had informed Agnes, a royal crimson ceiling, with hammered silver stars. No one had worshipped in this chapel since its erection. The lawyer opined that Agnes might care to, holding, it seemed, to the common belief that the higher-class female destitute soon learned a rigid habit of prayer.

Now, amid the candlelight before the fire, Agnes observed, in her cousin, a pure example of the redundancy of praying.

Genevieve was a being of gold. She might have stepped from the heart of the sun. From her head poured loops and coils of golden hair, shining like the flames of the hearth. Her eyes, the colour of chestnuts, had each a golden sequin, that could have been caused by the candles, or by some inner, ever-present combustion. Her flawless skin was softly flushed as if gilded. She glowed, she gleamed. While her dress of gold-leaf satin had been fashioned to match all.

Agnes, sitting in her one shabby, dark, 'dinner gown,' her hair pulled tight, could only smile her twisted, little, invisible smile.

"This must be amusing for you, Agnes," said Genevieve. "Do you like Italian wine? I expect the French vintage was too dry for you. Or do you like dry things?"

Agnes, used to the quips and cuts of numerous employers, answered only when needful. Genevieve was patently furious that her cousin had dared to come. Genevieve had already made quite clear the fact that Agnes was normally to dine in her own sitting-room upstairs. Genevieve had explained that, while hairdressers and dressmakers and other slaves might arrive regularly at the house, and Agnes must feel at liberty to engage them as and when she wished, Genevieve did not predict Agnes to wish for very much. Agnes would have simple tastes. Agnes, unused to opulence, would intend, circumspectly, to avoid it. And so, to the frequent dinner parties, to the evenings of dancing, she must naturally consider herself, under the post-mortem avuncular law, invited — but Genevieve would not be offended by her absence.

"I made quite sure, Agnes," said Genevieve, as she ate the chocolate fruits, "a Bible was put beside your bed." Raising her dessert wine, golden as she, Genevieve declared, "I've no doubt you have several favorite passages in the Godly Book. Do tell me one. I'm sure it would admonish me to be virtuous, and I'm sure I need reminding."

"I seldom read the Bible," said Agnes.

"Oh, your weak eyes. How thoughtless of me. But then, doubtless you have large portions of the holy work by heart."

Agnes sipped the wine. It was sweet as the pain of

toothache she had so often experienced. She said quietly, *"Curse God, and die."*

Genevieve started. She seemed shocked, or perhaps only behaved as if she were so. "What ever is that?"

"The Bible. You will find it in *Job*."

Genevieve smiled. "What a serpent you are, in your dark dress. You must have something brighter. We must see your true colours."

Upstairs, in the large bedchamber which was now hers, Agnes looked from her window and beheld night upon the park, the huge, blazing autumnal oaks and beeches put out, and crowned solely with midnight. Stars shone, dull as hammered silver. Below, to her left, she made out the chapel, stretching away from the side of the house. It had seven long windows, each caught in a spiderweb of iron, and through these nothing was visible. The chapel seemed to Agnes more like an orangery than anything else, the skittish styles of the house here mixed to an extreme of unlikeliness.

On impulse, before blowing out her candle, Agnes opened the Bible at random. Running her finger down the page, she read this: *All wickedness is but little to the wickedness of a woman.*

A WEEK passed. Agnes Drale became re-acquainted with familiar, anticipated things. Firstly, her despisement by the servants, and their carelessness with her, manifested in their short replies, the cold and muddled food brought to her rooms, the way in which her furniture, of all the building, was left undusted. Secondly, her exclusion from the life of the mistress of the house, Lady Genevieve.

There were, however, new, and quite unknown, comforts — the softness of the bed, even undusted and not well-made, the tastiness and variety of breakfasts, luncheons, teas, and dinners, even tardily and untidily presented. To have her own private place at last, and somewhere to put her books, allied to the chance that she might purchase more. Soon enough she barred the sneering or glowering maids from her sanctum, and herself, not reluctantly, made up her own bed, her fire, and dusted the fine old chests and chairs. The park, too, with its massing of fiery dying colours, afforded her long and fascinating opportunities for exercise. Agnes did not know any more, it is true, how to be happy, but she had never had before a life such as this.

She met, during that week, only once with Genevieve. This was in a lower hall, near dusk. Genevieve was returning aflame, in a riding habit of Prussian Burgundy, with two or three gallant young men.

"Oh, Agnes, if you wish to join us for dinner . . . but I don't suppose you do. She is most retiring," Genevieve added to her court, and they laughed, a laugh that such women as Agnes have had from such women and men as these, since humankind was evicted from Eden.

Needless to relate, Agnes did not attend the dinner. Nor did she have plans to intrude upon the other, more lavish, dinner Genevieve proposed to give, to dignify her eighteenth birthday. This celebration had been carried from its correct date in August, due to the business of her having come just then into the inheritance of the manor. She was a child, unsurprisingly, of Leo. Agnes, whose Virgoean birthdate fell curiously on the very day of Genevieve's extravaganza, imagined only that the onset of her thirty-fourth year would pass without notice among Genevieve's birthday flambeaux and fireworks.

This was not, however, exactly the case. Five days before the event, one of the maids rapped harshly on Agnes' door.

"Lady Genevieve says you are to go down. Lawyer's come."

Agnes felt a clutch at her heart. From her past history, she knew at once a trepidation that some successful act had been made to exile her, after all, from her anchorage, despite all self-effacement.

Grey and rigid, she entered the drawing-room, and there posed Genevieve, herself like a ray of the sunshine which burst in at the casements, the lawyer fawning and sunning himself in her contemptuous light.

"It seems there's some box Uncle left for us, to mark our birthdays. Apparently he believed they lay closer together than they do." She expressed a glitter of distaste at such a notion. "This gentleman," the word spoke volumes of disdain, "has said that we must be present when the box is unlocked."

The lawyer uttered, trying — in vain — to impress by privy knowledge. "As I have said, my lady, the receptacle has never been opened, not since it was brought to his estate by your Uncle. But the documents assert that it contains a most valuable, indeed unique piece of jewelry, as I believe, of Eastern origin."

All this was rather lost upon Agnes, who, flooded by relief, had blushed a sudden, unbecoming red.

Nevertheless she went, as instructed by the lawyer, and stood nearby, while the container was produced and a key set in its lock.

The box was of some black wood, and intensely carved with coiled and embracing designs. The lock was horrible, although well-oiled, and gave out such a screech that Agnes' hair rose on her neck. Inside the box, alone on a nest of papers, shone out the roar of gold.

Agnes did not, immediately, determine what this golden article might be. But strangely it came to her, how different this was, this deep, hot, heavy, and mysterious alchemical metal, how unlike the golden gildedness of Genevieve, which even she, Agnes Drale, had confused with it.

"A bracelet," said Genevieve. She seemed amused, idle, neither impressed nor curious.

But as the lawyer lifted it out, and held it for her, ready, the rich lushness of its gold drained the sunlight, drained even, for a moment, Genevieve.

Genevieve said, maliciously sweetly, "Come and see, Agnes. Which of us can he have meant it for?"

"Evidently, for you," said Agnes, in a leaden voice.

It was only her now-ingrained servitude that spoke, her resignation. And yet, her voice sounded ominous, and cold as a bell.

Genevieve took the jewelry, an intricately-worked band, having in the midst of its circle a sunburst. With no scruple or hesitation, Genevieve undid the clasp and fitted and secured it to her wrist, the right one, brushing aside the lawyer's offers of assistance.

Slinking back, he said, "The papers relating to the ornament are here."

"Yes, no doubt. Reading of any sort bores me terribly. It harms the eyes, you know, and makes them dull, and blind."

She drifted to the window once more, holding her trophy — who could think of it as other than hers? — before her, outstretched the length of her creamy, rounded, lower arm.

The lawyer took from the box a paper, and put it on the table. Agnes leaned, almost involuntarily, to see. The writing was highly decorative, and did not look like the rather slovenly script of her late Uncle.

*This wrist-ring, or bracelet, is known as the **Fraanghi** or **Frengeh**. Although very beautiful, in the land from which it was taken, it was thought to convey a curse.*

The lawyer sucked his lower lip. "Dear me."

At the window, seethed in light, Genevieve, the lion's daughter, did not seem to hear.

Agnes read on, with her dull and blinded and bespectacled eyes.

*A wise king, having this jewel, lived a full, long, and sanguine life. But, once the adornment passed to his son, this son, boastful and proud, made many enemies. It happened that he was found, then, the arrogant one, with the gem upon his wrist, but he was torn asunder. Then arose another king, a braggart, a cruel man, and he, wearing the jewel, was also found, **stripped to his bones** in the forest. Beware then, for not randomly does the object keep its name.*

Agnes turned to the lawyer. "What language is it, what does it mean? *Frengeh — Fraanghi —?*"

The lawyer glanced at her. He said, "Your Uncle was a great traveller in India, Persia, and the East."

Agnes said, "There is another paper."

This time, he took it out and handed it to her.

She read aloud, *"The gemstone is purported to be that Fata Morgana, a yellow ruby, of which there are few or no examples. Those who have conversely suspected the jewel to be a topaz, of the red variety, amend that such stones are not often found in that region."*

There was nothing else in the box, but for a deep shadow. Agnes said, "There is no jewel. The gold is plain."

"It seems so," replied the lawyer.

Genevieve spoke in the incandescence of her window. "A jewel? Is there a jewel in it?"

"No, my lady. It must be that it has lost the jewel — "

Agnes looked, and the flash from the bracelet blinded her for sure. The light had sprung from its central part, the sunburst. Before the darkness cleared from her eyes, she heard herself speak distinctly. "Perhaps the boss opens."

"Let me *see*."

For an instant, Agnes beheld her glorious cousin clawing at her own wrist, the way a cat will at something it does not like, or likes too well.

There was a loud click. It was a noise a clock might make, in the moment before it stops.

"Oh! Agnes, come and see — "

No malice was apparent now. Genevieve cried out, as had the precocious, lovely, repellent, and greedy child she had been at fourteen years of age, the day her Uncle had visited her and brought her such wonderful presents, and she had danced for him the 'Dance of the Pretty Fairy,' and recited some sentimental ode, and everyone had sighed, and clapped, but he had only gazed, with his thin, brown face and narrow, evil eyes — that she, the fool, had been too young and too self-enamoured to interpret.

Agnes moved to Genevieve across the room. She entered the flaming crystal of the light. And in the light, Genevieve became the palest ghost, but on her wrist, freed now from its cover, there scorched, amid the curve of gold, a gem, the red topaz or yellow ruby, just as the paper had specified.

Agnes, once more, heard from her throat the voice arise, as if another uttered within her. "It might have been made with you in mind, Genevieve."

On THE EVENING of Genevieve's deferred birthday
party, which was really her own, Agnes Drale descended
the main stairway in good time.

Most of the upper house had been decked with gilt
ribbons and swags of velvet roses. Tall, ivory candles
burned at every turn, as if gas had never been invented.

A few heads were rotated as Agnes came into the
reception room. Not at her beauty, nor in mockery, in
mere perplexity. In the past slender number of days she
had called upon the harassed dressmakers and coif-
feurs, and had so changed her appearance that
Genevieve, in the midst of admirers, did not for some
time recognize her. Agnes had not aimed for the impos-
sibility of charm or the veneer of sweetness. She wore an
expensive gown of jet black silk, whose tailored
shawling collar quite concealed the upper curve of her
spine. On this was pinned a watch of finest silver, with
seed pearls, tiny and of impeccable design. Her hair had
been re-invented in a style more classic and less severely
placatory, and had given her face, now mildly powdered, the stern and implacable look of the Roman dig-
nitaries found on antique coins. Agnes, who had been,
seemingly, bowed and apologetic, now looked more
what she secretly was, formidable and unforgiving. As
her eyes passed over the assembly, assisted by her
improved and gold-rimmed spectacles, no one was
moved to laugh at her. Best be wary, was the instinctive
if hidden thought. They took her not for a governess, or
poor relation, but some steely aunt, ready to despoil
their pleasure if they were not careful, to cast them
down. If one cannot ever be loved, it may be better, in
the interests of self-preservation, to be feared.

In some way, Agnes perfectly understood this. Her
glance, fortified also by a glass of malt-coloured sherry,

was unwavering. Although she could not have said exactly how she had come by her abrupt assurance.

It was only Genevieve who, recognizing her cousin suddenly, burst into a peal of mirth. Genevieve, herself in a dress of saffron, her hair raised like golden fruits in a basket of combs, half spilling on her enamel shoulders, was even then extending her fair arm, for everyone wished to study her bracelet — the single ornament she had put on. Agnes, despite seeing the jewel on its emergence, was also drawn to do so once again.

"Why, Agnes, how magnificent you are!" But Genevieve's sparkling voice passed over Agnes' bending head.

There in its socket of gold, the huge, polished gem, substance of the wristlet called the *Frengeh:* Yellow ruby or not, one could not mistake what it was like. The clear reddish upper water that melted through the tinge of nasturtiums, to a base the shade, perhaps, of a Harvest Moon. And over its face, a flaw, which must, being so remarkable, have made it even more valuable and curious, more esoteric, bizarre, and even sinister. This flaw showed itself as three soft bars of shadow, that were, unmistakably, like three stripes upon the pelt of a tiger.

"A tigerish stone," said the plump young lord who stood at Genevieve's elbow. "A tiger for a lioness, since her birthday, you know, falls more properly in Leo."

"The tiger abhors the lion," said someone.

"Does it not suit me, then?" asked Genevieve, playfully.

Her gallants laughed loudly. They laughed with countenances angled aside — they did not wish to dispute with the grim and elegant aunt who had spoken such ill-omened words.

As Genevieve glided away, they passed with her, like a

cloud clinging to a sunrise. And Agnes remained alone, wondering what she had said. It was strange, was it not, that the golden bracelet, which had closely fitted the strong arms of kings, would be small enough to cling to the slim wrist of Genevieve. But men in the East were often small of bone.

Agnes turned her head, and saw, as if her reverie had conjured it, an apparition. Against one wall, was positioned a small and slender man, clad in garments that, to Agnes, suggested the East, his head bound in a scarlet cloth. His skin was smoky, his eyes as black as her dress. Seeing that she looked at him, he bowed, his hands beneath his chin.

But then the crowd of Genevieve's guests washed between them, he was gone, and all that was left, for a moment, was the impression of a woman's amber-coloured gown, moving away, as it almost appeared, with no one inside it.

The dinner was held in the Old Hall. As decreed, torches burned. Gilded candles pointed from garlands of autumn leaves and forced red flowers. An artifice, a palm tree with gilt fronds, dominated the table's centre.

Through the many courses, the soups and meats and side dishes, the desserts and savouries, the selections of wines, Genevieve was Queen. Her radiance beamed the table's length. As Agnes sat, eating her sparing, precise mouthfuls, she felt swell within her her own murderous hate, that which never before had she been able truly to acknowledge. As the gaiety and high spirits emblazoned the hot, fragrant, and over-powering air, Agnes mused inwardly on all the mean cruelties inflicted upon, and the careless wrongs done to her. A host of horrors marched across her mind, and in their wake swept Genevieve, a sun in splendour, putting all other light, all other slight, to shame.

After the feast, out they went, on to the terraces above the descending lawns, and watched as, garnet and diamond, fireworks were let off against the backdrop of black trees and night.

Agnes Drale noted the little slender man in his turban, hurrying about the pitch, ordering the incendiary shows. While, as the fireworks soared, bursting with sharp bangs like artillery into their kaleidoscopes of flame, Agnes beheld how they reflected in the lines of the windows of her Uncle's unused chapel, unsanctified by prayer, throwing up crimson flares on its ceiling, where the still stars hung, as if it too were burning.

It was later yet, after midnight, when the cold champagne was served in the Old Hall, back into which they had mobbed to get warm, that the Eastern man approached Genevieve, and bowing low, hands joined, produced from thin air a yellow rose, unlike all the other madder roses, and put it at her feet.

"Oh, bravo!" exclaimed her lovers, who had arranged presumably for his participation. "Shall he read your future, Jenny?"

"Do say 'yes,' " cried the ladies, who wanted to have read their own.

Then Genevieve sat in a chair, the pivot of all things, a golden lamp; and Agnes waited in the distance, like a shadow. The Eastern man crouched by Genevieve's knee. He stared into her palm. He said, in a rhythm fluctuating like an autumn wind, "You are walking your true path, lady. Before you is your Fate."

A woman shrilled, tipsy and excited, "What is it to be?"

"It is shining," said the man, "like the morning. It

turns towards you its golden eyes. Your Destiny is beautiful, lady, and you will not fail to meet with it. It purrs, like a cat."

Genevieve clapped her hands. The *Frengeh* flashed, another firework, its gold, the astonishing stone that ran from ruby to topaz, and was striped like a tiger.

"What about that, eh?" asked the lordling, "Cursed, ain't it?" He grinned.

The man from the East smiled, his eyes lowered to the floor where, applauded but untended, the yellow rose had been trampled.

"The jewel will have caused the death of mighty kings," he said. "But what need this lady fear? She is in England."

At that they howled with proud laughter. And Agnes Drale stood watching, smiling a little, just as he did. Yet through the smirch and haze of sinking lights, she saw now, deep inside the crowd, a woman in an amber dress. Her hair was dark, springing and trailing all around her face and throat. Her skin was tawny, and the lights ran on it like water. Her eyes seemed to come and go, now pale and flame-like, and now dark as the sky beyond the house, as if fireworks went on in them still. And as she turned a little, her gown might be seen to be striped, barred, an unusual pattern, just before she was gone.

Agnes shivered in the scalding room. And raising her sour and flat champagne, she drank it down. She was in the grip of that most primal and appalling and triumphant fright, which the ancients knew to call Terror. She was aware that all things were altered now, and that the drab world held more than she had thought, and that God, in some form, some fierce and unimaginable and awful form, existed.

"THERE IS a wretch of a gypsy in my park," said Genevieve, peevishly, shedding her riding gloves. "She wore a dress of dull orange, and her dark hair all loose. I shall have men scour the grounds. She must be evicted."

Agnes did not argue with this statement. She ate her breakfast, there in the dining-room with its marble and velvet, where now she took her early meals. But as she bit into her kedgeree, Agnes recollected how, even prior to Genevieve's ride, she, Agnes Drale, had walked in the manor woods, and sensed that something was slinking behind her, hot in the frosty morning, something that smouldered on and off between the trees. And on the lake, the ducks kept to their island, while now and then, above, the song of the over-wintering finches fell mysteriously quiet.

Two grooms and three footmen were sent out from the house; they left jesting, and returned silent. Seeking for the gypsy they had found nothing at all, save the burnt leaves down from the trees, the berries like blood, and feathers of some bird a fox had taken.

THE SERVANTS were different now, in their attentions to Agnes Drale. In a matter of a month, they had come to respect her. As the last leaves scattered from the trees, so were discarded the prejudices and the glee of certain ill-used things for another ill-used creature supposed more vulnerable. Agnes was not as she had seemed.

When she brought back the surly young women to clean and tidy her suite of rooms, they took one fresh look at her, this Agnes seeming taller in her faultless black, straight and hard as the winter trees were coming to be, strong and impervious. And when their first efforts were not good enough, then she brought them back again by a couple of clipped words, to re-make her bed, to replace her higgledy-piggled ornaments in a reasonable order. They said, presently, she was obdurate, but just. After all, she knew what was right.

They did not say they had formerly sought to jibe at and prey on her weakness. They said they had mistaken her, been misled by a temporary loss of character on her part, and so not initially discerned that she was a lady and so she expected — and deserved — their best.

It was Genevieve now they took to task, Genevieve who had always been capable of viciousness, throwing at them her hairbrushes, retracting their wages, her unsuitable whims and extravagances, her manner that had, they now affirmed, no dignity. She had hardly worn mourning black for her Uncle, and that was a disgrace, he had been dead only half a year. She slept most of the day, until eleven o'clock, like a pig, and then was out gadding in the town, or rode about the park until the poor horse was lathered, and carried marks on its side of her wicked little whip, so the head groom frowned and cursed under his breath. She said something had frightened her in the park, under the oak trees, something, some vagrant, a cry or call or sound — but she was profligate and drank too much for a lady, a bottle of wine now at her luncheon, and two or more at night. With these sudden unaristocratic humours and alarms, a look had come into the exquisite face of Genevieve, that puffed it out and dredged away its lovely colour. She appeared more human now, standing in her hallway, under the chandelier which tinkled and faintly glinted in the cold October afternoon dimness, twisting her whip in her hands, her eyes roving, screeching like a fish-wife for lights, like that guilty king in that clever play Miss Agnes had mentioned.

And now Genevieve, their *Lady,* had lashed them all with her tongue. She swore they had a criminal here — she had seen the woman, she, Genevieve, had seen the gypsy bitch — such a word! No lady would use it, Miss Agnes would not — seen her in an upper corridor. Not only some no doubt impecunious and thievish relation of the servants taken in secretly under her ladyship's roof, but permitted to steal about the rooms of their betters, pilfering. In vain they protested, scandalized themselves, for they laid claim, the servants, only to relatives of the purest sort, and with here and there merely the by-blow of some exalted person who had loved their grandmothers or their great aunts unwisely but extremely well.

As the girl nightly brushed Agnes' hair, found to be long and strong and wiry, with its strands of steel, and the sparks flew off it, she told Agnes of Genevieve's strange, new, and troublous ways.

"I think, Miss Agnes, if you'll excuse me — "

"And what is that, Beryl?"

"I think she may've taken her Uncle's own road."

"Which road would that be, Beryl?"

"It was — *Hump,* Miss Agnes."

"Hump . . . ? Oh, hemp. I see. Opium."

"He was haddicked, Miss. Terribly so. The drug makes you mad."

"So I've heard."

"She ups and screams at me, Miss, yesterday, as I was going through the lower hall — '*Look! Look there!*' She gives me a proper turn. I dropped all the napkins. And then she struck me. 'Can't you even smell it, you stupid — ' Well, then she called me a nasty name. I said I couldn't smell nothing but for the fire burning in the little sitting-room, which was smoking. She says, 'Beryl, you — , that name again — and she hit me across the face. '*It's a dog,*' she cries. *'One of the dogs is in — that filthy orange one — fetch someone to put it out!'"*

Beryl brushed, and Agnes Drale's hair crackled. The sparks flew past the lamp, and the little clock chimed eleven.

"But there *was* a smell. I *did* catch it. A whiff; like the zoological gardens in the city. It seemed — beg your pardon — to come from her ladyship. Perhaps something picked up on her skirt — "

Agnes thanked Beryl, and Beryl put down the brush, and drew open the neat and perfect bed. Inside the hour, lying on the laundered sheets, Agnes slept her now-usual sound and dreamless sleep, which as a rule continued until seven in the morning.

However, about four, something woke her. She did not know what it was, but yet she was impelled to rise at once, and seek the window.

How icy the panes of glass were behind the thickness of the curtains, and beyond this flimsy barrier, lay the great park, stripped bare now to its black bones, and holding up a canopy of stars. Her eyes, her neck, her head — turned, and Agnes looked towards the star-hung chapel that ran out from the house.

She was bemused by sleep, and yet awake. She saw calmly, clearly, the long black window-spaces in their iron webs, and next, faint and glowing, how some occult light passed up and down inside. It was the shade of a dying lamp, reddish or ochre. It reminded her of how she had seen the reflected fireworks display upon the crimson ceiling. Yet, conversely, it moved low down.

"What can this be? Who's there? Oh, what?" Agnes murmured. She trembled and her heart beat wildly, and yet she was removed from her own self; from the expressive emotion of her familiar body. She sat high up within the walled chamber of her skull, and watched the moving glow, now yellowish, now red, until it ceased to move and faded away like a dying, or a sleeping, fire.

Then, returning to the bed, she too regained her sleep and in the morning, perhaps, had quite forgotten.

THAT EVENING, Agnes Drale was summoned by her cousin Genevieve, to dine in the Old Hall. Here every night Genevieve had partaken of her dinner, alone or in noisy, festive company. While Agnes had kept to her modest if luxurious rooms, now her own meal was always served hot, and decorously arranged.

No one but Genevieve waited in the Hall. Of all things, a cold repast, on this frigid night that conceivably promised snow, was laid beneath the illumination of a mere ten candles. The gas was out. The fire burned sluggishly about a handful of logs.

"The heat — the smell of recently cooked food," said Genevieve, turning rapidly to Agnes, "excites — something." She added, feverishly, "Animals in the park — come to the windows."

"As the wolves do, in Russia," supplied Agnes, coolly.

"Just so. Indeed. What an isolate place this is. I may remove to town. Lord E—, you recall him, I expect, has offered me the use of his Small House, only fifty rooms, but I must manage. You, of course, won't mind remaining here."

"No, I should think it very cozy," said Agnes, amenably.

They went to the table, its waste of white cloth, and helped themselves from the dishes.

"The servants . . . " said Genevieve. "It's because I must speak to you very privately, Agnes. No prying ears or eyes. They gossip about me — " Genevieve was pallid, her face, on another, might have been described as engorged, swollen. Her grasp was unsteady upon the silver utensils, and three times they dropped from her fingers.

Agnes ate at a slow and even pace, and sipped from her crystal glass the apricot-coloured wine. Genevieve ate nothing, but drank eagerly. On her wrist was a dull mark; perhaps the bracelet, the *Frengeh*, had bruised her. Occasionally Genevieve would encircle this bruise with her other hand. At last she said, "Do you remember the jewel, Uncle's silly foreign bangle — it's so heavy ... those times when I put it on. But the gemstone is spoiled. Three dark scorings across it — surely there's no such thing as a yellow ruby."

Agnes ate a tartlet. It was cold in the vast room, the fire soaking ever lower, casting a dark cinnabar glare, the candles flickering. The voluminous curtains were drawn fast at the long windows, to close out any wild beasts that might be gathering in the park.

"Agnes," said Genevieve, "I don't suppose you were ever — fanciful."

"In what way?"

"In — the way — oh, of ghosts, nightmares. Such things."

"Perhaps," said Agnes quietly.

"It is stupid of me," said Genevieve. "Never in my life — something is following me about, Agnes."

"Something is following — "

"Some *thing.*"

"How exactly do you mean?"

Genevieve drained her glass, rose abruptly, and flung it from her. It smashed in stars at the edge of the hearth.

"It is preposterous and absurd. But — I know that it happens. I *hear* it. I — *smell* it. I see it pass, sometimes near and sometimes at a distance."

"But what do you see — or hear or smell?"

"I can never be sure what it *is* — the smell is hot and pungent. Spicy. Or — a dirty smell. Or there is a noise — soft, like — a cat, walking over the floors, but a big cat, Agnes, very big. And sometimes —" Genevieve stared at Agnes' face, not seeing her, "I hear it — *breathing.*"

"You're overwrought," said Agnes.

Genevieve gave a squeal of laughter, "I am *terrified!*"

"How could there be such a thing?"

"The bracelet," said Genevieve. She wilted suddenly; she drooped. Such a stance, over thirty-three years, had brought about Agnes' stoop. To Genevieve it was a posture novel as darkness to one who had never beheld the night.

"The bracelet Uncle left for you," clarified Agnes, diligently.

"Yes, yes that horrible, gaudy gew-gaw. Oh God! I shut it up in its box again. I hid it in my dressing-room. And still — still — Oh, Agnes, I can't eat or sleep. I think I'll wake to find it crouching on my breast. I *dream* of it. It — *purrs.* Such a dreadful purr, rasping — like nails tearing velvet. I shall go mad!"

Agnes drank another mouthful of wine. She said, "You're unnerved, my dear cousin. Naturally, no such thing exists. But if you're in this state of mind, there is, after all, a certain recourse."

"Tell me! Quickly! Agnes — I beg you — "

"You must," said Agnes, raising her eyes, her spectacles gleaming bright, "turn to God. No other, my dear, can help you. Pray, Genevieve."

"Pray? *Pray?* Do you think — "

"I know it, Genevieve. God is attentive to every sincere plea. And only recollect, our Uncle built here a chapel, consecrated and ready for the most urgent use."

"The chapel," said Genevieve. And she spun about in

the direction of that narrow door which led from the Old Hall, out into the angled passage, and so to the folly of the chapel with its orangery windows and ceiling of stars.

At this moment, the most curious sound stirred against the huge room. It might have come from outside the walls, or down the chimney or out of the very air itself. It was indescribable, but as Genevieve heard it, she uttered a shriek, and Agnes rose to her feet, the skin crawling on her bones.

"Take a candle, Genevieve," said Agnes.

"Oh, Agnes — I'm too afraid — in the darkness — "

"Then I'll go before you. I'll go and see, and ignite the gas lamps that I've been told are fitted there, as here."

"But the light — " cried Genevieve, " — may attract — "

"It is," said Agnes, in an iron voice, "the place of God."

"Yes. Yes, then. I will. If you — will go there first."

"Stay here, and I'll return for you," said Agnes.

And taking up one of the faltering candle-branches, she walked across the Hall, her spine erect as if fletched with the quills of lizards, her hands colder than the promised snow.

At the narrow door she paused. The sweat started icily on Agnes' brow. She said, "Take courage, Genevieve. All will be well." And passed into the corridor beyond.

PERHAPS, because it had no windows, the corridor, that ran between other rooms unseen, was close and warm. It had a scent of fruits dried for cake — raisins, prunes, such items. At the turn, Agnes halted. The candles dipped and lifted up again their nervous flames. She went on.

The right-angle of the passage was only some four or five yards in length. At the end was a large door, secured only by a simple latch.

As Agnes approached it, she seemed to hear a strange,

muted noise, like tiny tinsel bells. She shivered again, touched the latch, and opened the door wide.

The chapel stretched before her, long and dim, its elongated windows dark, lit sidelong in a peculiar manner, by the vague, curtained lamps of the house. It was a slender oblong in shape, this chamber, and at its extremity a carved lectern stood, and before that, to either side, three carven pews with their backs to her. On the floor lay a red runner, velvet perhaps, and above soared the red arch of the ceiling where the silver stars winked back the candlelight.

Possibly it was the apprehension of Agnes Drale that made the atmosphere seem to tremble and ring. She had had so often to be brave in the face of many humiliations, attacks, and reversals, that courage was habitual with her.

Nevertheless, she moved stiffly, and put up her hand like a stick to the gas fitment she had perceived on the wall.

The gas fluttered and popped, and slowly the flame bloomed up, spreading down the aisle of the chapel and polishing the carvings on the backs of the pews. The second fitment was set adjacent to the lectern, and Agnes gathered herself to go there and attend to it. For she was not yet quite ready.

Beyond the long windows only the night finally showed, the glim of the manor put out. Around the lectern shadows clung, ascending into the crimson roof. It is now and then to be seen, this phenomenon, how a light, placed in an unexpected or unaccustomed position, may seem to throw a shadow that bears no relation to anything revealed by its rays.

Agnes stared, and then, intuitively, her glance descended and rested on the last of the right-hand pews, that which stood the nearest to the lectern. Its back was high, and nothing was to be seen, but the air was now so very hot, so intensely smothering, as if before some tropical storm. And in this choking, shimmering air, the quivering bells rang on, making dizzy Agnes Drale, so that she swayed, and her candles sank and died in her hand.

Something was rising after all, over the back of the last pew. Something was sitting up, a curve, a hump of darkness that rose into the light. Its colour slowly changed to amber, rich and royal, and over the amber scored the dark streaks and bars, and a stream of gold that ran from the lamps, on silk, or fur. It was the back — of an enormous beast, of a tiger, and yet, and yet, it was turning now, the golden sheen shifting, turning its head, to look at her.

Agnes Drale opened her mouth, but no sound came from her. She slumped against the wall, and was pinned there, unable to drop down.

It is a woman's face, but a woman's face that is the face of a beast, a face of amber, with human eyes that are the eyes of a demon, yellow as topaz, red as ruby, eyes that are not windows, for no soul is behind them, yet *something* is behind them, and looks out. And the jaws are wide, and the long teeth, brown and stronger than steel, protrude from it. The dark hair falls that might be mistaken for a woman's hair, but not now. And a hand that is a paw rests on the edge of the holy seat, and the claws unsheathe, and they draw one thin line along the wood, delicate, soft, and never, never will be forgotten the noise they make, as this is done, nor the rasping ripple of a speechless voice, coaxing and impatient. *And the thud, the lash of the tail.*

It is hot now as the centre of a furnace, or a dying sun.

Come, Agnes Drale, leave your candles where they lie, go backwards slowly and with caution, feel for the door, slip out, and close it carefully once more, behind you.

AGNES RE-ENTERED the Hall, firm, not breathless, and Genevieve sprang up at once.

"Everything is ready," said Agnes.

"The gaslight — "

"There is light," said Agnes. "And God is there, awaiting you."

Genevieve draws herself up, haughtily. "Then I shall go alone." If it is between her and God, no other is needed.

Ten minutes after, Agnes is in her bedroom, while Beryl brushes her hair. Across the park, once, twice, three or four or five times, they have heard an odd note, a shrill, distorted, soulless scream.

"It must be an owl," says Beryl. "There it is again. It does go on so. I hope it won't disturb you, Miss."

"Not at all," says Agnes.

IN THE SOMBRE MONTH of November, when the white snow was down about the manor, the lawyer finished his work for Agnes Drale, the legal proceedings necessary now that the house, and its estate, were hers. As she sat like a queen in her black tussore, he offered her a last paper.

"You were curious, I remember, Lady Agnes," he said, making intent use, as he had throughout, of her inherited title, "about that bracelet your Uncle had brought from the East. I confess I was a little, too, myself."

"An unlucky gem, as prophesied," said Agnes. "It's locked away, and no longer in my keeping."

"I hope, my lady," said the lawyer, "that you also affixed the golden sun-shaped cap once more over the stone?" He chuckled frivolously. "You will see why, when you regard this document I have procured from the city museum."

"Oh, yes. I did do that. My servants were very uneasy. They had learned the jewel was cursed. Poor Genevieve."

The lawyer touched his heart in an affectation of feeling. "And the criminal is still at large — ! A madman. Such a terrible, such an unthinkable end — eviscerated, rent, ripped, the blood splattered — the face torn off—" He displayed the purest ghoulishness of his time, or most times.

"There is a general belief," said Agnes, "that gypsies and their ferocious dogs — "

"Several had been seen, I gather," agreed the lawyer. "But to enter the chapel — "

"No one can explain," said Agnes. She nodded. The subject was closed; one did not argue with her.

She unfolded her palms and took the paper, and read it. As she did so, the lawyer, a true slave, and generously remunerated, stood respectfully smiling, to show how he was aware what nonsense he had just handed her.

This piece of jewelry is mentioned in several ancient texts, and seems to date from the fourteenth century. The jewel is itself not mooted as a mineral but as a living energy, or animal. *When let loose in particular conditions, it may evoke, it is thought, violent and horrible death, the ingredients for this seeming to involve the emotions of hatred and jealousy, in opposition to callous greed. In the case of one ruler said to have died through it, the matter is proposed as the actual opposition of the two elements of the stone itself — vividity and hardness.*

The bracelet, which is formed of gold, also entails an enclosement over the stone, which, if the. wrong or provoking elements are present, should in no circumstance be removed.

*Thus, it is the bracelet, the **setting** of the jewel, which is named **Frengeh,** or **Fraanghi,** deriving of course from the Musselman word, meaning, **A Cage.***

THE EYE IN THE HEART

From an idea by John Kaiine

THE LAST PLACE I saw was Venice. He said he wanted it to be somewhere special — and it was. The memories are so perfect, and whenever I want, I can take them out of the cupboards of my mind and look at them. The malachite green canals, the greenish blue of the Italian skies, the gleaming domes, the white pigeons. And my husband, standing brown and smiling, his eyes full of pride in me, and love — and, yes, sexual love as well. How thoughtful he was. They were a magical two weeks.

Our holiday was marred only by one brief episode. I don't know why I think of it, but sometimes I do. To belong to our Sect of course sets us apart. All persons of deep convictions experience these odd occasional slights. One mustn't dwell on them or feel bitterness, because bitterness does no one any good.

But there. She was a young woman in a white dress, tanned, and apparently happy as we were. Impulsively I went up to her, and asked if she would take a photo of us, my husband and I. I could imagine him, in the future, looking at it fondly, remembering our delight and oneness. But the girl edged away a little. Firmly she said "No." And then, blushing and frowning, to cover her bluntness, "I'm no good with cameras. Excuse me." Then she hurried off.

My husband, seeing I was slightly upset, at once found a man, who was much more amenable, and took the shot of us, which I've seen. It's a nice photograph. Perhaps the girl was only truthful and didn't want to let us down. Yet . . . I think she had realized we were people of a sect, our particular Sect, and our beliefs offended her. And somehow, now, I sometimes see her face, with my mind's eye, its blush, its frown, the sort of — terror — in it. So, using my special computer, I'm trying to explain.

THERE WAS ONE other thing about Venice, and other places we went through. I did feel so sorry for the older women, the married ones. I noticed especially, their eyes were so dull and heavy and troubled. But I haven't been much outside our Town, and so I'm used to our own married women, whose eyes are always clear and sparkling.

When I was a child, a lot of girls, including me, used to pretend to be married. My mother sometimes told me off for using so many of her scarves, and losing them in the woods. That was before we started Domestic Classes. Then, of course we had to practice properly. There were a few accidents, the worst one when a girl fell down the school steps and broke her ankle. Otherwise we laughed so much. But soon you get very proficient. I was, well, I'm boasting but it's a fact, one of the best. And it's stood me in good stead. Later, once they've allocated your house in Town, for a month before you marry, you have individual training. My husband told me I was an absolute star, but then I showed off to him. I demonstrated what I could do. We sneaked in the house alone, when we weren't supposed to, you see. I think quite a few people guessed, actually. His smile didn't help, it was so broad afterward you could count all his white teeth!

The only thing I never had quite right was the cooker — I'm still working on that, but the splash-screen gets pretty dirty. Just so you know, I'm not saying I'm faultless at anything — heaven forbid.

Some people, I've heard, sometimes ask why. I mean, why we do this.

It's so obvious that it's quite hard to explain. It's that thing about bitterness again. Bitterness, and being hurt — worrying over what you can't do anything about — and then hurting others, worrying others, making a mess. And then — you're left with nothing.

We marry for life. Marriage is sacred. And everyone wants to be happy.

My mother had the bluest eyes. I used to stare and stare at them, so clear and darting as she spoke to me. Aquamarines. I can still see them, though she died last year. It was a sad time. Dad may marry again, though. He's still strong and young-sounding. I take flowers to her grave, and once I tripped, and this young girl, about twelve, ran over and helped me up. I could almost hear Mom laughing. *And you such a star!* She was sweet, my mother, but she was very down-to-earth, too.

I can recall quite well what she said to me, when I was about five, and she explained. So maybe I should just use her explanation, instead of trying to find the words myself.

"Women are so sensitive, darling. They have to be. They have to be aware what a man wants, what their children want. They have antennae all over them, whiskers of feeling. And unfortunately that has a down side. It means they get hurt so easily. And then they doubt. And soon they just can't believe. She'll say to her husband, 'You don't love me anymore. I can see it in your face.' Maybe he's just tired — or maybe his love is tired. But she'll read something so awful into it. And then she'll nag and rave on, and drive him crazy. And in the end he won't be able to stand it. He'll slap her — or worse, he'll leave her. And what good will that do her? And men, you see, honey, sometimes they do little things . . . little things it's better for a wife not to know. It's much nicer if she needn't worry about if she can forgive him. Do you remember that silly song, 'Lipstick on your Collar'? Well, the women here in Town don't ever have to bother about that. Most of all, the thing they always see, with the eye of the heart, is how he looked at them last. All that wanting and care, that love. And when he tells you he loves you, why, he does. Oh darling, we're so lucky."

WHEN WE came back from Venice, I went straight into our hospital. I had the loveliest doctor. He was the kindest man. He assured me, there isn't a single scar, and he let me feel, so I know. "You're pretty as a picture," he said. He even flirted, and I must have looked nothing at all after the op. "Your eyes are green as grapes, Missy. I could look and look at those green eyes. I could eat them up."

My husband bought them for me. Dad would have, but he just insisted. They are truly beautiful, I cried out when I saw them, in their velvet box. We displayed them with the wedding presents. I'm sorry to say I think there was a bit of jealousy here and there. Well, I'm sorry to say I enjoyed it, too.

And now we live so happily — all but for the cooker! Never mind. I've got years and years to master that.

In my mind, I can see my husband as clear as a painting, and the love and wanting in his face. And when he kisses me, that's what I see, that's what I'll always see.

Oh, I know there are people out there, deluded people who perhaps even mean well, who try and try to get us stopped, or hounded out of the state, but if only I could tell them how wrong they are. Though I'm blind now, because

I'm blind, like every married woman in Town, I know I need never be afraid.

It was my twenty-first birthday last week, and my husband was a little bit late — only an hour or so. And I might well have started to worry, searching his face, trying to trap him in some lie . . . But no, he wasn't lying about all that at the office. I only have to remember his face, the way he looked in Venice. And I take his hand, and his lips are warm.

After all, as my mother said, "What the eye doesn't see, the heart doesn't grieve over."

And I've some wonderful news to give him when he gets back tonight. I'll wait up, even until three or four in the morning. I'm pregnant.

I wonder if it will be a girl?

VERMILIA

HE WROTE: "She is a vampire. Now I know. I thought I was alone."

He felt the inevitable amalgam. Shock and excitement, jealous resentment, unease.

He would never have said, "The city is mine." How could it be? There must be several others, like himself. But he had never met one, here. Not here. And, otherwise, none for half a century.

They kept to themselves. Like certain of the big cats, they did not live easily together, the vampires. They drew together for sex, sometimes even for love. Then parted, eventually.

And if one was sensed, then generally, they would be avoided — by their own kind.

But now, now he wondered if he had wanted . . . ? The one who said no man was an island, was quite wrong. Every man is, every woman is, both prey and predator. Alone.

And she was an island lit by gorgeous lamps, smooth and lustrous in her approach, her hidden depths and heights alive with unknown temptations.

Of course. She was a vampire.

Flirtatiously he wrote: "What now?"

THE FIRST TIME he saw her, was across a crowded bar. It was just after sunset, vampire dawn. She had that fresh look a vampire had, waking to the prospect of a pleasant "day." Obviously, there were others who had it, too — certain night-workers who enjoyed their jobs. But vampires loved their employment. Most of them. The stories of guilt and angst were generally spurious — or poetic.

She moved about the bar, sometimes sitting, crossing and uncrossing her long pale legs in their sheaths of silk. She had black hair with a hint of red, and a bright red dress with a hint of blue, sleeveless and body-clinging, the sort that only a woman with a perfect figure could wear. And her figure was perfect.

The face was something else again — sly and secretive, with elusive eyes. The mouth crayoned the colour of the dress. For this vermilion colour, he coined a name for her almost at once: Vermilia.

She would be pleased, he later thought, once he had seen her at work. Vampires tended to obscure their true names, at least from each other. The invented name he would offer her, like a first gift.

Why she had initially caught his attention he was not so sure. Possibly vampiric telepathy, empathy . . . For there were other attractive women in the bar, even with perfect forms, and faces that were actually beautiful, if only in the synthetic contemporary manner.

Naturally, she did not look like that. She would have appeared as well in a sweeping Renaissance gown, or corseted crinoline.

From involuntary observation, he began to watch her. It was soon apparent she was there to secure company. But, she was selective. She would speak to men, engage their interest — even allowing a couple to buy her a drink — but then she would drift away. Not for a moment did he take her for a hooker. She was not — businesslike. You could see, she liked what she was doing. For her, it was foreplay.

That night, himself, he had no rush. He had taken rich sustenance for three consecutive nights, draining his source with civilized slow thoroughness. She had died, happily, in the hour before sunrise. Tonight, then, was a leisurely reconnoitre, no more. He would not need blood again for seventy-two hours at least.

He felt nothing for his prey, or very little. He was seldom rough or cruel — there was seldom any need. To seduce, to entrance, was second nature to his kind. Was he thinking Vermilia might be a worthy successor to the last dish? Probably not. After someone so lovely as the last young woman who had died, he would have preferred a very different type, perhaps even ugly. You did not want always the same flavour.

Besides, he soon began to realize about Vermilia.

She was drinking red wine. It was a human myth that vampires could not eat, or imbibe any fluid save one. They did not need to, certainly, but they could. He himself disliked alcohol, and drank mineral water, but that was his personal taste. He understood also she did not favour red wine because it reminded her of blood. What else was ever like blood?

Finally, she was with a boy, standing right up to the bar now, across from him as he watched her. For a second even, her eyes slid over his face. Did she see him? Sense him, as he had begun to sense her? Maybe not. She was intent on her prey.

The boy — he was a boy, though probably forty years of age, arrested in some odd gauche slim adolescence of human immaturity — was fascinated at once. He bought her another wine. Then another.

"Yes," he wrote, "right then I did truly suspect. I was

sure she was not a professional. Therefore, and in any case, why fasten on this oddball character, plainly not rich, not handsome, and not wise. A new flavour?"

They were there for about twenty minutes more. He even caught phrases from their conversation. "You do? Wow." And she, "Let me show you. Would you like that?" They were not talking about sex. It was a building, the building where she lived. Some old-style architecture, that had been used in a movie, she said. He did not catch the name of the director or actors in the movie. Conceivably she made it up. He was almost sure by then.

When they left the bar, he left also, sidling out into the hot night, to follow them unseen.

The city was black, jeweled but not lit up by its coruscating terraces of lights. Humanity idled by, skimpily clad, drinking beers and snorting drugs from cones of paper. Police cars shrilled through the canyons, rock music thumped.

They reached the famous building. It rose high above, and did look extremely gothic, with some sort of gargoyles leaning out from the fortieth floor.

The foyer was open to anyone, at least to any vampire, dim and shadowed, with carven girls holding up pots of fern, and the doorman watching a TV. Either he waved to Vermilia, or thought he waved to some other woman he knew to reside there. To *him*, the doorman said, not turning, "Hot night, Mr Engel."

"It is."

Vermilia did not turn either. She was showing her boy the statues and the cornice, and summoning an elevator.

He got in with them. Vermilia did not glance. The boy looked slightly embarrassed, then forgot, the way a vampire could always make a human forget.

They got off at the fifty-first floor. He rode up to fifty-two. When he came back down the stairs, they were still outside her apartment.

The corridor was dimmer even than the foyer. The doors were wide spaced and no one was there. He stood like an invisible shadow by the stair door, and looked.

"Oh — I forgot my key. Or I lost it."

"Maybe I can pry it open with this — " The credit card twiddled in boyish old fingers.

"Honey," said Vermilia.

It occurred to him she did not live here at all, liked the chancy stuff of doing it right now, in the corridor.

She had her arms round the boy's neck. The boy kissed her, sloppily, the way you would expect. Then she put her face into his neck.

He gave a little squeal.

"Ssh," she said softly. "It's sexy. You'll like it." Then a pause, and then, "Don't you like it?"

"Ye-aah, I guess . . . ."

It did not last long.

As she pulled away, a vermilion thread was on her chin. It might only have been smeared lipstick.

The boy breathed fast. He turned to try to open the door.

She said, "Oh, leave that. Let's go out. I'd rather go out."

"But I thought maybe — " She was already by the elevator again.

The boy shambled after her, pressing a surprised handkerchief to his bleeding neck. "Hey — you drew blood — "

"Sorry, honey."

The elevator came.

He knew she would lose the boy somewhere in the crowds. He let her go.

He went back to his living space, and wrote about it in the book he kept. He wrote, "She did not relish his blood. She only took a little. Must then have gone looking for someone else."

And then, flirtatiously again, "What now?"

But he knew. He would go after her. As no one else could, he could find her. Hunt her down. Oh, Vermilia . . .

HE HAD NEVER thought of them much as victims, the ones he took. Some he even allowed to recover and forget him. The best, he drained over three, four, five nights, at the end eking it out. There was no other pleasure in the world like it. Sex, the closest, was anaemic beside it. He would never have tried to describe the delight, the power and the glory. There were no words in any language, or from any time.

The night after he saw Vermilia in the bar, he took a girl off the sidewalk near the park. Perhaps it was Vermilia's fault, in some incoherent way. He did not control himself, and drained the girl, among the trees . . . Her passage from slight surprise to thrill to ecstasy to delirium and oblivion, was encompassed in two hours. Because he had been incautious, he had then to obscure her death, to cut her throat — almost bloodless — and roll her down the 3 A.M. slope into the kids' wading pool. One more puzzle for all those whirling car-bound cops.

The next night he began the hunt.

He was very perplexed not to find her at once, Vermilia.

But the reason he did not was very stupid. He had never thought she would return instantly to the bar, and do exactly the same there as before.

When she left with her new beau, a muscled moron, he let her have him. Did not even bother to go in the building with them — the same building.

Presently, about half an hour after, the moron came plunging out, looking both smug and unnerved.

He went up to him. "Say, are you OK, son?"

"Sure, sure — some weird babe."

"You gotta be careful."

"Yeah, old man, I guess you do."

He knew that the moron, who had a surgical dressing now on his thick neck, saw him as some cobwebby, bent old guy, leaning on a cane.

The moron swaggered off, proud of his youth. She must have let him have some sex, in payment. Perhaps the blood had been good, he looked strong. But it was not always that way; sometimes the puny ones had the nicest taste.

He went in, and the doorman, watching TV, called out, "Mind the floor, Mr. Korowitcz. Woman spilled the wash bucket, still damp."

The elevator took him up to fifty-one, and he walked along to her door. Presumably it was her door. Of course, she might have taken the stairs, as he had, last time. But why would she? Unless she had seen him — there was always that.

He tried the door.

He was thinking, she might assume it was the moron back, angry maybe, or just wanting another helping.

Or she merely might not answer.

Then the door opened.

She looked right up at him in a cool still amazement that made him aware she had, somehow, not sensed him at all, not properly seen him, until that moment.

LATER, writing, he wrote: "Should I have been more careful? I? I was innocent after all, worse than the boy in the bar. How could I guess?"

She said, "Who are you?"

"A. . . kindred spirit."

"Really?"

She looked glad enough to have him there. But that was usual. To the one he focused on, he was everything, a prince among men. With his own kind, it was not quite the same. Even so. He was all her conquests had not been, and more. What struck him was that she did not seem at all wary. No, she was inviting — if not exactly yielding.

"May I come in?"

She laughed. "I see. I have to ask you over the threshold."

"I think you know better than that."

"Do I?"

"We," he said, peremptorily, "decide. Asked or not."

"My." She pivoted. "Come on in, then."

As he passed her, she ran her hand lightly along his arm. Even through the summer jacket, he felt the life of her.

The apartment was in keeping with its grand façade and foyer, and just as dimly lit. What startled him was its total ambience of cliché. Velvet draperies hung, and tall white candles burned, dark perfumes wafted, Byzantine chant murmured, stained glass obscured the windows. There were no mirrors he could see. This room was exactly what *humans* expected a vampire's apartment to be. Yes, even to the skull on the real marble mantel, the ancient dusty books, and the chess-set in ivory and ebony standing ornately to one side.

He had never come across, on the rare occasions that he met them, any vampire who lived like this, and he himself certainly did not. His room was inexpensive and plain, without curios. Without, really, anything.

She had a piano too.

Now she walked over to it, and ran her fingers over the keys, clashing with the chanting. He could tell from the way she did that, too, she could not play the thing at all. Show, then. Just for show.

"Like a drink?" she said. "Or am I being forward?" And she snapped her teeth.

He smiled. Grimly. Her vulgarity — he would have preferred to leave. But something — herself, obviously — held him there.

A drink. . . She was perverse, kinky, a freak. Vampires did sometimes like such games together. He too had done so, long, long ago. Acting prey-predator, drinking each other's blood. It could be amusing, as a novelty. But that was all it was. She, though, he could tell from some infinitesimal quivering in her, found the idea a turn-on.

Was it just possible she did not believe he was what he was — one of her own kind?

He walked over to the sofa and sat down, sinking miles deep. She moved about him, round the room, prowling like a cat, and now, to his disgust, lit some sort of incense. She must be very young. She looked about twenty-five — maybe less than a hundred, then. For vampires, though immortal, did age, in their own way. No sags or wrinkles, but something in the line of the bones, the way they were.

"But tell me about yourself," she coyly said.

And she came and sat down beside him, leaning back a little, displaying herself, her eyes gleaming now, yet still elusive — *reflective*, like the mirrors she did not have.

"Nothing to tell," he said. "You know that. Our lives are all very much the same."

"Why are you here?" she asked.

He looked at her. Why was he?

"You," he said.

"I've put my spell on you. I did that the other night, didn't I? Across the bar. I thought, my oh my."

"Did you."

"Yes. I bet you spied on me with Puddie."

"With whom?"

"Puddie. That guy."

"Which one?"

She smiled, and her teeth glinted. He could see their sharpness. She was not being careful. Of course, with him, that would be a futile precaution.

"You know what I do. And I know what you do," she said. "Come on, let's do it."

"You want that with me."

"You bet I do. Oh yes. So much."

He did not want to drink from her. Later, he wrote, "I wanted nothing less than her blood. That was my fatal mistake. But she had — as she said so naively, fooling me further — cast a spell on me of some sort. And for me, Vermilia was the first of my kind for all that time."

He lay back, almost bored. "Ladies first."

"Oh, how sweet. Yes, then."

As she leaned over him, he had — he afterwards told himself — a premonition. But he was too indolent to heed it.

She smelled wonderful too, new scents; fresh-baked bread and fresh-cut melon, and this perfume, and the incense smoke which had caught in her hair.

Her bite was clumsy. She hurt him and he swore.

Why put up with this? He was thinking, he would give her one minute.

He wrote, "Suddenly something happened to me. Unprepared — how could I be otherwise — I was flooded, overwhelmed. The — no other word is legitimate — *rapture*."

He did not, writing, compare it at all to sex. But again, probably, that was the nearest comparable thing. The tingling, surging, racing — And presently, the pleasure-gallop exploded as if it hit some crystal ceiling of the brain — a kind of orgasm. He blacked out.

When he came to, which, that first time, was only a few seconds later, she was sitting back, looking at him, licking her lips.

"Sorry I hurt you," she said. "I need them sharpened again. The teeth, I mean. But my little Chinese guy, who does it for me — he's off someplace. He's a great dentist, too."

He was thinking, *Is that what they feel, when I —* dizzy and wondering, when she put her hand up to her lips. She slipped the two eye-teeth out of her mouth. They were removable caps. Her own teeth — were blunt, ordinary.

"Did you like that, honey?" she asked, needlessly. "I'll make some coffee."

While she was gone, somehow he found the strength to get up, and get out of the apartment.

In the elevator, he almost passed out a second time.

As he wandered across the foyer, the doorman said, "You don't look too good, Mr. O'Connor."

He thought doubtless he did not.

HAVING no intention of going back, the next night he hunted among the bars many blocks away from the gothic building.

He took three women, and each time found he had killed them, which was a nuisance in the matter of disposal. The last one he did not bother to hide, leaving her among the trash cans in an alley. Despite the excess of blood, he felt enervated, and depressed.

The following night he overslept, waking two hours before midnight. This was not unheard of for a vampire. But it was rare.

Vermilia.

He found himself in some nightclub, sipping a mineral water that cost seven dollars, saying her name in his head — the name he had given her.

He kept thinking about what had happened to him, with her. He was pretty sure he had also dreamed of it. Again, vampires did dream. But not much.

He wrote, "I am like some little virgin bride after her first night. I infuriate myself."

He discovered that now, when he took the blood from his prey, he did not enjoy it so much. At first, desperate for the blood, he had not noticed.

Did he, then, want the blood of Vermilia? Somehow, that thought revolted him. Almost made him, in fact, retch. Why was that? The blood of another vampire could not properly nourish. But, it was not repulsive, or poisonous —

He thought of her leaning to him, and piercing his throat with the peculiar caps she needed because somehow her teeth had grown deformed and useless. He thought of the rhythm beginning, and his head went round.

He bought a bottle of Jack Daniels. Drank some. Threw up.

The next night, he threw up the blood he had taken from his prey. Twice.

He lay in the dark of his bare room, cursing her.

What was it? What had happened to him? A human might have feared some disease, but he, a vampire, was immune to such diseases. And she, a vampire, would not carry any disease.

The next night, he went to the gothic building. And in the foyer the TV-doorman turned morosely and said, "Hey, bud, who the hell are you?"

He stood there, made stupid. Never before had he been seen like this, when he had not meant to be.

He mumbled, "Number fifty-one. The lady."

"Oh, who's that?"

Who indeed.

"She knows me."

"OK, bud. No funny stuff. Get outta here."

He walked out, and there was Vermilia, like in the best movie, dawdling towards him up the street. She wore black tonight, but her mouth was still the proper colour.

"Honey!" she cried. She ran and hugged him. "You look beat."

They walked by the doorman, who now seemed to see neither of them.

In the elevator she jabbered about some idiotic thing, he did not grasp what she said. Why was he here — with her?

In the apartment, she lit the candles, the incense. He stood coughing and trembling.

"Like a beer?"

"I'd like you to do what you did last time."

"Oh sure. But let's get in the mood."

He fell down on the sofa. She caressed him. He writhed with need and dragged her mouth to his neck. "Do it. For God's sake — "

She did it.

It was the same as before. Ecstasy, racing, explosion. Out.

This time he was unconscious for an hour. She said so

anyway, shaking him. "Come on. You always fall asleep. If you weren't so beautiful . . . I need my bed. I have to be at work in the mornings."

New stupefaction only hit him as he reeled towards the elevator. *Mornings?*

THREE MORE TIMES he went to her. Between, he was able to take a little blood, here and there. It was no longer easy to do this. Partly because he did not properly want it, and besides sometimes got sick when he had taken it. Also partly because his ability to seduce seemed strangely less. In the past, he had needed only to look, perhaps to touch or speak. That was enough. Even at the moment of impact, if there was a struggle, his great strength could subdue at once, but, more likely he could still them with a brushing of his lips, a whisper.

Now some of the prey got cold feet. Some fought with him.

And he did not have the energy to pursue these ones. And any way, he knew, he was losing it. Losing it all.

He thought he had said to her, the third time, "What have you done to me, what are you?"

And she had said, "I'm a vampire, honey. Just like you. Only you just like to play it one way, don't you? But that's fine by me. I like it best this way. Sometimes."

More than the terrifying pleasure, it was something else that brought him back, and back. The spell. But what was the spell?

"How old are you?" he said.

"You're no gentleman," she said. Then she said, "Oh, hundreds of years, of course." She lied. He knew she lied.

It was worse than that. She was losing interest in him.

She had by now told the doorman to let him up, but when he was with her now, she said, "You might do something for me."

What was she talking about? Exhausted, he closed his eyes. Exhausted, he begged her to do what she did.

That night, when he came around, he knew she was killing him.

It had to stop.

But he was hooked.

"OK," she said. "Come tomorrow. I may have a friend here. You'll like her."

"Will you — "

"Yes. Go on now. It's so late. You were asleep for *four* hours and I couldn't wake you."

"You have work in the morning," he drearily remarked.

"Sure do. My stinking job."

"But the sun," he said.

"Oh, get out of here," she said, laughing and impatient.

Outside — he leaned on her door and then he began to see. Swimming down in the nauseated elevator, he saw more.

The doorman stared. "Hey, you on drugs or something, mister?"

He got to his bare room, and lay down.

Tomorrow night. He would go. He could not help himself. No one could help him. But he thought now he understood . . . And tomorrow, before he left, he would write it in his book. In case in the future, to some other this same thing might happen, as well it might.

As well it might.

"This is Raven," she said.

Raven had long black hair and a face made up white as

a clown's. At the corner of her mouth she had painted a ruby drop, but her lipstick was black.

"My," said Raven, and she curtseyed to him, leering. But Raven was the same as Vermilia — the same kind and species.

Tonight it was to be different, Vermilia said. They would take off all their clothes. They took them off.

He stared at their bodies, Vermilia's perfect, Raven's not, both irrelevant.

In turn they ogled him.

Then they all lay down on the wide sofa. The girls drank wine, and tongued him, and all he could smell was hair and flesh and perfume and wine, and all he wanted was for them to have his blood and he knew this time would be the last, and he cursed himself and them and the world and all his hundreds of years that had not saved him. Consumed with fear, he shook with desire.

"He likes to be the subserve," said Vermilia. He hated her accent. Hated her. "Go on, Rave, he'll like it."

Raven picked up his wrist. She sank in her teeth, also caps, he supposed. The pain was horrible. He wished he could kill her. Then, it began, even so, began —

And Vermilia's lips were on his neck, and then the bite, sharper, better — her dentist must be back in town.

Like an express train, a locomotive of fire, the surge rose up in him. He forgot he would die. Forgot he had been alive.

The fireworks erupted through gold to red and white and to vermilion.

As his brain and heart burst he screamed for joy.

Leaving him, Raven and Vermilia, whose true name was Sheila — but who called herself on such nights Flamea, which he had never bothered to learn — turned to each other.

When they were through, they got up. "He sleeps for hours."

"He's great-looking. But what a drag."

They left him and went to get some chocolate cake.

While they were in the kitchen, since he had died and was a vampire, he disintegrated quickly and completely to the finest white dust, which presently blew off through the air, coating the apartment lightly, and making Sheila-Flamea sneeze for days.

Some human myths of vampires were true.

When the girls came back, they commented on his absence, and that he had rudely got up and gone.

"But look, he left his clothes."

They raised their brows, and shrugged.

EARLIER, he had written in his book:

"I know now. She is no vampire. She is a human. A woman playing at being a vampire. This is how she has her fun. Pretending she is our kind. Acting it out.

"But why it should do *this* to me, I have no notion. Perhaps it is only me, but such a scenario may affect others of my kind in the same fashion, and to them I leave this warning.

"We have taken the blood of humans all these millennia. Now, unknowing, they are prepared to take ours — by accident, thinking we are the same as they — or not recognizing us — or not thinking there is any difference between us and them. And when they do take our blood — *this* may be the result. I have no answer as to why. I have no resistance to it. Perhaps it has evolved, this power, naturally. Like some virus or germ. Perhaps this is now their *natural* means of protecting themselves against us."

His last lines were these:

"Her kind have always killed my kind. That used to be with stakes and garlic, honed swords, sunlight and fire. Now, is it this way? Her kind kills my kind with . . . kindness."

FLOWER WATER

LADY EMERALDINE MORROW vanished, or died, yesterday; and the circumstances were reported in many of the papers. It was the bizarre nature of events and their number of witnesses, which led to the publicity.

In the midst of a private festival, as the sun began to set, Lady Emeraldine was rowed across her small private lake, to her small private island. Just visible from shore, she there commenced to regale her three hundred guests with vivid torrents of music on her harp.

Her many accomplishments, coupled to her great beauty, have been well known and much publicized for years. Also her enormous good humor, her happy, light-hearted disposition. And, in some circles, her apparent callousness.

The music rang out, chords, glissandi, and the sun sank into the woods, and the sky turned from crimson to the coolest mauve.

It was at this moment, in the last of the twilight, that Lady Emeraldine ceased playing, in the very middle of a spirited improvisation. As startled applause broke forth, a loud cry soared upwards from the island. Then came a burst of flame, a sort of explosion. Something quite small, dark and hard, shot into the air, then fell down into the lake, and with a sizzle, disappeared.

Guests swam or rowed in swarms to the island. They found a charred place beside the harp, which was itself unscathed. Of Lady Emeraldine there was no evidence at all.

There was of course talk of spontaneous combustion, or of abduction by fiery creatures from some other world.

Myself, I am strongly inclined to think that Lady Emeraldine was one of us.

UNTIL I MET HIM, under the coloured lamps of the Public Gardens, I had had an unpleasant life. My story is all too common. Father a drunkard. Mother a washerwoman. Put out at fifteen on the streets. Here I unoriginally plied my trade in the oldest profession on earth, and with very limited success, being neither very attractive, nor very enthusiastic, and by no means a talented actress.

As the years passed, I had been also beaten and abused. I had thieved and been thieved from. I developed the expected passion for gin, and lost the last of my slight looks. Some of my teeth dropped out, my eyes were dim, my balance unpredictable. In this state, at twenty-four, here I was in the Gardens, not looking for custom, certainly, but tottering up and down, blearily eyeing the paper lanterns in mawkish solitude, before a police constable should behold and move me along.

When he spoke to me, indeed I took him for the police.

"Can't a poor girl come in and joy herself for five minutes for no cost, without she gets herded away?" I whined, in traditional, useless obstinacy.

"I don't suggest you go," he said, with a voice too educated for any of the police I had come across, which had been many. "No, stay with me."

"What, you want to walk with me, do you?" I croaked. I said, I was no actress, and though I had been trying, for at least five years, to act the pathetic sodden old harlot I had become, I was really no good at it.

"I'd like to hear your story," said he.

"Soon told. For the price of a gin."

"Champagne," said he.

At that I felt I should straighten up. "For the likes of me? What are you after? What's your game?"

He was young, rich, and handsome. He shone with health and wealth and grooming. He must therefore have some perverted whim. Fill me with expensive liquor and then slice me in scallops.

"We can remain at all times in the general gaze," he said. "I was only moved by your plight." But when he said that, he suddenly burst out laughing. I could see, in fact, he had the most carefree face I had ever looked at. I have seen one more such, since then. But I will come to that.

"Lead on then, Charlie," I said, thinking he was truly mad.

"My name is Raphael Pemberton. And yours?"

"Lizzie Lines."

We shook hands, and all about, very likely, the fashionable persons in the park glanced askance at us.

He took me to the open ballroom in the Centre of the Gardens, and straight off ordered two bottles of a famous champagne, on ice, also plates of oysters, bits of geese in aspic, jellies, cakes, and heaven knows what.

As I sat there I thought, *He must be going to poison me, slip something in my glass. Blame my demise on my weak condition.* I racked my brains to remember strange deaths of blowsy, nasty whores in public thoroughfares, with a handsome gentleman nearby. Probably I had only missed hearing of them.

In any event, my life was not so grand I yearned that much to keep it, or so it seemed after a couple draughts of the champagne.

Raphael Pemberton, meanwhile, began to question me. He wanted to learn about this vile existence I had had. He could see, he told me, that I had suffered.

As I regaled him with my history, thickly laying on all the horrors, and inventing several new ones — my dying mother's bedside with the non-existent little ones snivelling in my skirts, my noble father renouncing the drink, and dying of want of it — actually he had been squashed by a runaway beer barrel — Raphael stared at me, his face working as if with grief until, every few moments, he burst out laughing again.

With the champagne I too began to see the funny side of me, and soon we were rolling in the aisles, a sideshow for the adjoining tables.

Additionally, I forgot to act my part. I became myself.

At last he said, between our gulps and hiccups, "You seem improved, Lizzie."

"Well," I said, "both my parents trod the boards — the stage, that is — before their luck changed. I had no talent, but I learned how to speak. Is that," I added, "why you're so amused?"

His pretty face fell. "No. Oh no, Lizzie." Then he bloomed, I have to say, like the rose in his buttonhole. "What a beautiful night!"

"Not bad," said I.

"Tell me, Lizzie," said Raphael Pemberton, as we began upon the third bottle, "would you like to be young and lovely again?"

"I'm not so old as I look. It's the gin wot's done for me, guv'nor. I was *never* lovely."

"For the first, then, Lizzie. How about it?"

"If you're buying."

"Selling, in a way. How old would you say *I* was?"

I squinted. Strong drink, by removing all pretense at focus, had oddly improved my vision. "Twenty-one," I said.

"Wrong, Lizzie. Seventy-one would be nearer the mark."

I smiled. Humour the fool. We were, as he had said, in the general gaze. And it seemed he had not poisoned me yet.

"You don't believe me, Lizzie Lines. Of course not. I look young. I'm handsome. And, evidently well-off. The latter springs from the former. It can for you. I feel so happy, Lizzie. How do you feel?"

"I feel splendid. When the drink wears off, I'll be back where I was."

"Just imagine," said Raphael Pemberton, "there was a drink that never wore off."

"Oh yes?"

"A drink that, after one swallow, made you feel so well, so glad, as if — as if your heart was full of stars. Always just a little tipsy. Never a bad day. Never a sad night. No pain. No sorrow. Think of that, Lizzie."

"I am."

"Does it appeal?"

"What do you think? Besides, obviously it makes you young. Twenty-one, seventy-one. And good-looking. And it makes you rich, too?"

"Wealth comes from the rest. If you're utterly healthy, completely attractive, and your mind sharp, and your attitude merry at all times — you can't avoid riches, Lizzie, getting to be rich. Just think what you could have done, with all that."

"Well, Ralphie, I didn't have the chance, did I?"

"You have it now."

He gazed at me soberly for all of three seconds. Then

he grinned. Well-being flashed and flamed from him. You could never think a blazing torch looked sick.

"This is a drink," I said.

"Yes, Lizzie. And I offer it to you."

"Why?"

"I have just one dose, and I must give it to someone."

"And why is that?"

"Because, outside the human frame, it's indestructible. I can't pour it away. Not down a drain. Not into the sea. I don't even want to lock it up because, in a thousand years, someone might find it. But you. I think you deserve it, Lizzie."

"Oh, yes. And why is *that?* For my terrible life?"

"Because you're such a bitch."

HE TOLD ME THEN, as the dancers cavorted on the ballroom floor and the lamps burned lower in the trees, and the fourth bottle came; and I knew that, jolly as a jack-rabbit, in the morning I was going to wish I was dead — he told me about Aquaflora.

Someone had found a hidden spring, it transpired, beneath a temple in Italy dedicated, in pagan times, to the goddess of nature, Flora.

This someone, whose name Raphael Pemberton claimed not to know, had drawn from the spring — reputed, according to a Latin inscription about the fount, to restore, heal, and bless — one flask. An ancient legend declared that barren women had sought the fount and drunk there in order to bear children, also that cripples had washed in it and grown whole, elderly men got back their youth, and many other such tales. What had become of all these recipients of miracles had never been said, but in the end, the spring was shut away by the priestess for reasons of spite.

The modern explorer who found the spring did not think for a moment it possessed any unusual qualities. He took the water as a curiosity. A day later, returning to the spot on other exploratory business, he found the spring had mysteriously dried up again. With the other excitements of his trip, he forgot the matter.

It was over a year later, once more at home, that the traveler again took notice of the flask from Flora's spring. By this time he desired to impress a young lady, and so he bore the flask into her house, told her that here was the wine of the goddess of flowers, and she, out of bravura, poured a few drops into her tea cup, and drank them.

Within a quarter of an hour, a change became apparent. Her undeniable prettiness had escalated into a potent glamour. A strain in her left foot, that had been annoying her for days, vanished. Her hair, which was not very thick, took such a turn towards the luxuriant that all the pins fell out in a downpour. Within the day she could see farther than the most far-sighted man in her father's regiment, could hear a bat squeak, and had mastered the piano forte, which so far had eluded her, to the point of rendering the "Minute Waltz" in forty seconds. Her skin was like cream, her grace that of a swan, and two missing teeth had grown back.

Her unnamed swain, the traveler, lost no time himself in sampling the juice from the holy spring.

Presently two of the most attractive people in the country walked to the altar.

"And lived happily ever after," said I. "I suppose, in *fact*, for ever?"

"No," said Raphael Pemberton.

It seemed that the fortunate couple somehow slipped from the annals of history, and after them only the flask remained, its contents next portioned out in several equal measures.

"How many?" I asked.

"That I can't say. The last will and testament which brought me mine, informed me of nothing but the basic tale, and that the fluid, which might be called the Elixir of Life, but which was only named as Aquaflora, would give me health, youth, physical glory, luck, and perpetual happiness." At which Raphael Pemberton lifted his marvelous face to the sky "And it has! Oh God, it has!"

"But there are others?"

"Many. How many I have no idea. Sometimes — I believe I have unearthed one. People of great beauty and talent. People who are never for a moment sad. I read once of a fellow screaming with mirth at a funeral. I sought him out. I'd been wrong — he was only subject to a rare laughing disease."

We drank a little more champagne. The sixth bottle now, I thought.

"You said," I said, "that you reckoned me a bitch."

"Well you are, aren't you?" said my host, smiling lovingly at me. "All around me I can see the poor and ill and needy and broken. But you're a clown, Lizzie. You mock us all and you mean no one any good, not even yourself."

"Fine words for a gentleman," squawked I.

But, "Look," said Raphael. And from his coat he drew out a tiny phial full of a muddy brown mess. "With my own mouthful of the water came this other one. It may be that these were the last two measures from the flask. One for me. One for someone of my choosing."

"So you want to waste it on me. On a bitch. What about your mother? Your wife? Your mistress? Your fancy boy?"

"All of those," said Raphael, careless, light of heart, "are long dead. You see, when I took my dram, I was aging and almost alone. I didn't hesitate. And when I looked into my mirror, what a roar I sent up. I've been roaring every since. Oh, Lizzie. The worst news can't shake me. When I learned my only son had died, I had to hide my habitual, genuine smiles with a copy of the *Times*. If the world came to an end, there I'd be in space, charming as a comet, spinning with pleasure. *Nothing*, Lizzie, can bring me down. Think of it, Lizzie."

"But you want it for me as a *punishment?*"

"Not quite. It will suit you, Lizzie. You laugh at us all. It's in you already."

"There must be some catch."

"Can you think of one?" he asked.

I looked at him. After all the booze, I did believe the story, and the filthy-looking muck in the glass phial might well be a magic potion. My days had been devoid of any nice thing. Was I not due for some colossal change in fortune?

"It's poison," I said.

"It's water of flowers."

I had a strange notion then. I remembered some flowers in a vase in a public house where I had been sitting on a sailor's lap, and the flowers were past their best. In the obligatory fight that followed, the vase was knocked down and the flowers spilled and the water ran out on the edge of my dress. What a stink it had, that flower water.

But the lights were growing dull; and I bethought me of the Last Chance, the Final Risk, which, in fairy stories and in the silly dramas my parents had acted on the stage, must be taken or lost for ever.

So I uncorked the phial, sniffed it — it had actually no odour — and sipped. I waited a little after that, to see if there were any burning or discomfort. Nothing happened. So I tipped the contents, the Aquaflora, down my throat. "Cheers."

"Cheers, Lizzie," said Raphael.

And then he got up, and we went onto the floor, and danced a polka.

I knew I was drunk enough to try, but soon enough I understood that now I had a mastery of this polka that is not given to many. And by the time they cleared the floor to watch us, and by the time the orchestra itself surrendered and stood applauding, and I felt my back was straight, and my corset loose at my waist, and my hair tumbling down the colour of polished coal, and my hand white on his sleeve, and I could see every tree to the termination of the mile-long avenue, and hear every individual hand clapping, I knew he had not lied.

The champagne was gone. I would never need a drink again. The world — was my oyster.

"I feel quite wonderful," I cried to Raphael.

"So do we all," he said, and his voice, for a moment, was black as iron from the pit, before he burst out laughing, and I with him, in ecstatic joy.

WHEN I WENT HOME with Raphael Pemberton to his fine home in the square, I believed I was going there for the eternal reason, and for the first time in my life, I was looking forward to it. And, perhaps, even more than that, to the bathroom he promised with the enormous mirror, where I could see to the full what so far I could only feel.

The servants were in bed — or perhaps dismissed, I now sometimes conclude — and he led me up the stairs by low light, and opened the door of the bathing apartment, which led off his chamber.

I left that door ajar, and outside I heard him in his vast

bachelor bedroom, talking to me as I stripped under the gas-lamps and showed myself the new Lizzie Lines.

I am accustomed to her now, this paragon of raven hair and hand-span waist and skin like lilies. But then I could not see enough, turning this way, that way. And licking all around my new growing teeth, and admiring my corn-less feet, washing myself the while in delicious pomades that now I could have for myself simply by smiling at a man — and to smile, when one is feeling so incredibly well and strong, and brave — and victorious — and safe and confident — is *easy*.

Meanwhile, Raphael went on with a sort of monologue.

To start, I scarcely listened.

But now, I piece it together somewhat, for in the end, I heard the end.

He spoke of all his shining days of happiness, not one with any flaw. And of his nights of blissful sleep unmarred even by any unappealing dream.

He spoke of his rise to wealth. Of all those idyllic spots he had visited and all those impossible conquests he had made. Of business ventures of pure success. Of the realization that, whatever he wished for, would soon be his.

And laughing, sometimes breaking into snatches of happy music and song, unable to restrain the sweeping delight of all and everything, which I too now had within me, Raphael now related how he had observed the miseries of the world, had looked upon its torments and its tears, even on its blood, and futile sacrifice, and never once had their shadows touched him.

"I've seen a woman hoarsely weeping at her husband's grave, I've seen the dead brought up in hundreds from a mine, I've seen a hopping child wasted by plague, and a city under a flood, and I've sung this very song, Lizzie.

"Lizzie, do you hear any strain in my voice? Do you, Lizzie. Regret, guilt, pain? No? I'm enwrapt in sweetness. For ever and a day."

I went out then, naked, in my exquisite flesh, and there he stood, Raphael Pemberton.

"Have you heard of the Last Straw, Lizzie? The one that breaks the back of the camel much overloaded? You, Lizzie, are it."

I laughed. I always laugh, now. Show me your wounds, I will lave them with laughter. If heaven falls, I shall fly above heaven. I cannot do otherwise.

"Perhaps you won't believe me, Lizzie Lines. I've offered this single phial of the elixir of life, this Aquaflora, seven hundred and eighty times, before I came to you. To the drunk I've offered it, and to the sober. To the rich and the destitute. To the sick, the dying, the agonized, and the mad. They all refused. This gave me some hope, Lizzie. But then, tonight, you crossed my path. I knew you at once. She'll take it, thought I. As so you did, Lizzie, you bitch."

And then Raphael Pemberton convulsed in a paean of hilarity, content, and pleasure, and as he did so, there broke from him one howl of anger louder than any thunder. Then he was on fire. He went up like a firework. Vanished in a few seconds. Lightnings, sparks, and gushes — I jumped back — laughing, of course laughing.

It took about a minute for him to be consumed in the golden detonation. And out of it there showered down only a veil of slightest ash, to touch the carpet scorched merely where he had stood. But one, tiny wizened black thing there was, that shot up and fell back, and lay there, which might have been his heart. All, that is, that a lifetime of fulfillment, happiness, and perfect peace had left of his heart.

THERE IS NO other phial of Aquaflora in existence; at least, I have none. Enviously, I deduce, you would read of the delirious wonders of my life, if I paused to repeat them. I have had all I want. More. A cornucopia. And, with good reason, I have never been sad. But, more to the point, even in the presence of the darkest and most awful, rent and desolate horror of this earth, never have I felt the faintest hint of hurt or sorrow. As for despair; I cannot even recall that angel with its sallow, leaden wings.

I look at you, without pity, for pity grows from fear. Your sufferings. Your endings.

With my heart brim-full of melody, I say, I the smiling, beautiful, and blessed, you cannot be more envious than I.

Your lovely pain, your tortures, and your anguish that I cannot even in a dream recapture. Your loss, your rage, expressed in the poetry of words and souls, tragedy, romance — cheated, I.

Melody and laughter have shrivelled, by now, my heart, little as a raisin, like the heart of Raphael Pemberton, who gave me this.

Far, far off like a mist glimpsed fading on a hill, I think I see — nights when I sobbed or stormed, the glories of agony. The power of riven love. And my destitution, and my bad sight, and how my teeth left my mouth. My triumph over these paltry terrible things. My dignity. My inheritance, my rights, the sword's edge, honing me, telling me of my life. But perhaps it did not, and I was only what he said, and deserved only what I got from him.

One day I too will flare up and be gone. Like Emeraldine Morrow, whose withered heart dropped in a lake.

For now, all is lovely. All is well. It cannot be otherwise. Aquaflora. Stinking water from those stagnant flowers.

I have only had ten years of it. One was enough.

What will bring *me* the explosion of release, and let Lizzie from her prison of interminable, heavenly joy?

For me, as for all of them, perhaps, though quite unfelt, it is that last being freed from a Pandora's box of human truth. *Exasperation.*

DOLL SKULLS

But I, being poor, have only my dreams;
I have spread my dreams under your feet;
Tread softly because you tread on my dreams.
Yeats

IT WAS the last evening of the old year, but also of the century. As the winter dusk fell like gray powder, a million lights appeared across the city, the rich glow of oil lamps and the fainter bluish glim of gas, the cold bold electric windows, and the electric pods that marched along the higher streets, the rouged neons of the cafés, the soft blush of candles. With such a massing of lit eyes, Paradis meant to watch nightlong, to make sure the ship of the city should sail through that terrifying gate, into her future.

On the boulevards there was, too, some frenetic hilarity already, crowds that surged and laughed and blew whistles, and a scatter of motorcars that rattled by with their own great lamps alight, charged with shouting revelers. From the large mansions about the Obelisk, an occasional premature firework escaped. Children ran through the avenues, half unaware of the momentum of the time, yet primed to it, calling and shrieking.

The cathedral on its hill was bright as a jewel box, its glorious windows like cut fruits on fire, signaling God for protection, perhaps.

Fear and festival were in the air.

The mother, as she trudged homeward, however, paid small attention to all this.

Ten years before she had been a young girl herself, and would have laughed and been whirled about in a fashionable frock, willing to drink wine, and to perch in the back of a polished car. But since then she had been in love, and been in abandonment, and next in pregnancy, and so in childbirth. As the moon changes, so did she. Her slender shining nights were gone. Now she was thin and worn, and in her hair something had clawed out the color in long strands. She was drab, weary; at twenty-seven years, old.

As she walked up the long hill toward the clockmakers, she thought of her child. This child it was who had taken away her life, stopped her, the young girl, and gradually yet quickly altered her into this withered, partly stooping crone. Despite that, the mother — which was all she had become, there was no other name for her save drudge — loved the child very deeply, loved the child with all her soul. And the child, a girl of nine years, loved her mother in return with so much love that the whole city could not really hold it, and so it had escaped like the fireworks, up into the sky.

It was a fact that, when together, the mother and the child blossomed a little, were increased and better. But all else in their lives was difficult and unyielding. And, through that too, they were often apart for long hours, during which, lacking each other, they were also exposed to strangers who mistreated each of them in crass or subtle ways.

The mother slaved underpaid in a shop, for instance, where her fellow workers were cruel and stupid, mocking not only their intolerant customers, their base employers, but also each other and all the world. They took delight in playing quite dangerous practical jokes, such as filling dusters with pepper, or making the winter roadway out-side extra slippery with spilled liquid. They sneered at the elderly and courteous woman who came there to buy laces for her stays, overcharged her, and kept the money, saying she could afford it. They laughed openly at the flushed girl sent to purchase intimate underclothing. (Abashed, the mother had tried to be especially helpful to both of these victims.) Everything the assistants did, all told, was revolting, and the mother shunned them as best she could. Even so they stuck pins upside down into her tray of rib-bons, put salt into her water glass, and called her to her face, the Imbecile.

The child, conversely, had been sent by law to school, and here her thinness and pallor, her lack of energy and her dim sight, had won her the reputation, too, of being a simpleton. Both larger and smaller children tormented her, called her foul names, and sometimes beat her — although not often, for the mere threat of violence elicited from her such utter terror, indeed to the point of vomiting, that it was enough for them. Her teachers regarded her with disgust, for she was not seen to be intelligent, and since she could not always make out what they wrote on their blackboards, or through fright, assimilate what they said, they either ignored her, or rapped her with a ruler on her thin white knuckles, and put her to stand in corners.

In such a nightmare, mother and child existed. For either of them there seemed no end, no rescue. At home, nevertheless, they did not speak of the agonies of that out-side world, called by fools, real. They shut it from them with the strength of the embattled warriors they were.

Their home was a tenement which leaned. The stairs were partially rotten, the roof leaked, and sometimes a rat would arrive in their apartment. But the mother said they should not fear the rats, which were living things as they were. So she gave a little food to them, and each of the rats, three or four of them, became as docile and soft as a kitten, one tusker especially, who would sit, pale as snow, on the mother's knee, and allow her to feed him crumbs of bread and cheese, or suck milk from her fingers.

Actually the child, so afraid, and with such cause, of human beings, had no fear of any other creature. She found beetles as fascinating as birds, and did not shy away from huge carriage horses on the street, only looking up at them in admiration. At school, one day, when the bullies hid a large spider in the child's hat, she coaxed it out on her palm and carried it to a window, where she let it go carefully into some ivy. This earned her their respect for a week. (Of course, had she been afraid of spiders, the shock might have sent her into hysterics.)

The mother earned little enough, and she and the child, the rats and beetles, ate very meagerly. Tonight, the mother had wished things to be different. It had come to her that she and her daughter were to see the turning over of one century into another, and that this was a remarkable occasion. The child, to whom the mother frequently told beautiful stories of a magic world that, fortunately, made the 'real world' truly appear a thing of sawdust and lies, became filled by her mother's excitement. And so they planned a small feast. To this end the mother had saved, and this evening, released early from her hell, she had gone about the shop and market eagerly. There was now in her basket fresh bread and a portion of butter, some cheese, and cold meats, an onion, herbs and apples; milk and chocolate. This was satisfactory, but still all was not quite well. She had wanted to buy the child a gift. In vain, the mother had looked into the glass walls, like prisms of ice, the windows of the better shops. She had seen velvet dresses and sequined fans, and toys without number, brilliant and entrancing. And all of them as far beyond her means as the Milky Way.

At last she turned to go back, knowing she must not be too late, or the child would be frightened, aware too of the storybook cliché; she had become the poor slattern who cannot afford, for her bastard child, a starry present. And now a benign witch should step down from thin air, and offer her this present, because it was the hour for it, the moment, this sinister and sorceress night between two vast rifts of time. And the mother laughed a bitter tiny laugh. Her dreams were full of loveliness, and this she had imparted, unsullied, to her child, her poor, skinny, ugly little child that she loved so much. But though she might pass the wonder on, in her heart it had died. She had been forced to believe at last in reality.

Halfway up the hill, the mother paused. The sky was all dark now and she saw the old clock tower in this darkness, lit too with a misty light in its crown. Nearby, at the gates of a little park, by the glimmer of lanterns, a few persons were selling things.

The mother went closer, unsure, not wanting to linger. There were pictures in cheap frames, not well-painted, and this made her quite sad, for either the artists had not troubled, or else they had no talent for this work, and had not yet found out their proper talent. Also there was various bric-a-brac, and some rickety chairs despoiled from some lost home. At the end of the line waited an old man, shabby and bent over, with long gray hair. Before him on the ground stood a box, and out of it, as the mother drew close, he produced two bright small objects. These he held out to her, and as he did so, his face lifted from the shadow. She had been about to flinch aside, but the look of him stayed her inadvertently. How handsome he was, he must in his youth have been a prince among men. Her heart actually fluttered because ten years before, she had been something of a gem herself.

"Dolls for you, madame. Two lovely ladies. For your children."

The mother looked down, and there they were, the dolls. Plainly they were sisters, and she saw at once one was a few years older than the other. Their sweet faces were pale, and shaped as the faces of two cats, and their great smoky eyes had been rimmed by gilt. From two gilt hats furled long milky plumes. Their dainty china hands were an iota larger than their perfect little feet encased in charcoal shoes with gilded heels. Around their throats were somber ruffs edged with glitter. The elder had dark curls and a dress of rose satin. The younger was blond, and clad in aquamarine silk. Beneath the skirts glimpsed some creamy layers of lace.

"Yes, madame. Now, how can you refuse? Think how your children will delight in them."

"Just my daughter, monsieur," said the mother, surprising herself. She did not often now confide in anyone.

"Ah, just your daughter," repeated the old man. One of his eyes had a drooping lid, a sort of wink. It seemed to say: I knew all along but we must pretend, mustn't we?

"She would love them," said the mother.

"Then surely she should have them. The world teaches that denial is good, but this is one of the great lies. Fulfillment is good, providing no one is harmed. And the truly happy do no harm."

The mother's eyes burnt as if they had filled with tears, but they had not. She said, tentatively, "How much is it you're asking?"

The old man spoke a price. It was quite cheap.

The mother thought she could go without stockings for another month. What did stockings matter?

"Then I could afford one of them."

"Ah now, madame. Could you be so heartless as to part them? They're sisters, as you can see."

"I can only afford one doll," said the mother, firming herself, as she forever had to.

The old man said, "Well, tomorrow is another century, or perhaps we shall be swallowed by a star, as some have predicted. So, I'll give you both my dolls for the price of one. My box is empty. These are the last. Tomorrow I go far away. Two for one."

"Are you certain?" said the mother.

The old man looked at her again. His winking eye said, Come now, you know I don't say what I don't mean. Don't you remember, three hundred years ago, when you and I, both of us young and fair, danced on a floor like ice, with champagne in our blood and wings on our feet?

The mother blushed faintly. She fumbled for her purse, and found the money and handed it to him. He bowed to her as a count would do to a princess. Then he put the two dolls gently down into her basket, laying them between the bread and chocolate, between the staff of life and the sweet unneeded comfort that life makes so necessary.

As he did this, she beheld an odd ring on his hand. It was set with a miniature skull, carved presumably from bone. Sallow and ominous. She did not care for it and wondered if this meant some bad thing, and she should beware. Her embarrassment altered into slight fearfulness, and she thanked him and quickly turned away.

She was almost apprehensive as she went on, that he would now call loudly after her, demanding more money, perhaps with a harsh and sneering laugh. He did not. And as she turned upward into the leaning canted rows of ancient houses, slums now, mostly all darkened after the carnival of lights below, she saw the stars visible overhead. She pulled her skimpy scarf from her neck to cover the dolls, lest some thief notice their finery. She had the urge, as she did so, to explain to them what she did. But she had learned not to talk to inanimate objects.

W̲HEN SHE reached home, she found the child anxiously waiting in the larger of their two rooms, but the anxiety was, this time, more of impatience than unease, because the child too had been busy.

She had washed and dressed herself in her best frock, and undone her long rat's tails of hair, and combed them. Then she had laid the table with the embroidered cloth kept for birthdays, and put out the cutlery and the plates and cups. Obviously, too, the child had been setting aside some of her slight allowance of money, which was meant to gain her a glass of milk and a piece of bread during the school day, or a fruit or cake on her days of holiday. In the middle of the table, stuck to an azure saucer, was a tall vanilla candle marked with the hours from eight until midnight. And by it, some primroses gleamed in a bottle. All the shabby furniture had been dusted and the cushions plumped up and a painted shawl spread on the best chair. Their two pictures, one of which showed knights riding beneath a balcony of graceful women, and the other one, a lion asleep, had been decorated by paper bows. Best of all perhaps, in the narrow window hung a string of paper birds, superbly cut out and colored by the child herself, in secret, with sequins winking on their wings.

"Oh," said the mother.

"Do you like it? Do you?" asked the child. Her mother was the only one in the world to whom she ever dared to offer anything of herself.

"Oh yes— oh yes. It's so pretty—it's so exactly right.

And the candle! And the wonderful birds. But you didn't have your milk—"

"Yes," said the child, "every other day."

They regarded each other solemnly. Man has never lived by bread alone, and these two both knew it very well. The mother conceded the child's common sense, and better yet, her uncrushed imagination, her ability to ascend. Then the child darted to her and they embraced. It had been a terrible blow to them both that, due to the dangerous nature of the house stairs, the child was no longer able to fly down them and meet her mother at the lower door.

"I have a surprise for you," said the mother presently, "but I want to take it into the bedroom and wrap it up for you. You must have it at midnight. And after dinner you should have an hour's sleep, so you're awake when the century crosses over."

"Oh no," said the child. "I won't need to sleep before. There's no school in the morning. You promised not."

"So I did. No, no horrid school. No horrible shop. We'll stay up until one in the morning, and then we'll sleep until ten."

They gave a mutual cry of happiness and victory. For a moment the foulness of Reality fell down and was trampled underfoot by two pairs of slender feet, both in ill-fitting shoes.

As the mother wrapped the two dolls carefully in silvery paper, in the cramped, damp-darkened bedroom, she heard the child bustling about, washing the salad of herbs in a basin, cutting up the onion and apple and heating the oil in the pan.

The dolls were so beautiful, and so pleasant to touch, to eye and fingers like lakoum to the mouth, honeyed, soothing, voluptuous, nearly drugged. The child would love them utterly, for she loved beautiful things. The mother acknowledged, with vague shame, that her child thought she too, the mother, very beautiful. But the mother knew that she was not, and knew that the child was not, except to her mother.

However, when the apple and onion were fried, and put with meat and cheese, and the bread and butter set out, and the hour candle duly lit, and the cranky gas lowered, they sat there in a sort of glow, eyes luminous and cheeks warm, laughing and telling silly stories that made them shake with mirth. And when the hot chocolate was prepared for dessert, and the mother added a dash of brandy, they became quite drunk and began to talk to each other of kings and enchantresses, as if they knew them well, which in a way they did.

(Only once or twice, did the mother think of the curious skull ring the old man had worn. She had been taught fairly remorselessly that nothing good could ultimately come of anything, even of joy. With great skill she still tried to push this lesson from her. The old man did not matter at all. Only the present of the two beautiful dolls.)

They found it really quite easy to keep awake, although both had had to rise about six that morning. It was after all a night that arrived only once in a hundred years. They sang, and danced even, pecking round on the worn carpet to three hummed waltz tunes. When a wind blew up over the city, as if responding to the speed with which now — it was after eleven — Paradis rushed toward the future, the paper birds flew about on their strings. And the mother realized that perhaps her child could have been clever if she had been given some chance. And it seemed to her that possibly she could save to have the child's eyes looked at, and glasses prescribed, and, even if this should mean more cruelty and invective for the child to endure, it might also permit her to learn more. And the mother would not remember just then that the teachers in the poor school were ignorant and useless, at best stupid and at worst monsters, and glasses might not help at all since there was not much of worth to be seen with them.

By five minutes to midnight, when they had made a second chocolate with a second wisp of brandy, the mother was childishly dreaming that there was a way to be found through the labyrinth of terrors. It was the food and the chocolate, the brandy and the flying birds. But she did not remind herself of that.

Tonight they were a queen and a princess. They could feast and stay up late, and tomorrow sleep on, regardless of the dictates of the world.

"Mama — it's true. The bells are ringing!"

They went to the window hand in hand, and looked out into the clustered dark which was, one moment dense and impenetrable, and next— alive, alight, blazing like a sudden morning. From somewhere a thousand extra lights were born, actually from the very meanest windows, where in a sudden unreasoning festival of amazement, the despairing doomed and damned had all at once thrown off the darkness and reached out to the promise of hope. And in the sky a thousand other lights were breaking, pink stars and gilded, hail of tinsel, fireworks like flakes of the moon. The clocks struck and the bells clamored, and up from the city rose all the pent screams of arrival and astonished greeting, as if every citizen was only in that instant born.

The threshold had been passed. The sky had not fallen and the earth still bore everything up. The moment had come — and was gone.

"Isn't it wonderful?" said the child.

"Yes," said the mother. "Yes."

And they opened the window to hear the noises better, the car horns and the whistles and trumpets, the dogs barking in front, the smashing of glasses for good luck.

"And now," said the mother. She put the silvery package into the palms of her child. The child parted the paper carefully.

The mother stood as if high up or faraway, watching her child. She saw a shadow spread over the face of the child. The child stood speechless. She was too old for dolls. The mother had misjudged. How could she have been so foolish as to buy them? They were shoddy, this was the reason for their inexpensiveness. An awful mistake.

The child said, stiffly, "They're more lovely than anything." She looked up at her mother. The child's face had changed with the passing of the century. What was it? "Their names," said the child, "are Miralda and Dianelle."

"Do you like them?"

"Yes," said the child.

Abruptly the mother saw what had happened. It was not disappointment. One of the great shocks of existence had occurred. The child was in love.

The mother went to her, and gently, almost timorously, touched her hair. The mother did not touch the dolls any more. They had become attached to the child, as if by strings of metal, and gone with the child away, into a cube of crystal.

ONE OF THE REASONS for festivals is the belief that through them, something may change for the better, that by toasting a new year it may bring different and kinder fortune, that a corner has been turned, a door gone through. Most humans hold to this dream stubbornly, and when it is finally, utterly lost, they grow old.

The mother credited herself with having grown up.

Yet, the festival had galvanized her, and when a couple of days later she found herself back in her awful place of work, with everything gray and abysmal about her still, some inner child in her that was herself, raged and wept. This is the price that hope extracts. Hope is one of the best gifts, but also one of the harshest masters.

Because she had returned a day late, on pretense of illness, her colleagues had a story that the Imbecile had been sick with drink. She had been seen, they jeered, soliciting sailors on the antique quay of the Angel, only the basest of whom would go with her because she was so unappealing.

The mother bore this because she had to. But as the days and weeks went by, and nothing improved, chalk was rubbed into her threadbare coat, and coins stolen from her purse, she found herself struggling with her own pain. This was much harder, for by now something had truly been changed, and for the worse.

There had always existed solace for the mother in her child. At this stage, without the child, the mother would probably have sunk much lower, even under the river, maybe. And the child too had needed the mother. Now however, the child was otherwise absorbed.

At first, the mother was captivated, on coming in, to find the child there playing with the two dolls, Miralda and Dianelle. This play involved the table, and the piling up of some books, or the placing of the fern from under the window, a lamp, cards, perhaps two thimbles of water, the painted shawl. The child greeted her mother affectionately, and did everything she was asked, even cleared the table instantly. But when they sat to their supper of bread and coffee or thin soup, the dolls sat with them.

By the lamp's low light, their smoky eyes gleamed, their curls, dark and blond, glistened and their finery shone.

The child did not speak very much, unless questioned about the dolls.

Then they had all three been walking in the park, by the great fountains, and here Miralda, the elder of the dolls, had spoken to a handsome duke, who much admired her, but Dianelle had been more interested in sporting with her little dog. Or they had been to a theater, where half the audience rose to glimpse them, and seen there a wonderful performance in five acts, and in the intervals they had eaten sugar almonds and marzipan, and drunk transparent wine. Sometimes they had stayed home, however, in their mansion, where marble statues held torches, and there was a domed conservatory up three hundred steps, from which it was possible to observe, through a telescope, the planets of other galaxies.

The mother listened, in delight herself, to the child's inventions. In the past, it had been she, the mother, who had told the stories. And for awhile the twenty-seven-year-old woman, bent and elderly and worn out as a glove, had been lifted from herself and floated there, her eyes fixed without focus on flighty Dianelle and wise Miralda, partaking of their freedoms, decorum, education, and opulence. Through a sort of shimmering haze she saw them, like candlelight. She almost fancied that their heads would graciously turn upon their white necks in the somber ruffs, or that, when the child lifted them to show them dance, they did so.

But in the end, the child grew more reticent. She would say now only that all was well, that tonight Miralda and Dianelle were to take her to another country. This, when pressed, she would explain to be a very cold one, with mountains diademed by ice, or a very hot one where enormous beasts prowled and parrots laughed in the cinnamon trees. Or there would be cities with minarets. Or a sea where temples came down into the waves.

"In your dreams," said the mother, at last.

"If you like," said the child.

And this cool little phrase turned the mother aside, as if now she had spoken in the wrong language, the language of a stranger.

Sometimes the mother would wake too, in the big bed, and see, as if miles away, the child quietly sleeping. Previously the child had been inclined to snore in her sleep from winter congestion, but now she was so still that, once or twice, with a pang of fear, the mother bent over her to see that she breathed. And on the pillow sat the dolls, Miralda, Dianelle, like two little fairies or angels set to act sentinel. How hard their eyes in the packed darkness, hard as tears that had become granite. The mother remembered that, unlike other dolls, they did not smile, and she recalled they had no color in their cheeks.

Somewhere away within her own skull, the child was dancing, boating, riding in bright carriages or on the backs of dove-skin horses. Miralda was introducing her to painters, poets, and musicians. Dianelle was guiding her through picnics of frosted sweetmeats and champagne. How old was the child in these dreams? Perhaps the timeless age of a doll, between maiden and baby.

"And what did you eat?" the mother asked of the great dinner, where every goblet and plate had been of sheerest glass. The child told her of dishes from the Arabian Nights.

"And what dress did you wear?"

"Oh, it was silk. And I had pearls in my hair, and feathers."

The mother knew that in her dreams, and in her playing when awake with Miralda and Dianelle, the child was not without beauty—or, now, accomplishments, for one evening she had entered the apartment to find the child singing in a hoarse thin voice some song, she said—when asked—she had composed to her imaginary guitar.

. This waking and sleeping dream-world, then, initially appealing to the mother, began to unnerve her as it closed her outside.

There is always this problem, just as the real world is so often determinedly confused with the Real, so it is difficult to differentiate between others that are fantasy, or maybe madness.

Christ Himself seemed to have found this an obstacle with some of his listeners.

The mother began to brood upon what went on now with her child and the two dolls, bought so easily, on the Night of Passage.

Surely the child's complete immersion in their invented life could not be healthy, might indeed be a danger—but then what was there to offer in return?

She became lonely, too, the mother. Her child was considerate to her, the way a loving daughter would be, as she went into the distance, with new inspiring others.

There was no one to seek out for advice. For ten years or more, the mother had had adult conversation only with horrors, and what humanity sometimes calls beasts, forgetting beasts do not merit such connections.

Sometimes she tried to tempt the child to different things. A book of pictures bought at some cost, an outing. But the books were received with gratitude, and carried off to furnish more fuel for the adventures of Miralda and Dianelle. The outing could not compete with them. And the mother noted as well, a politeness in the child, a patience —not to hurt the kind parent who meant so well and could provide — so very little. Only now and then, some element would attract the child. And she would say, "Oh, Miralda's swans are like that one!" Or, "Dianelle came down in a ball gown just the color of the sky."

One night, as the mother walked home, about two months after the start of the new century, like many other nights, she found she had begun to cry. And she leaned on a wall, out of sight, lost as a girl of nine whose mother has left her.

THE MONTHS WENT BY. Spring fluttered down into Paradis, the new moon of seasons. The mother did her accounts carefully, for now the time was coming when the expense of the winter stove would be balanced by the summer turning of milk, and the sometimes undrinkable quality of the common tap water.

At the shop, the assistants found a new game, remarking that something had begun to smell. It was of course untrue, unless they scented the stench of their own souls. The mother bore with it, as ever. But she sensed now, abruptly, a day was drawing near when they would manage to oust her and what then would she do? Perhaps she might find work in the poisonous laundries, but these would probably kill her in a year, she was no longer physically strong.

That evening she returned to the tenement, with some fruit and chocolate that was bought in a fit of recklessness, feeling her death, the death of everything, although the spring night was fresh and starred by buds.

When she opened the apartment door, fear leapt at her throat.

There at the table sat the child, still as stone, and down her face the tears were streaming, pouring, like rain.

"What is it?" cried the mother. And she ran forward,

and grasped the child, as if to get between her and whatever novel dreadful force was now at work

"No, Mama, I'm safe. I am. No, nothing happened to me." The child held the mother as protectively as the mother held the child. This the mother became aware of, and reassured somewhat, loosened her grip.

"What, then?"

The child indicated the table. The mother now saw it — she had seen nothing in the room but the child until that moment.

There, on the softest cushion, lay the elder doll, Miralda. She was stretched on her back with her arms at her sides. Her curls and the plumes of her hat framed her pale exquisite face. Beside her had been positioned the other doll, Dianelle, sitting stoically upright. The hard clear eyes of both of them reflected the lamp, but in a glassy, sightless way, like the eyes of a dead fish.

"Miralda died," said the child softly.

"But —" said the mother. She checked herself at once. "How terrible."

"She was very old," said the child, still weeping, but without any expression, and the mother noticed oddly that her nose did not run — she wept herself like a weeping doll. "Older than she seemed. Much, much."

"Yes," said the mother humbly. "And poor Dianelle must be so sad."

"Dianelle is dying too. She told me, when I found Miralda. Only a few hours."

"But can't she be saved?" said the mother, unaccountably, perhaps anxious now. "They're great ladies, Miralda, Dianelle. Some important physician — "

"There's no cure. They're so old. They've done such a lot," said the child.

The mother shuddered. She wondered, caught herself

wondering, if Dianelle would require a priest And, horribly, unavoidably, if she herself would want one, at her own deathbed.

As if the child knew what she thought, or some of it, she said, "There's no need for any fuss. They're not frightened. Dianelle told me, only the body dies. And she wants to be with Miralda. She always has been."

SUDDENLY THE MOTHER GLIMPSED — absurd, fearsome — what it was that alarmed her. The child, contained in this world of dream and fantasy, had become one with the two dolls. If they died — what did she expect for herself? Before she could resist the impulse, the mother touched the forehead of her child, to test for fever.

"No, no, Mama," the child said again, very gently. "I'm quite well."

The mother got up. She stood there, and did not know what to do. At length, she made the chocolate, and put the cup beside her daughter's hand. The child's tears had ceased.

"Drink what you can."

The child nodded, tasted the cup, and set it down.

The mother withdrew to the bedroom, and here she took out some stockings that needed to be darned. As she did this, she began to pray. She reckoned herself peculiar, foolish, an imbecile for sure, for, although she did not now believe in God, or thought Him wicked, she would always pray to Him in her direst moments. It seemed to her there had never been any answer, except perhaps further punishment. And yet, to speak to Him eased her. Of course, there was no one else to whom she could turn.

After about two hours, she stole out, and saw that the child was sitting as before, with the cold chocolate congealing beside her. Both dolls now lay on the cushion.

Mysteriously, aptly, the lamp was burning low. It was a room of shadows and mourning.

"Oh—" said the mother.

"It's over now," said the child, almost the words of the Cross. The mother clasped her hands together. "But we must bury them," said the child.

The mother cast about her mind wildly. She must not upset the child further. But what was to be done? And in the center of her confusion a voice rose in her, which said, What nonsense. Throw the things out with the rubbish. Or better still, sell them in the market. This voice, which had the exact tones of her colleagues' in the hell-shop, she recognized immediately and pushed from her with enormous invisible violence. And it seemed to her she saw the voice falling miles down, back into some pit.

"There's a paper box," said the mother. "Do you remember — I brought it from the shop to keep gloves in. It is only paper, but if they're wrapped in the painted shawl — will that do?" Her own voice was full of apology and pleading.

The child said, "Oh, yes."

"And tomorrow we can go to some place where there's — some open space. And I can put the box into the earth."

The child looked up now. She smiled at her mother. "We can keep the box," she said. "It will be all right. You see, really the funeral will have carriages made of glass and dark horses with plumes, and hundreds of people will walk behind. And there will be a mass, with two thousand candles."

"Yes," said the mother.

But then she fetched the box, and put into it the painted shawl, that was the only thing which remained of the colored, lighted days, ten years before. The child lifted the dolls into this cocoon, and quickly covered their faces. Then the lid was put down.

They lowered the box into the deepest drawer of their chest, where it need not be disturbed.

And then they stood there, in the gloom of the bedroom as mourners do, at a loss, once the coffin has gone down into its hole.

Later, when they had eaten their bread and cheese, and were in bed, the mother lay awake. She was not afraid, but full of an ominous sadness, a sickening uncertainty. Beside her the child slept, silently as now she always did.

Finally the dawn remade the sky and the noises of the day commenced in the street below. The child woke, and said softly, "Mama, may I have a book — a book with words to read?"

"Yes, my love. But you know how trying it is for your poor eyes —we'll go to see a doctor soon."

"My eyes are much better, Mama, I can even see the things on the blackboard at school."

The mother did not believe this, but she did not say so. She promised the book. She had partly noticed the child's knuckles were not so often split open and bruised by rulers, but she had put this down to a random upsurge of mislaid humanity in the teachers.

While they drank their coffee, she watched the child surreptitiously. The child seemed calm, no longer distressed or tearful.

She has forgotten it, the mother thought, hopefully. *And she has grown out of the dolls. That's good. It must be good.*

THE END CAME VERY SIMPLY.

By then it was summer, hot and steamy in the lower city as if Paradis lay in the heart of a primordial swamp, as once it had.

Entering the shop, at the usual early hour, the mother met one of the assistants skipping toward her, while the others waited, leering and sneering.

"*Monsieur* wants to see you."

It has come. Oh God, what shall I do?

But in the wooden bravery of despair, the mother went without delay to a dingy room, where the overseer of hell awaited her, his congested face swollen further with displeasure.

"You are to go and see someone. You're to go now. I don't like it. I won't be told what's what in this way."

The mother poised before him, astonished.

He thrust at her a letter, and she read it, but it made no sense. "Go on, go on," cried Monsieur, flapping her off.

Outside, the colleagues clustered. "Got shot of you, has he, Imbecile? Oh what a shame!"

The mother did not speak. She sat down on a chair, while they capered around her.

"Want some brandy, do you? You'll be lucky. You can have some of my snot if you like!" And at this witticism they were so convulsed they barely saw her pass out of the door, which perhaps peeved them later, for they were never to see her do it again, or pass in, for that matter.

At a small office on another street, the mother was treated more humanly, if with equal patronage. These, too, supposed her slow or retarded. At least the facts were persuaded into her.

Then she walked away, up through the city wandering, not knowing where she was, and as this went on she seemed to catch sight momentarily of bizarre things, a bird that flew about with wings of softest fire, an arching rainbow, pink and honey, that described the towers of the cathedral, a boat on the river with dragonfly sails, a car driven by a bear.

Finally she went into a café and ordered aniseed liqueur that she had not tasted in ten years. And this she drank, startled at herself. And when she burst into laughter, the waiters thought her tipsy, but only smiled, because she was a good-looking woman, worth a glance or two, and why should such an interesting woman not drink a liqueur at nine in the morning?

After the liqueur the mother knew where she must go and there she went, to the tumbling swarthy house that held her daughter's school.

The children had just been let out for some recreation, which entailed sitting in a shadeless yard with three stone walls to look at and, over one of those, the unswept street. A single child, however, was seated on a bench, and another girl was holding up over this child's head a dilapidated sunshade. Like a little queen she sat there, the favored one, and others sat at her feet, two cutting up an apple and a pear for her, and another begging for something, this was quite evident from her gestures. Then all the girls begged too. Suddenly the seated child began to sing. She had a sweet high voice, a voice like that of a well-tuned instrument. The song she sang the mother did not know, and yet it entranced her, as if it had come from some place where she had been in dreams, some marvelous country forgotten through amnesia, and now glimpsed once again with a pang of memory, nostalgia, and wild excitement.

The other children were also affected by this singing. They drew in close, craning, their eyes fixed on the child who had the bench. Even the rough boys, who played on, tussling, ceased to make any noise. Had they been older, they would have listened frankly.

When the song was over, there was a space of silence,

and then the mother, half-embarrassed, raised her own voice and called to her child.

The girl on the bench got up instantly, and came running over to her.

But as she came, the mother saw it all, all that she had not seen. How the child's hair was full and shining, her skin like porcelain, the soft flush at her cheeks, the deep shade of her eyes. And in those few seconds, like an hour of careful thought, the mother beheld not only how her child was changed, but saw through her, as if through clearest water, to what she would become. She saw her lifted up upon some spire of celebrity and dancing in the sky, with pale emeralds on her fingers, and Paradis at her feet; the world at her feet.

"I've something to tell you. It's wonderful."

"Yes," said the child. She was not surprised, only ready. She expected the best news.

"An elderly lady used to come into the shop. She was so courteous, old-fashioned. The others were so rude to her. Poor creature, she died. But oh — she's left me some money. A lot of money."

"Oh, yes," said the child, happy, not surprised.

"She didn't know me, you see. She said that I was kind to her."

As they looked at each other, the woman and her daughter, they were not privy to what else the elderly lady had bequeathed. The pretty little bow-tied presents soon to be delivered to all the remaining assistants in the shop. Which each contained the turds of dogs and other, even more prolific, animals.

They did not know, or need to know, the woman and her daughter. They were already quite busy talking of the small house they would inhabit, with milk-washed walls and polished floors, with mirrors having pictures of butterflies in their corners, and the knights and ladies, and the lion, in areas of honor above a piano, overlooking the walled garden with tea-roses. Nor had they forgotten the three or four rats, the white one particularly, and planned how they might be induced to move with them from the tenement.

As the mother and her child went away from that school, the pupils grouped by the wall, looking out like convicts, watching two freed prisoners escape. They had only the apple left to them, the convicts, and the pear. Which they ate, and so had no more.

LOVE CAN TAKE many forms. Even that of a perfect and beautiful man, abused and whipped, bleeding and asphyxiating on a cross. Love is bewildering.

In the night the young woman woke and got out of bed, leaving her daughter sleeping. She went by stealth to the chest and from it she took the coffin, the paper box, and carried it, closing the bedroom door behind her, into the outer room.

Here she lit the gas, and taking one breath, drew off the box's lid, and delicately pulled away the folds of her shawl.

Not much was left of Miralda and Dianelle. Some threads of their glamorous dresses, aquamarine, rosy, some sprinkles of gilt, their dainty shoes. And there was some sawdust, such as might be used to fill the interior parts of dolls. Other than this, there were only two tiny skulls, about the size of acorns, well-shaped, complete in every way, even to the minuscule teeth, which were charmingly clean and wholesome, like seed-pearls, though otherwise the bone had darkened.

QUEENS IN CRIMSON

WE CLIMB the steps of the castle, my husband and I.
We go slowly, for I am soon out of breath. Sometimes he
will forget and hurry up the steep stone treads two at a
time, leaving me to come on at my own pace. Then, courteously, he hesitates. In his face, as he watches me
approach him, is the familiar mingling of contempt and
pleasure. Ten years older than I, he still finds me very
beautiful, or so he says.

The castle is, of course, magnificent. Its enormous
walls and towers, barbaric, impenetrable, dominate the
border. Below the rocky slopes fall into the valley and the
city, whose roofs shine pale copper and paler green in the
slanted afternoon sun. To the south, the mountains rise
with combs of snow. And above, the sky. The castle is
almost like a natural thing but inside the stone rooms are
more recent modernizations of the fifteenth and sixteenth
centuries, carved furniture and stands of huge candles,
carpets from the East, windows of crystal, and opaque
glass, coloured like blue flowers, blood, and treacle.
Within, the castle is clearly an artifice. But what else could
it be, for it was formerly the house of a king.

Ahead of us, the guide moves, pointing out many
things, which the scatter of tourists, and my husband,
understand, for they speak the language of this country, as
I do not. I have often wished and tried to learn various lan-
guages, but have never been able to master more than a
few standard phrases, all of which I can only speak with a
stutter, although normally I do not stutter at all. Curiously,

my accent is often quite good, good enough that, here, once or twice, when I have been forced to utter one of my phrases, (at my husband's insistence) the person addressed has assumed that either I am indigenous or fluent, and broken into a torrent of words incomprehensible to me. I have then stood, shaking my head, smiling and blushing a redhead's blush, moving my hands helplessly as if searching out some support in mid-air. I am locked, it seems, inside my own language, which, to some extent, I can bend to my will. It is as if I am afraid to learn another tongue, in case, then, I lose my ability with the original. My husband thinks that I am lazy and do not apply myself. He thinks this of me also in other areas, even in the area of my failure to conceive a child. Indeed, I have not tried to become pregnant, except by the basic formula of entering into the sexual act with him. Nor have I tried to prevent pregnancy. However, I have never wanted to be pregnant, never wanted to give birth to another human being. The notion fills me with surprised alarm. But to my husband, a child, or rather children, preferably one of each gender, have been a goal of his since his twenties. When our marriage had been decided and we had begun to make love, he told me that we would have children, and I had not argued. On some level I think I knew I would not, and perhaps deceived myself that he might come to be philosophical. Did I love him madly, promising him by my silence or acquiescence that I would do whatever he desired? Did I mislead him because I in turn desired him so much? No, I could not say that. He was handsome and rich, clever, an intellectual man of forty, with a wide experience of the world. I found him interesting, fascinating, physically very attractive. He admired me and was kind to me. He said he loved me. Probably, confronted by such perfection of person and luck, I had felt I could not refuse.

In the middle of the South Tower of the castle, we reach the suite of rooms that once belonged to the king's wife.

Below had already been seen the splendour of the armoury with all its extraordinary weapons, mail and banners, the banquet hall, the king's own apartments — strangely — inconveniently? — far off from those of his spouse. In the king's rooms were services of gold and cups of glass, Bibles with covers of silver, intricate tapestries, musical instruments of bewildering variety, also swords and bows, complex obscure games, the least of which was chess, even a canvas that purportedly the king himself had painted. For he had been, I already knew, a man of stature and genius. Elsewhere, but not here, I had been shown his portrait. Although in his middle years, he was a tall, muscular man, with a gorgeous leonine face framed in tassels of ripe gold hair. His eyes were narrow with vision, and his lips sensual. Behind him in the picture poised an angel, a unicorn, a stag, a lion, an eagle. The sun and moon stood in the sky together as, sometimes at evening, they do. He was good at everything. His skill in war and diplomacy, in sword-play and dance, gaming and wise talk were unrivalled. Not a single report of him could praise him enough. Besides, he painted beautifully, profoundly, and composed exquisite music. One of the loveliest airs of any era or time was his, and even now recordings are made of it. It is called: *The Red Gown*.

In the suite of the queen everything is quite different. The furniture is light and delicate, the walls hung with pastel things, the bed dressed in silk and gauze. There is a tiring table based on a classical design, and with a mirror of subaqueous greenish glass. By a stool leans only a little guitar of wheat-coloured wood.

The guide speaks to us, and, as always, I find myself

stupidly nodding, although I have not recognized a syllable. My husband cranes over and whispers loudly in my ear. "He says that the lute belonged to the second wife."

"Oh, yes."

"But the bed was arranged like this for the third."

I want to ask what evidence remains of the first wife, but my husband does not tell me; possibly the guide has not said.

The tourists turn to glance at me disparagingly. This had happened below. I am a foreigner who, arrogantly, has not bothered to learn the language.

From the queen's suite, a door gives on an oddly contemporary creation, a roof garden, laid out (my husband says) for the third wife. Trees rise in terra cotta pots, their heads each round as a globe. They cannot be the trees that were here then. A balustrade cuts off the massive descent to the courtyard below.

In a bird-cage sits a stuffed yellow bird, representing the pet of the third queen. It, the guide — my husband — says, died on the morning of her execution.

As everyone clusters about the marble bench that had been carved with maenads for the queen, I wander to the balustrade, and look over. Down there, all of seventy, eighty feet — I am bad at judging such things — she had come out into the white winter snow, and placing her forehead into the scoop of that small stone block, had had her neck sheared through by a honed steel sword.

My husband taps me impatiently on the shoulder. "What are you doing?"

"Looking at the block."

"That isn't the block, of course."

"I see."

"If only," he says, "you had tried to grasp the language. But then, I knew I'd have to take charge of you."

If it is not the block, what is it? A mounting stone perhaps, used by the knights of the king in bounding on to their horses. Some had done this to get away, the three who had made love to the three wives of the king.

My husband draws me back towards the guide, who shoots at me a look of aversion. But I have also, from time to time, intercepted such looks from my husband. Whenever, in fact, I remonstrate at his wishes, which, naturally, I seldom do. If I had always crossed him, would he have grown accustomed and forbearing?

I had been poor when we met, and for a short time after. He had come into the place of business where I worked, to see one of the directors. In passing, by error, through that long and dismal chamber, he had glimpsed me, noticing me first, no doubt, because of the astonishingly red shade of my hair. He said nothing, but later one of the women of the upper offices came down, and handed me a note. I was invited to call a particular number. Bemused, I did so. I thought I had been selected for some secretarial duty, and did not relish it, since I was not especially competent. Instead I heard the voice of an educated man, my future husband, who inquired if I would meet him that evening for a cocktail. I agreed. I had never resisted the sexual advances of important men in my working life, for I had seen the trouble resistance could lead to. When I entered the shadowy lounge of the hotel, where white death lilies stood like phantoms, I was expecting nothing but something mildly unpleasant, like a visit to the dentist for a routine filling. But I was greeted by someone elegant and beautiful, who handed me into a little gilded chair, plied me with red champagne, and later took me away in a silver car to a dinner of tiny delicious endless courses. He did not then sleep with me. He told me that I must learn his life and he would help me. He thought it would become me, and we should both see. In parting he kissed my cheek, and handed me an orchid so transparent that in the morning it was dead, killed simply by being alive.

There were many dinners after this. And many other things. I was removed from my job to a wonderful flat that overlooked the great park with its birches, planes and fountains. I was fitted for clothes. My red hair was re-styled, though left as long as ever. He wished to give me a dog, but I begged him not to. I was afraid for it, after the orchid. Living things should not be awarded between us — for that reason, perhaps, I was sure I would never conceive his child.

But somehow he took my refusal of a dog as a need to have instead him, and now that I had been creamed and smoothed and shaped to receive him, he told me we would marry, and led me to his bed. He informed me there I could never leave him after that. I had known as much.

He knew nothing of me. I do not mean that he had not had me investigated, obviously he had done that and maybe still does. But of me, nothing. I was for him a dream he had had in his youth. He would cherish me. He would make me his own. He would change me. I should benefit.

Half a decade has passed since our wedding, in a Byzantine church at the foot of a mountain. I have failed him. I am not clever. I do not like the books or music he values or the food he prefers. I am ordinary in sensual matters. I fail to arouse him now by anything other than my looks, and indeed, for me, I have not experienced interest, let alone orgasm with him, for five years. Evidently, I pretend. I think that he believes in my response, but reckons it limited, uncouth, possibly tasteless. And I have not become pregnant. He knows he is not at fault. He underwent some tests and learned that he is potent and fertile. I too am supposed to be fertile, but then I bribed the doctor to tell my husband this, not wanting to undergo the medical examination.

Suddenly the guide says something which, startlingly, because I know most of the words, I can understand.

"A lover reached this garden, using a rope."

I suck in my breath, but no one else does. Have I misinterpreted? Surely I have. How could the queen's lover have scaled this terrible tower on a rope? He would have been seen, certainly. Or fallen.

I think of the three queens of the king who composed *The Red Gown*, a melody which has lasted five centuries.

In the past, and again before we came here (my husband has always insisted that I read books on all the countries to which we travel) I have found the history of the three queens. Each was a redhead — the king, it seems, was partial to this fiery colouring — all redheads, but all different. The first was voluptuous, heavy, with a skin like milk and golden eyes. Her hair was the dark red of mahogany, and, unbound, it hung to her hips. She could sing, and singing one of the king's songs, she won his heart. He married her, and for a few years they lived happily. But she gave him no heir, and finally he concluded that she had borne a premature child in secret, by another man. He ordered her tried, and she was found guilty. Her body showed the marks of pregnancy and birth. On the morning of her execution, she was dressed in crimson, as the custom was, not to show any blood. Her long hair was bound up into a tower of gold. She went to the block with her hands on a prayer-book. She did not speak a word, and when her head fell, flowers sprang from the spots of gore that scattered on the yard.

The second queen was a slender princess of another land. She was given to the king and he loved her at once.

Her skin was pink, her hair was the red of Eastern amber, so fine that it was like rosy golden rain, and her eyes green. For a few years he adored her, but she did not conceive his heir, and then she too took a lover, in order to have from him what she could not get from the king. She was tried and found guilty. She was dragged to the block screaming and puking with terror, and all her hair came loose over the crimson gown, so that they had to cut her locks in the courtyard, before they could successfully decapitate her.

The third queen was a plump and olive-skinned slattern of the kitchen. The king was older then, and not so discriminating. She had black eyes, and her hair was ginger, like the spice, and curled, and was so long it reached her knees. She would wrap the king's member in it and he would lose control. For a few years she kept him happy, but her belly stayed flat as a plate. He came to be told she was a witch who practised against him, had several lovers, including the Devil, and could not get with child since her womb had been neutralized by sorcerous intercourse. She was tried, found guilty, and sent to the block. She had already cut off her hair herself, and burned it on the fire, when she glided out upon the white snow in her crimson dress, and lay down on the block, smiling. It took four strokes of the honed sword to sever her neck. After she was dead, the executioner threw himself off the castle wall, ashamed at having botched the job, or nervous of demons.

"See, up there," says my husband, "that is the window from which the king watched the beheading of his wives. He contrived to have an exact image, the glass is magnified." He smirks strangely. Something in all this pleases him. I have never thought he liked women, only the way they look, the feel and scent of them, the fruit of their bodies. His total power upon and over them.

The window is extremely high, set with seemingly plain, cloudy glass. It reminds me of the windows in the street of shops where once I tried to buy him a present. It was something I was sure he would care for, a rare old book, and although I purchased it with money which he himself paid into my allowance, even so that money was supposed by then to be mine. However, my husband was not impressed by the book. He explained to me that he already had a copy of it in his library, a copy far older and more valuable, and that this any way might be a fake. Someone returned the book and I was given a cheque for the money I had spent.

It was in this same street, a month later, that I met a young man with wild dark hair. I forget his name, but I remember his white thin body very well. He was the first of my three lovers. I have only had three, and each only for one afternoon.

The guide is saying something about the view now. I recognize the word *view*.

We stare out across the valley and the city, with its pretty roofs, out at the mountains. Beyond them is another country, to which my husband says he wishes to go tomorrow. He turns now to look at me and I feel his eyes on my face, but make believe I do not know. I can picture his gaze. It is half evaluating. He says the new country is lawless and dangerous. This seems to inspire him. Last night he gave me a necklace of rubies, such crimson stones, and requested that I wear it as he performed the act of sex with me.

The guide has finished. The tourists are pressing tips into his hand, but my husband does not do so, he does not believe in tipping. Instead he graciously bows to the guide, and we return into the suite, and next begin to descend the stairs of the tower.

"How lovely you are," he says to me, quite loudly, the way he translated what the guide said, when he thought I should know it. "I could never let you go." His hand presses on the back of my neck like a blunt blade which may be sharpened.

We come down and out at last, into the awful courtyard. Some of them are staring at the block which my husband says is not the block of the executions. But it is sunny, and birds are calling over the castle tops.

"Wouldn't it be bizarre," he says, more quietly now, "if you had finally consented to become pregnant while we were here? That is, in the hotel," he adds, in case in my foolishness I might think he means it had happened without penetration, by magic, at the castle.

"Yes," I say. Recently, I never argue.

But I have not become pregnant and I never will, by my husband. Last night I dissolved, in his brandy and soda, the undetectable capsule my third lover, the doctor, told me how to obtain. I saw my husband drink it down. It takes twenty-four hours to work. After midnight, in his sleep most likely, my husband will suffer a fatal heart attack. I will find him dead beside me in the morning. Most of his wealth will presently be mine — if I want it, which I am not sure that I do.

A fresh wind blows the yellow flowers on the rocky slopes under the castle. Tendrils of my hair flutter across my eyes and I brush them back. Behind us someone shuts a door with a colossal clang.

ALL THE BIRDS OF HELL

1

ONCE THEY LEFT the city, the driver started to talk. He went on talking during the two-hour journey, almost without pause. His name was Argenty, but the dialogue was all about his wife. She suffered from what had become known as Twilight Sickness. She spent all day in their flat staring at the electric bulbs. At night she walked out into the streets and he would have to go and fetch her. She had had frostbite several times. He said she had been lovely twenty years ago, though she had always hated the cold.

Henrique Tchaikov listened. He made a few sympathetic sounds. It was as hopeless to try to communicate with the driver, Argenty, as to shut him up. Normally Argenty drove important men from the Bureau, to whom he would not be allowed to speak a word, probably not even Good-day. But Tchaikov was a minor bureaucrat. If Argenty had had a better education and more luck, he might have been where Tchaikov was.

Argenty's voice became like the landscape beyond the cindery cement blocks of the city, monotonous, inevitably irritating, depressing, useless, sad.

It was the fifteenth year of winter.

Now almost forty, Tchaikov could remember the other seasons of his childhood, even one long hot summer full of liquid colors and now-forgotten smells. By the time he was twelve years old, things were changing forever. In his twenties he saw them go, the palaces of summer, as Eynin called them in his poetry. Tchaikov had been twenty-four when he watched the last natural flower, sprung pale green out of the public lawn, die before him — as Argenty's wife was dying, in another way.

The Industrial Winter, so it was termed. The belching chimneys and the leaking stations with their cylinders of poison. The rotting hulks along the shore like deadly whales.

"The doctor says she'll ruin her eyes, staring at the lights all day," Argenty droned on.

"There's a new drug, isn't there — " Tchaikov tried.

But Argenty took no notice. Probably, when alone, he talked to himself.

Beyond the car, the snowscape spread like heaps of bedclothes, some soiled and some clean. The gray ceiling of the sky bulged low.

Argenty broke off. He said, "There's the wolf factory."

Tchaikov turned his head.

Against the grayness-whiteness, the jagged black of the deserted factory which had been taken over by wolves, was the only landmark.

"They howl often, sound like the old machinery. You'll hear them from the Dacha."

"Yes, they told me I would."

"Look, some of them running about there."

Tchaikov noted the black forms of the wolves, less black than the factory walls and gates, darting up and over the snow heaps, and away around the building. Although things did live out here, it was strange to see something alive.

Then they came down the slope, the chained snow tires grating and punching, and Tchaikov saw the mansion across the plain.

"The river came in here," said Argenty. "Under the ice now."

A plantation of pine trees remained about the house. Possibly they were dead, carved out only in frozen snow. The Dacha had two domed towers, a balustraded verandah above a flight of stairs that gleamed like white glass. When the car drove up, he could see two statues at the foot of the steps that had also been kept clear of snow. They were of a stained brownish marble, a god and goddess, both naked and smiling through the brown stains that spread from their mouths.

There were electric lights on in the Dacha, from top to bottom, three or four floors of them, in long, arched windows.

But as the car growled to a halt, Argenty gave a grunt. "Look," he said again, "look. Up there."

They got out and stood on the snow. The cold broke round them like sheer disbelief, but they knew it by now. They stared up. As happened only very occasionally, a lacuna had opened in the low cloud. A dim pink island of sky appeared, and over it floated a dulled lemon slice, dissolving, half transparent, the sun.

Argenty and Tchaikov waited, transfixed, watching in silence. Presently the cloud folded together again and the sky, the sun, vanished.

"I can't tell her," said Argenty. "My wife. I can't tell her I saw the sun. Once it happened in the street. She began to scream. I had to take her to the hospital. She wasn't the only case."

"I'm sorry," said Tchaikov.

He had said this before, but now for the first time Argenty seemed to hear him. "Thank you."

Argenty insisted on carrying Tchaikov's bag to the top of the slippery gleaming stair, then he pressed the buzzer. The door was of steel and wood, with a glass panel of octuple glazing, almost opaque. Through it, in the bluish yellow light, a vast hall could just be made out, with a floor of black and white marble.

A voice spoke through the door apparatus.

"Give your name."

"Henrique Tchaikov. Number sixteen stroke Y."

"You're late."

Tchaikov stood on the top step, explaining to a door. He was enigmatic. There was always a great deal of this.

"The road from Kroy was blocked by an avalanche. It had to be cleared."

"All right. Come in. Mind the dog, she may be down there."

"Dog," said Argenty. He put his hand into his coat for his gun.

"It's all right," said Tchaikov. "They always keep a dog here."

"Why?" said Argenty blankly.

Tchaikov said, "A guard dog. And for company, I suppose."

Argenty glanced up, toward the domed towers. The walls were reinforced by black cement. The domes were tiled black, mortared by snow. After the glimpse of sun, there was again little color in their world.

"Are they — is it up there?"

"I don't know. Perhaps."

"Take care," said Argenty surprisingly as the door made its unlocking noise.

Argenty was not allowed to loiter. Tchaikov watched him get back into the car, undo the dash panel and take a swig of vodka. The car turned and drove slowly away, back across the plain.

The previous curator did not give Tchaikov his name. He was a tall thin man with slicked, black hair. Tchaikov knew he was known as Ouperin.

Ouperin showed Tchaikov the map of the mansion, and the pamphlet of house rules. He only mentioned one, that the solarium must not be used for more than one hour per day; it was expensive. He asked if Tchaikov had any questions, wanted to see anything. Tchaikov said it would be fine.

They met the dog in the corridor outside the ballroom, near where Ouperin located what he called his office.

She was a big dog, perhaps part Cuvahl and part Husky, muscular and well-covered, with a thick silken coat like the thick pile carpets, ebony and fawn, with white round her muzzle and on her belly and paws, and two gold eyes that merely slanted at them for a second as she galloped by.

"Dog! Here, dog!" Ouperin called, but she ignored him, prancing on, with balletic shakes of her fringed fur, into the ballroom, where the crystal chandeliers hung down twenty feet on ropes of bronze. "She only comes when she's hungry. There are plenty of steaks for her in the cold room. She goes out a lot," said Ouperin. "Her door's down in the kitchen. Electronic. Nothing else can get in."

They visited the cold room, which was very long and massively shelved, behind a sort of airlock. The room was frigid, the natural weather was permitted to sustain it. The ice on high windows looked like armor.

Ouperin took two bottles of vodka, and a bunch of red grapes, frozen peerless in a wedge of ice.

They sat in his office, along from the ballroom. A fire blazed on the hearth.

"I won't say I've enjoyed it here," said Ouperin. "But there are advantages. There are some — videos and magazines in the suite. You know what I mean. Apart from the library. If you get . . . hot."

Tchaikov nodded politely.

Ouperin said, "The first thing you'll do, when I go. You'll go up and look at them, won't you?"

"Probably," said Tchaikov.

"You know," said Ouperin, "you get bored with them. At first, they remind you of the fairy story, what is it? The princess who sleeps. Then, you just get bored."

Tchaikov said nothing. They drank the vodka, and at seventeen hours, five o'clock, as the white world outside began to turn glowing blue, a helicopter came and landed on the plain. Ouperin took his bags and went out to the front door of the Dacha, and the stair. "Have some fun," he said.

He ran sliding down the steps and up to the helicopter. He scrambled in like a boy on holiday. It rose as it had descended in a storm of displaced snow. When its noise finally faded through the sky, Tchaikov heard the wolves from the wolf factory howling over the slopes. The sky was dark blue now, navy, without a star. If ever the moon appeared, the moon was blue. The pines settled. A few black boughs showed where the helicopter's winds had scoured off the snow. They were alive. But soon the snow began to come down again, to cover them.

Tchaikov returned to the cold room. He selected a chicken and two steaks and vegetables, and took them to the old stone-floored kitchen down the narrow steps. The new kitchen was very small, a little bright cubicle inside the larger one. He put the food into the thawing cabinet, and then set the program on the cooker. The dog came in as he was doing this, and stood outside the lighted box. Once they had thawed, he put the bloody steaks down for her on a dish, and touched her ruffed head as she bent to eat. She was a beautiful dog but wholly uninterested in him. She might be there in case of trouble, but there never would be trouble. No one stayed longer than six or eight months. The curatorship at the Dacha was a privilege, and an endurance test.

When his meal was ready, Tchaikov carried it to the card room or office, and ate, with the television showing him in color the black and white scenes of the snow and the cities. The card room fire burned on its synthetic logs, the gas cylinder faintly whistling. He drank vodka and red wine. Sometimes, in spaces of sound, he heard the wolves. And once, looking from the ballroom, he saw the dog lit by all the windows, trotting along the ice below the pines.

AT MIDNIGHT, when the television stations were shut down to conserve power, and most of the lights in the cities, although not here, would be dimmed, Tchaikov got into the manually operated elevator, and went up into the second dome, to the top floor.

He had put on again his greatcoat, his hat and gloves.

The elevator stopped at another little airlock. Beyond, only the cold-pressure lights could burn, glacial blue. Sometimes they blinked, flickered. An angled stair led to a corridor, which was wide, and shone as if highly polished. At the end of the corridor was an annex and the two broad high doors of glass. It was possible to look through the glass, and for a while he stood there, in the winter of the dome, staring in like a child.

It had been and still was a bedroom, about ten meters by eleven. His flat in the city would fit easily inside it.

The bedroom had always been white, the carpets and the silken drapes, even the tassels had been a mottled white, like milk, edged with gilt. And the bed was white. So that now, just as the snow-world outside resembled a white tumbled bed, the bed was like the tumbled snow.

The long windows were black with night, but a black

silvered by ice. Ice had formed too, in the room, in long spears that hung from the ceiling, where once a sky had been painted, a sky-blue sky with rosy clouds, but they had darkened and died, so now the sky was like old gray paint with flecks of rimy plaster showing through.

The mirrors in the room had cracked from the cold and formed strange abstract patterns that seemed to mean something. Even the glass doors had cracked, and were reinforced.

From here you could not properly see the little details of the room, the meal held perfect under ice, the ruined ornaments and paintings. Nor, properly, the couple on the bed.

Tchaikov drew the electronic key from his pocket and placed it in the mechanism of the doors. It took a long time to work, the cold-current not entirely reliable. The lighting blinked again, a whole second of black. Then the doors opened and the lights steadied, and Tchaikov went through.

The carpet, full of ice crystals, crunched under his feet, which left faint marks that would dissipate. His breath was smoke.

On a chest with painted panels, where the paint had scattered out, stood a white statue, about a meter high, that had broken from the cold, and an apple of rouged glass that had also broken, and somehow bled.

The pictures on the walls were done for. Here and there, a half of a face peeped out from the mossy corrosion, like the sun he had seen earlier in the cloud. Hothouse roses in a vase had turned to black coals, petrified, petals not fallen.

Their meal stood on the little mosaic table. It had been a beautiful meal, and neatly served. An amber fish, set with dark jade fruits, a salad that had blackened like the roses but kept its shape of dainty leaves and fronds. A flawless cream round, with two slivers cut from it, reminding him of the quartering of an elegant clock. The champagne was all gone, but for the beads of palest gold left at the bottom of the two goblets rimmed with silver. The bottle of tablets was mostly full. They had taken enough only to sleep, then turned off the heating, leaving the cold to do the rest.

The Last Supper of Love, Eynin had called it, in his poem, "This Place."

Tchaikov went over to the bed and looked down at them.

The man, Xander, wore evening dress, a tuxedo, a silk shirt with a tunic collar. On the jacket were pinned two military ribbons and a Knight's Cross. His tawny hair was sleeked back. His face was grave and very strong, a very masculine face, a very clean, calm face. His eyes, apparently, were green, but invisible behind the marble lids.

She, the woman, Tamura, was exquisite, not beautiful but immaculate, and so delicate and slender. She could have danced on air, just as Eynin said, in her sequined pumps. Her long white dress clung to a slight and nearly adolescent body, with the firm full breasts of a young woman. Her brunette hair spread on the pillows with the long stream of pearls from her neck. On the middle finger of her left hand, she wore a burnished ruby the color and size of a cherry.

Like Xander, Tamura was calm, quite serene.

It seemed they had had no second thoughts, eating their last meal, drinking their wine, perhaps making love. Then swallowing the pills and lying back for the sleep of winter, the long cold that encased and preserved them like perfect candy in a globe of ice.

They had been here nine years. It was not so very long.

Tchaikov looked at them. After a few minutes he turned and went back across the room, and again his footmarks temporarily disturbed the carpet. He locked the doors behind him.

IN THE CURATOR'S SUITE below, he put on the ordinary dimmed yellow lamp, and read Eynin's poem again, sipping black tea, while the synthetic fire crackled at the foot of his hard bed.

> *We watched the summer palaces*
> *Sail from this place,*
> *Like liners to the sea*
> *Of yesterday.*

Tchaikov put the book aside and switched off the light and fire. The fire died quite slowly, as if real.

Outside he heard the wolves howling like the old factory machinery.

Behind his closed eyelids, he saw Tamura's ruby, red as the cherries and roses in the elite florist's shops of the city. Her eyes, apparently, were dark.

Above him, as he lay on his back, the lovers slept on in their bubble of loving snow.

THE FIRST MONTH was not eventful. Each day, Henrique Tchaikov made a tour of the Dacha, noting any discrepancies, a fissure in the plaster, a chipped tile, noises in the pipes of the heating system — conscious, rather, of the fissured plaster and tiles, the thumps of the radiators, in his own apartment building. He replaced fuses and valves. In the library he noted the books which would need renovation. And took a general inventory of the stores the house had accumulated. Every curator did this. Evidently, some items were overlooked. The books, for example, the cornice in the ballroom, while lavatory tissue and oil for the generator were regularly renewed.

He used the hot tub, but only every three or four days. In the city, bathing was rationed. For the same reason he did not go into the solarium, except once a week to check the thermostat and to water the extraordinary black-green plants which rose in storeys of foliage to the roof.

Most of the afternoon he sat reading in the library, or listening to the music machine. He heard, for the first time, recordings of Prokofiev and Rachmaninov playing inside their own piano concertos, and Shostakovich conducting his own symphony, and Lirabez singing, in a slightly flat but swarthy baritone, a cycle of his own songs.

For those who liked these things, the Dacha provided wonderful experiences.

Tchaikov also watched films, and the recordings of historical events.

Sometimes in the mornings he slept an hour late, letting the coffee-plate prepare a sticky brew, with thick cream from the cold room.

Usually he kept in mind these treats were his only for eight months at the most, less than a year. Then he would have to go back.

The dog became more sociable, though not exactly friendly. He stroked her fur, even brushed her twice a week. He called her Bella, because she was beautiful. Probably this was not the right thing, as again, when he left, some other person would be the curator, who might not even like dogs.

Bella, the dog, each evening lay before the fire in the card room, sometimes even in the suite. But normally she would only stay an hour or two. Then she wanted to go down through the house and out by the electronic dog-door.

He began to realize that the wolf howling was often very close to the mansion. At last he saw the indigo form of a wolf on the night snow. The wolf howled on and on, until the dog went out. Then the wolf and the dog played together in the snow.

The first time he saw this, Tchaikov was assailed by a heart-wringing pang of hope.

The house manual told him that the wolves had invaded the factory, and remained there, because they lived off the rats which still infested it. The rats in turn lived off the dung of the wolves. It was a disgusting but divinely inspired cycle. Bella and the wolf must have met out upon the frozen ice of the ancient river buried below the Dacha and the pines. Although there would be females of the wolf kind for the wolf to choose from, instead he took to Bella. An individualist. Tchaikov did not see them join in the sexual act, but he accepted that they too were lovers. This seemed to symbolize the vigor still clinging in the threatened world, its basic tenacity, its magic. But he put such thoughts aside. Magic was illusion. Sex was only that, just like the "hot" magazines Ouperin, or someone, had secreted in the suite, and which Tchaikov did not bother with. For him, sensuality was connected to personality. He preferred memory to invention.

Of course, occasionally he pondered Tamura and Xander, their intrinsic meaning. But never for long. And he did not go up again to look at them.

In THE FIRST DAY of the second month, a fax came through from the city computer, informing him a party would be arriving at midday.

He shut the dog Bella in the kitchen, and put on his suit and tie.

At sixteen hours, or four o'clock — they were late, another avalanche — the party drew up in two big buses with leviathan snow tires.

Tchaikov understood he was unreasonably resentful at the stupid intrusion, for which the place was intended. He wanted the Dacha to himself. But he courteously welcomed the party, twenty-three people, who stared about the hall with wide, red-rimmed eyes, their noses running, because the heating in the buses was not very good.

They had their own guide, who led them, following Tchaikov, up the stairs to the manually operated lift. Tchaikov and the guide took them in two groups of eleven and twelve up into the dome.

They seemed frightened on the narrow stair, and in the corridor, as though extreme cold still unsettled — startled — them. They peered through the glass doors, exactly as Tchaikov had. When he and the bossy guide ushered them through, they wandered about the bedroom. Told not to touch anything, they made tactile motions in the air over ornaments and furnishings, with their gloved hands.

One woman, seeing the lovers, Tamura, Xander, on the bed, began to cry. No one took any notice. She pulled quantities of paper handkerchiefs from her pocket; possibly she had come prepared for emotion.

Downstairs in the ballroom, the guide lectured everybody on the Dacha. They stood glassy-eyed and blank. The significance of Tamura and Xander was elusive but overpowering. Tchaikov too did not listen. Instead he organized the coffee-plate in the card room, and brought the party coffee in relays, laced with vodka, before its return to the city in the two drafty buses.

When they had gone, about six, Bella was whining

from the kitchen. He fed her quickly, knowing she wanted to be off to her lover. He gave her that night two extra steaks, in case she should want to take them out as a gift, but she left them on the plate. Oddly, from this, he deduced she would eventually desert the Dacha for her wolf partner. Instinctively she knew not to accustom him to extra food, and to prepare herself for future hardship. But doubtless this was fanciful. Besides, she might by now be pregnant with the wolf's children.

BELLA LAY before the synthetic log fire, her gold eyes burning golden-red. Her belly looked more full than it had. It was about twenty-two hours, ten o'clock.

Tchaikov read aloud to her from the poem "This Place."

> I dreamed once, of this place.
> When I was young.
> But then I woke —
> When I was young.

It was five nights since the bus party had visited. Once the dog had got up, shaken herself, and padded from the room, Tchaikov went upstairs and stepped into the elevator.

The night was extra cold, minus several more degrees on the gauge, and the great bedroom had a silvery fog in it.

He could look at the couple now quite passively, as if they were only waxworks. A man and a woman who had not wanted to remain inside the sinking winter world. But was it merely that? Was their mystical suicide cowardice — or bravura? Did they think, in dying, that they had somewhere warm to go?

The Bureau had not advanced any records on them,

and probably their names were not even those they had gone by in life.

Again, he asked himself what they meant. But it did not really matter. They were, that was all.

In the night, about four A.M., an unearthly noise woke him from a deep sleep, where he had been dreaming of swimming in a warm sea jeweled by fish.

The sound had occurred outside, he thought, outside both the dream and the room. He got up and went to the window, and looked out through the triple glazing which was all the suite provided.

The snowscape spread from the pines, along the plain, and in the distance billowed up to the higher land, and the black sky massed with the broken edges of stars. Far away to the right, where the plain was its most level and long, a black mark had appeared in the snow. It must stretch for nearly twenty meters, he thought, a jagged, ink-black crack in the terrain.

Tchaikov stared, and saw a vapor rising out of the crack, caused by the disparity between the bitter set of the air and some different temperature below.

The sound had been a crack. Like a gigantic piece of wood snapped suddenly in half — a bark of breakage.

But new snow was already drifting faintly down from the stars, smoothing and obscuring the black tear in the whiteness. As Tchaikov watched, it began to vanish.

Probably it was nothing. In the city, apertures sometimes appeared in the top-snow of streets, where thermolated pipes still ran beneath. Somebody had told Tchaikov there had been a river here, passing below the house. The driver had mentioned it too. Perhaps the disturbance had to do with that.

Tchaikov went back to bed, and lay for a while listening, expectant and tensed. Then he recalled that once, in his early childhood, he had heard such a crack roar out across a frozen lake in the country. Instinctively, hearing it now, he had unconsciously remembered the springs of long-ago, the waxing of the sun, the rains, the melting of the ice. But spring was forever over.

He drifted back down into sleep, numb and calm.

THE NEXT MORNING as he was coming from the solarium, having switched off the sprinklers, he heard the sound of a vehicle on the plain. He went into the ballroom and looked down at the snow, half noticing as he did so that the curious mark of the previous night had completely disappeared. A large black car was now parked by the Dacha's steps, near the statues. After a moment, Tchaikov recognized the car which had brought him here. Puzzled, he waited, and saw the driver, Argenty, get out, and then a smaller figure in a long coat of gray synthetic fur.

They came up the steps, Argenty pausing for the smaller figure, which was that of a woman.

After a minute the house door made a noise.

There had been no communication from the city computer, but sometimes messages were delayed. In any case, you could not leave them standing in the cold.

Tchaikov opened the door without interrogation. Argenty shot him a quick look under his hat.

"It's all right, isn't it?"

"I expect so," said Tchaikov.

He let them come in, and the door shut.

Argenty took off his hat, and stood almost to attention. He said, "There aren't visitors due, are there?"

"Not that I know of."

"I thought not. There's been another power failure. I shouldn't think anyone would be going anywhere today."

"Apart from you."

"Yes," said Argenty. He turned, and looked at the woman.

She too had taken off her hat, a fake fur shako to match the coat. She had a small pale slender face, without, he thought, any makeup beyond a dusting of powder. Her eyes were dark and smoky, with long lashes of a lighter darkness. Her dark hair seemed recently washed and brushed and fell in soft waves to her shoulders. Just under her right cheekbone had been applied a little diamanté flower. She met his eyes and touched the flower with a gloved fingertip. She said quietly, "A frostbite scar."

"This is my wife," said Argenty. "Tanya."

Then she smiled at Tchaikov, a placating smile, like a child's when it wants to show it is undeserving of punishment. She was like a child, a girl, despite the two thin lines cut under her large eyes and at either side of her soft mouth.

He remembered how Argenty had talked on and on about her, her light-deprived Twilight Sickness, her wanderings in the night and cries. She had been lovely, he said, twenty years ago. In a way she still was.

Unauthorized, they should not be here. It could cost Argenty a serious demotion. What had happened? The power failure? The electricity off in their flat, gloom, and the refrigerator failing, and Argenty saying Leave all that, I'll take you somewhere nice. As you might, to stop a miserable and frightened child crying.

Tchaikov said, "Come into the card room. There's a fire."

They went through with him, Argenty still stiff and formal, absolutely knowing what he had risked, but she was all smiles now, reassured.

In the warm room, Argenty removed his greatcoat,

and helped her off with her fur. Tchaikov looked at them, slightly surprised. Argenty wore the uniform of his city service, with an honor ribbon pinned by the collar. While she — she wore a long, old evening gown of faded pastel crimson, which left her shoulders and arms and some of her white back and breast bare. On her left hand, under the woolen glove, was another little glove of lace. She indicated it again at once, laughed and said, "Frostbite. I've been careless, you see."

Tchaikov switched on the coffee-plate. He said, "I usually have lunch in about an hour. I hope you'll join me."

Argenty nodded politely. She began to walk about the room, inspecting the antique oil paintings and the restored damask wall covering. Argenty took out a brand of expensive cigarettes and came to Tchaikov, offering them.

Argenty murmured, very low, "Thank you, for being so good. I can't tell you what it means to her."

"That's all right. You may even get away with it, if the computer's out."

Argenty shrugged. "Perhaps. What does it matter anyway?"

After the coffee, Tchaikov showed them the ballroom, then went to organize a lunch. He selected caviar and pork, the type of vegetables and little side dishes he did not, himself, bother with, fruit and biscuits, and a chocolate dessert he thought she would like. He took vodka and two bottles of champagne from the liquor compartment. For God's sake, they might as well enjoy the visit.

He opened up the parlor off the ballroom. It too had a chandelier dripping prisms. He turned on the fire and lit the tall white candles in the priceless candelabra. He was not supposed to do this. But against Argenty's tremendous gamble it was a small gesture.

"Why don't you stay tonight?" said Tchaikov. "Leave early in the morning. There's another bedroom in the suite. Quite a good one—I think it's for visiting VIPs. By tomorrow the power failure will be over, probably."

"That's kind . . . you've been kind . . . but we'd better get back."

They looked at the sleeping woman, at the sleeping dog and the fire.

"Why did this happen?" asked Argenty. His voice was gentle and unemphatic. "Couldn't they have seen —why did they give up all the best things, let them go — they could have — something — surely — "

Tchaikov said nothing and Argenty fell silent.

And in the silence there came a dense low rumble.

For a moment Tchaikov took it for some fluctuation of the gas jet in the fire, and then, as it grew louder, for the noise of snow dislodged and tumbling from a roof of the mansion.

But then the rumbling became very loud, running in toward them over the plain.

"What is it?" said Argenty. He had gone pale.

"I don't know. An earth tremor, perhaps."

The rumbling was now so vehement he had to raise his voice. On the table the silver and the glasses tinkled and rattled, something fell and broke, and on the walls the pictures trembled and swayed. The floor beneath their chairs was churning.

The dog had woken, sat up, her coat bristling and ears laid flat, a white ring showing round each eye.

Argenty and Tchaikov rose, and in her sleep the woman stretched out one hand, in its lace glove, as if to snatch hold of something.

Then came a thunderclap, a sort of ejection of sound

that ripped splintering from earth and sky, hit the barrier of the house, exploded, dropped back in enormous echoing shards.

The windows grated and shook. No doubt some of the external glass had ruptured.

"Is it a bomb?" cried Argenty.

Tanya had started from sleep and the chair, and he caught her in his arms. She was speechless with shock and terror. The dog was growling.

"1 don't know. It's stopped now. Not a bomb, I think. There was no light flash." Tchaikov moved to the door. "Stay here."

Outside, he ran across the ballroom, and to the nearer window which looked out to the plain.

What he saw made him hesitate mentally, stumble in his mind, at a loss. He could not decipher what he was looking at. It was a sight theoretically familiar enough. Yet knowing what it was, he stood immobile for several minutes, staring without comprehension at the enormous coal-black dragon which had crashed upward through the dead ice of the frozen river, showering off panes of the marble land, like the black and white concrete blocks of a collapsed building. In the puddle of bubbling iron water, the submarine settled now, tall, motionless, less than thirty-five meters beyond the Dacha, while clouds of stony steam rose in a tumult on the steel sky.

3

THEY MARCHED STEADILY to the mansion, over the snow. Henrique Tchaikov watched them come, black shapes on the whiteness.

Reaching the steps, they climbed them, and arrived at the door. He could see their uniforms by then, the decorations of rank and authority. They did not seem to feel the cold. They did not bother with the buzzer.

He spoke through the door apparatus.

"You must identify yourselves."

"You'll let us in." The one who spoke then gave a key word and number. And Tchaikov opened the door.

The cold gushed in with them, in a special way.

"You're the current Bureau man," said the commander to Tchaikov. He was about~thirty-six, athletic, tanned by a solarium, his hair cut too short, not a pore in his face. His teeth were winter white. "We won't give you much trouble. We've come for the couple."

Tchaikov did not answer. His heart kicked, but it was a reflex. He stood very still. He had taken Tanya and Argenty down to the kitchen, with the dog, and shut them all in.

The commander vocalized again. "We don't need any red tape, do we? My men will go straight up. It'll only take the briefest while. The dome, right?"

Tchaikov said slowly, "You mean Tamura and Xander."

"Are those the names? Yes. The pair in the state bedroom. Here's the confirmation disc."

Tchaikov accepted the disc and put it in the analyzer by the door. After ten seconds an affirmative lit up, the key number, and the little message: *Comply with all conditions.* The commander took back his disc. "Where would we be," he said, "without our machines." Then he gave an order, and the four other men ran off and up the stair, like hounds let from a leash, toward the upper floors and the elevator. Obviously they had been primed with the layout of the mansion. Tchaikov saw that two of them carried each a rolled rain-colored thermolated bag. They would have some means of opening the upper doors.

He said, "Why are you taking them away? Where are they going?"

The commander showed all his pristine, repulsive teeth. "Quite a comfortable stint here, I'd say, yes? Don't worry, they won't recall you until your time's up. Messes up the files. Seven months to go. You can just relax."

Tchaikov grasped it would be useless to question the commander further. He had had his orders, which were to remove the frozen lovers in cold-bags, take them into the submarine, go away with them, somewhere.

Tchaikov said, "It was impressive, the way you surfaced."

"That river," said the commander, "it runs deep. So far down, you know, the water still moves. We came in from the sea, thirteen kilometers. Must have given you a surprise."

"Yes."

"There's nothing like her," said the commander, as though he boasted about a selected woman, or his mother. "The X 2 M's. Ice-breakers, power-hives. Worlds in themselves. You'd be amazed. We could stay under for a hundred years. We have everything. Clean reusable air, foolproof heating, cuisine prepared by master chefs, games rooms, weaponry. See how brown I am," he added, dancing his narrow eyes, flirting now. "Have you ever tasted eggs?"

"No."

"I have one every day. And fresh meat. Salads. My little boat has everything I'll ever need."

There was a wooden, flat sound, repeated on and on.

The commander frowned.

"It's only the dog," Tchaikov said. "I shut her in, below. In case she annoyed you."

"Dog? Oh, yes. Animals don't interest me, except of course to eat."

Tchaikov thought he heard the lift cranking up the tower, going to the dome.

The commander looked about now, and laughed at the old regal house, the old country Dacha with its sleeping white candy dead.

They stood in silence in the hall, until the other four men ran down again, carrying, not particularly cautiously, the two thermolated bags, upright and unpliable. Filled and out of the dome, the material had misted over. Tchaikov could not see Tamura or Xander in these cocoons, although he found himself staring, thinking for a second he caught the scorch of her ruby ring.

"Well done," the commander said to him. "All over." It was like the dentists in childhood. "You can go back to all those cozy duties." He grinned at Tchaikov. But his use of jargon was somehow unwieldy and out of date. Did they speak another tongue on the submarine? "A nice number. Happy days."

The dog had suddenly stopped barking.

The door let the men out. Tchaikov watched them returning over the snow, toward their black dragon-whale. Already the ice was forming round the submarine's casing, but that would not be much of an inconvenience. He wondered where they had been, how far out in jet black seas, where maybe fish still swam. When the vessel was gone, the ice would swiftly close, and tonight's fresh snowfall heal the wound it had made, as snow had healed the preface to the wound last night.

Tamura and Xander, preserved from the submarine's warmth in some refrigerated cubicle. He did not know, could not imagine for what purpose. Although the nagging line from some book — was it a Bible? — began to twitter in his head . . . *And He said: Make thee an ark —*

Above, the dome was void. The great polar room with its stalactites of ice, the footsteps already smoothing from the carpet.

He descended quickly to the kitchen. He had told Argenty where the medicine cabinet was, and suggested that he dial some sedative tablets for his wife. Tchaikov was unsure what he would find.

Yet when he reached the lower floor, there was only quietness. Opening the kitchen door, he found the two of them seated urbanely at the long table.

The dog Bella had gone. But Tanya sat in her red dress, and looking up, she met Tchaikov only with her lambent eyes.

She said to him, reciting from memory from Eynin's poem that he too knew so well:

> *In Hell the birds are made of fire;*
> *If all the birds of Hell flew to this place,*
> *And settled on the snow,*
> *Still darkness would prevail,*
> *And utter cold.*

"She knows it by heart," said Argenty.

"So do I, most of it," Tchaikov answered.

"The dog went out," said Argenty. "We thought we heard a wolf."

"Yes. They've mated."

The kitchen was bathed in vague ochre heat, only the light of the new cooking area was raw and too bright.

Tanya's eyes shone.

"You were very good, to hide us away."

"It's all right," he said. "The military are shortsighted. They came for something else."

In a while they heard the strange, sluggish hollow suction of the submarine, its motors, diving down again below the ice. The house gave now only a little shudder, and on its shelf one ancient plate turned askew.

Tanya laughed. She lifted her dark springy hair in her hands.

Tchaikov saw that Argenty's hair, under the polishing light, was a rich dull gold.

HE SLEPT a deep leaden sleep, and dreamed of the submarine. It was taller than the tallest architecture of the city, the Bureau building. It clove forward, black, ice and steam and boiling water spraying away from it, rending. the land with a vicious hull like the blade of some enormous iceskate. In the dark sky above, red and yellow burning birds wheeled to and fro, cawing and calling, striking sparks from the clouds. The birds of Hell.

When the submarine reached the Dacha, it stopped just outside the wall of the suite, which in the dream was made of glass. The wall shattered and fell down, and looking up the mile of iron, steel and night that was the tower of the submarine, Tchaikov noticed a tiny bluish porthole set abnormally in the side, and there they sat, the lovers, gazing down with cold, closed eyes.

Waking, he got up and made black tea on the plate. From the other bedroom of the suite, across the inner room, came no sound. When he looked out, there was no longer a light beneath their door. If they had switched off the optional lamp, perhaps they slept.

When the afternoon darkened, they had sat on with him in the kitchen, drinking a little, talking idly. There was the subtle ease of remaining; he realized before Argenty asked, that they did after all mean to stay a night at the house.

Later the dog came in again. Tchaikov fed her. She lay by the hot pipes for half an hour before going out once more.

During the interval, Tanya suddenly sang a strange old song in her light girl's voice, "Oh my dog is such a clever dog — "

Bella listened. Her tail wagged slowly. She came to Tanya to be caressed before padding off into the star-spiked night.

They ate cold pork and bread for supper and finished the champagne. Argenty thanked Tchaikov, shaking his hand, throwing his arm around him. The girl-woman did not kiss Tchaikov as he had half expected — hoped? — she would. She only said shyly, "It's been a wonderful day. Better than a birthday!"

By the time he concluded his nocturnal check of the Dacha, they had gone up, and just the lamp showed softly under the door.

But they were in full darkness now, so Tchaikov walked almost on tiptoe from the suite. He did not want to wake them if they slept. He wished her not to dream as he had, of the triumphant submarine.

Outside, the ice had superficially closed over again. Snow fell in gentle pitiless flakes.

The elevator seemed particularly sluggish. He had to work at the lever with great firmness.

Above, in the icy corridor, Tchaikov shivered, only his trousers and greatcoat on over his nightshirt. As he walked toward the glass doors, he had a sense of imminence. What was it? Was it loss?

As formerly, he hesitated, and stood at the doors, staring in through the glacial light, the glacial glass, the cracks, the fog of ice.

He experienced a moment of dislocation, pure bewilderment, just as he had with the submarine. He had previously seen the bed clothed by two forms. Now they were removed and the bed was vacant. But there were two forms on the bed.

The bed was clothed.

Tchaikov opened the doors with the electronic key they had so noiselessly replaced on the chest in his room, before going up again. Of course, the key, lying there, had been obvious for what it was. Like the house map in the card room. There would have been no difficulty in deciding.

The bedroom, when he entered it now, did not strike him as so frozen. The breath of the living seemed finally to have stirred it, like the fluid of the deepest coldest pool, stirred by a golden wand.

Tchaikov went across to the bed. Two bottles had fallen on the thick carpet. He looked down, at the couple.

They lay hand in hand, side by side. Their faces were peaceful, almost smiling, the eyes fast shut. Like the faces, the eyes, of Xander and Tamura. Yet these two lovers had needed to be brave. Despite the vodka they had swallowed and the tablets from the medicine cabinet, they had had to face the cold, had had to lie down in the cold. He in his well-brushed uniform with its single honor, and she in her pale red sleeveless gown.

But there had been no struggle. They seemed to have found it very simple, very consoling, if not easy. Perhaps it had been easy, too.

Her somber hair, his gilded hair, both smoked now by the rime. And on the diamanté flower that gemmed her cheek, a single mote of crystal like a tear.

Tchaikov backed slowly and carefully away. It was possible they were not quite dead yet, still in the process of dying. He tiptoed out, not to disturb their death.

By THE END of the ninth month, when the Bureau at last recalled him, the dog was long gone. He had seen her at first sometimes, out on the snow, playing with the wolf and their three pups. But the wolf was a king wolf, made her queen over the wolf pack, and in the end, she went away to the factory with them.

When he heard the howling in the still night, he thought of her. Once, the moon appeared incredibly for a quarter of an hour, sapphire blue, and the wolves' chanting rose to a crescendo. Her children would be very strong, cross-bred from an alpha male and such a well-nourished mother.

His faxed report had been acknowledged, but that was all. Tchaikov never commented upon or thought about the aspects of what had occurred, he detailed and visualized the events only in memorized images.

The night of the blue moon, which was two nights before his return to the city, and to his cramped flat with its thudding radiators, the tepid bath once a week, the rationing, the dark, he wrote in the back of the book of Eynin's poetry, on the blank page which followed the poem called "The Place."

Here too he set out the facts sparely, as he had done for the Bureau. Under the facts he wrote a few further lines.

"I have puzzled all this time over what is their meaning, the lovers in the ice, whoever they are, whether right or wrong in their action, and even if they change, their bodies constantly taken and replaced by others. And I think their meaning is this: Love, courage, defiance — the mystery of the human spirit, still blooming, always blooming, like the last flower in the winter world."

THE PERSECUTION MACHINE

Dedicated to the Matchless Edward Gorey

I: Uncle

MY FATHER galloped into the library with a look of terror.

"Your uncle is coming!"

"My — uncle? Who do you mean?"

"Constant."

"But I thought—"

"No," said my father, running to the window and glaring out nervously. "He isn't dead. Only mad."

"I see."

"Of course you don't." My father spared a look of distaste for me. As his son, I had had certain duties never properly explained, one of which had been to become a perfect replica of himself in the city of business. Instead I had metamorphosed into a fashionable writer, and it was not in him to forgive me. "Well," he said now, "since you're so clever, I'll leave you to entertain him. Try telling him who you are."

"We've discussed this previously. I'm not clever, only a genius. As for Uncle Constant, if he's calling here, presumably he wishes to see you. After all, does he even know of my existence? I'm sure I didn't know of his."

"It was kept from you. I expect he will have learned. Twenty years since I saw him. Horrible."

"Is he deformed?" I inquired with pleasant anticipation.

"No. Only his mind. Stall the wretch. Get him to leave if possible."

I shrugged. "Does mother share your aversion?"

"Your mother will faint," said my father, "if he so much as touches the panels of her parlour door."

My mother tended to faint continually when confronted by annoyance. She had already fainted once at my arrival. My father had had the grace only to offer to throw me out. A recent short novel of mine, dealing with forbidden love, very I may say, tastefully, had caused their latest dislike of me. I, meanwhile, came to visit them from a sense of responsibility, since they were always in want of money.

But what was the motive for mad Constant's arrival?

The doorbell rang below. My father shrieked and rushed from the room.

When Steppings appeared presently in the library door, I accordingly asked him to show the visitor up.

A moment later, my Uncle Constant was revealed to me.

He was a man of about fifty-eight or sixty, corpulent but pale, with a mane of grey hair and disordered clothes. He seemed out of breath, as if he had been running, and he darted a wild look about the room.

"Are we alone?" he demanded.

"I believe so."

"Who are you?"

"Your nephew, Charles."

"Who? Oh, never mind it. Only let me sit down. I'm exhausted. They've pursued me all day. Not a second's peace." He fell noisily into a large chair.

Steppings reappeared, mostly from nosiness, but I sent

him off to bring some of my father's Madeira. I had no qualms in this, since I had supplied the wine myself.

"Well, uncle. How may I help you?"

"Help? Impossible. No one can help. I ask only a minute's respite." His breathing quieted a little and he blew his nose into a gigantic handkerchief. "It's no use my explaining. Only I understand what I suffer."

"This may be said of each of us."

"I see you're a philosopher, sir. Did you say we are related? My God, I've run into my brother's house, haven't I?"

"Didn't you know?"

"I will run in anywhere I am able when they are after me."

"Who? Do you mean the police?"

My Uncle Constant was racked with melodramatic laughter.

Steppings came in with the wine and a tray of biscuits.

Constant struck the tray and the biscuits flew in all directions. Steppings did not flinch, merely put on the expression — of a surprised chicken — which has seen such good service over the years. I rescued the Madeira and poured two glasses, waving the chicken away as I did so.

"Drink this."

"Is it poison?"

"I don't think so."

"Nothing short of poison is any use to me. I pant to be released from my suffering. But suicide is a sin." He reminded me of my father. Uncle Constant drank the Madeira at a gulp and I refilled his glass. "They're after me, worse than ever. Their weapons — If only you knew."

He, as my father had done, bustled to the window. He stared out, I assumed, at the peaceful street.

"Not yet," he muttered. "But soon."

"And you have no matters to consult my father upon?" I asked.

"Who? Who is your father?"

"Your brother."

"I have no brother," said Uncle Constant. "I am cast out into the wilderness." Then his face contorted. It grew red, then blue. "I hear it!" he cried. And flinging the goblet on the ground, or rather the carpet, he sprang away and was gone. I heard his cascade down the stair and the crash of the street door.

I stood by the window and presently saw him emerge and scuttle fatly down the street. He disappeared from view.

2: Uncle's Story

Aᴌᴛʜᴏᴜɢʜ I questioned my father and mother about my Uncle Constant, neither told me anything. My father ranted and my mother fainted. Steppings looked like a chicken, and when I tried to enlist his help, only importuned me to persuade my parents to use a new sort of cheese in the mouse-traps. I told him that I disapproved of mouse-traps. Steppings confided that he himself ate the cheese. It was a harmless perversion, during which he sometimes emitted small squeaks.

I was touched by his trust, but it did not help me to discover my uncle.

However, a month later, endless searching led me to a tall gaunt house in the south of the Capital. Here a gentleman bearing my uncle's name resided. The instant I beheld the house, I knew it must be he.

Large bars were on all the windows, and a sort of portcullis was let down outside the door.

On my ringing the door bell, through the portcullis, no one came.

It was a sunny day, and I sat down across the street on a low wall, to watch and wait.

Presently a maid came out of the house with the low wall.

She attempted some ineffectual dusting of the privet hedge, and then bent to my ear.

"He's a madman, that one. You after him for a debt?"

"Not at all. I am a long lost lover of his, come to call on him."

"You're one of them preeverts," said the maid, and ran in.

Half an hour later, two somberly-clad women, with the figures but not the charm of pigeons, came down the street, mounted my uncle's steps, and banged on the portcullis.

I could tell at a glance they were religious persons, and that a lack of response would not put them off. It did not. Getting no reply, they banged the louder. And the larger lady began to cry: "Open the doors of your hearts, O ye lost children of the Lord. Hear the word of the Master!"

I expected a window to be raised and some missile inserted through the bars and thrown.

Instead, to my surprise and delight, sounds of vast unlockings eventually echoed over the street, the portcullis lifted, and my uncle appeared in the doorway.

He wore a yellow dressing-gown and a look of fear and loathing.

"Be off," he yelled at the two ladies, "I know your tricks. Where is it? Is it near? I won't be decoyed."

"Repent," said the large lady. "Here is a tract — "

But Uncle Constant swept the article from her gloved hand.

"Away!" howled uncle, and thrust her down the steps.

The lady fell upon the other one and both toppled to the ground. There was the hideous noise of bursting corsets.

Before my uncle could shut the door and the portcullis I leapt across the street, over the wallowing ladies, and up the steps. I seized Uncle Constant's hand.

"Uncle Constant!"

"Aah! Villain! Unhand me."

"I am your nephew, Charles," I intimated, as he tried to run me through with his sword-stick.

"Who?"

"Your nephew. We met a month ago."

"You're not one of their spies?" He peered at me. "No. Your hair's too long and you have no moustache. Come in then. Quickly. Let me lock the house. I am in deadly peril. If they should once gain a foothold— There! Do you hear it? No. No, you would never hear it."

He slammed the door against the world and we were in a dark hall papered with a design of large red bats, or perhaps prehistoric birds.

"But I did hear — " I began. My uncle took no notice.

Once he had let down the portcullis by means of a switch, locked the door three times and bolted it twice, my uncle led me up a carpeted stair and into a small dim room. The bat wall-paper persisted, but otherwise there were chairs and a sofa and some brandy on a stand. Through the bars of the windows and heavy dusty lace, little was visible, and I imagined that he preferred this to be so.

"Sit down," said my uncle, "whoever you are."

"Uncle Constant, I did hear a noise. Perhaps a train?"

My uncle looked at me strangely. He frowned. Then,

going to the stand, he poured out two generous brandies.

He did not, though, give either one to me, or take one himself, he left them where they were as a decoration.

"I will tell you my terrible tale," said my uncle.

"Thank you."

"You must not interrupt."

I nodded mutely.

Assuaged, perhaps, my uncle seated himself in a vast armchair that rather resembled a pig.

"In my youth," he began, "I had no cares. I did very much as I wanted. I had been thought too clever for school, and so a number of tutors had taught me at home. I had no friends and wished for none. My only interest, as I grew older, was collecting young actresses. Then one evening, on my way home from the theatre, I was met by a messenger in the street. My parents had perished in a fire at the house of an ice-cream manufacturer, and I had now inherited the family fortune."

Although I knew that my grandparents were not dead, and that there had never been a family fortune, I did not argue with Uncle Constant at this point. I felt that probably he was instinctually lying in order to give some framework to what might follow.

"I fell," he continued, as if gratified by my sensitive abstention, "into a melancholy. I stayed indoors and only wandered from room to room of the house, recalling the unhappy hours I had spent there with my parents, who were both obtuse and ugly. The prettiness of my actress collection came to repel me, and I saw these girls no more. After some months, I ventured out at night, and walked the nastiest thoroughfares of the city, until it was almost dawn. Gradually, as I was returning to the house, I became aware that I was being, and had indeed been for some while, followed, by a number of mysterious shadowy figures. At length, a peculiar noise resounded distantly behind the smoking chimneys and smouldering refuse pits of the alleys."

My uncle looked at me expectantly, but, true to his wish, I did not interrupt. Consoled, he went on.

"I can only describe this noise as that of some curious engine, which also whistled, rather like a factory hooter. **Chug chug,** it went, and then **Whoop! Whoop!** Alarmed, I hastened home, but after I was indoors I heard something move down the street and a shadow was cast upon my windows."

My uncle got up, and going to the brandy glasses, he poured their contents into an aspidistra, then refilled them carefully from the decanter. He left them on the stand, and resumed his chair and his tale.

"Soon after this, when I had gone out once more on some necessary business, I was again followed, and after a time I heard repeated the ominous chugging and whooping of the sinister engine. I hurried at once on to a busy thoroughfare, and there the din of the crowd somewhat mitigated the sound of the pursuit. After a few minutes, however, a frightful shooting pain began in my right knee. And then another, worse, in my right arm. I fell against a lamppost, and an old gentleman came up and smote me in the face, accusing me of being drunk. As I partly lay there, I saw, through the ranks of the oblivious and jeering crowd, a fearful thing rolling slowly and mightily down from the end of the street. It was a sort of carriage, yet it had no horses, and from it protruded all manner of pipes and coils, wheels that whirred and the nozzles of what could only be guns. Suddenly one of these flashed with a cold green fire, and a new pain lanced through my belly. Atop the device was a crew of men clad like explorers in long coats, goggles, and unlikely hats. They had moustaches and their lips were thin and cruel. From the midst of them a funnel glowed and steamed and out came the noise. **Chug, chug.** And then **Whoop, whoop.** No one in the street but I could see this evil equipage. I turned; and, as best I could for my hurts, I ran. The more distance I could put between myself and the engine of torment, the more relief I gained, and finally I shut myself into the house and knew an end to my pain. Its four walls, imbued as they were with boring memories of my parents, protected me. But as I crouched behind the door, the machine passed down the street. Its shadow fell again inside the house. From that day, I have not been free of it."

My uncle rose once more and paced to an empty parrot cage. He stared into it and shook his head.

"So far, they have not gained access to my home. Now and then their spies seek me. The machine never lies in wait for me outside the house . . . a sporting chance is allowed me — although they are not really fair. If ever the machine can by stealth enter these premises, I am lost."

A vague rumbling sounded in the street. A faint shadow crossed the window and next the ceiling. I got up and went to look out. The street was empty but for another maid dusting a hedge, and two porters carrying a stuffed bear. The religious ladies had picked themselves up and gone away.

"You may speak now," said my uncle.

"Have you," I asked, "approached no one for help?"

"In the beginning, ceaselessly. I went to the police, and then to private companies. But all laughed me to scorn. An eminent doctor has certified that I am harmlessly mad."

"The engine or machine is invisible to all others but yourself?"

My uncle returned to the brandy stand and drank both

glasses of brandy. "I am doomed." He then showed me out of the house.

3: Uncle Pursued

AFTER that second meeting, I took to following my Uncle Constant.

He went out, as can be imagined from his fears, very seldom, and so my vigils were frequently long, dull and unrewarded — except by the emergence of the privet-dusting maid, who seemed to think that, despite my 'preeversion,' I fancied her person.

This was rather trying. However.

Finally, my uncle began to slip cautiously out of the house on hobbled rapid errands.

He would first of all open the door a crack, having of course noisily unlocked and unbolted it, and raised the portcullis. He would then gaze fixedly at each side of the street in turn. He never noticed me, even when I had not taken the trouble of obscuring myself behind the hedge. And I noted presently that, even if he looked at me on the street, he never recalled who I was or that I was anyone but a complete stranger.

Having perused both directions, Uncle Constant would leap forth and bolt one way or the other. Being portly, his quickness soon flagged, but he kept up what pace he could, his arms clutched to his chest, rather in the manner of a squirrel. Now and then he would break into a run. And frequently, he would glare behind him. In doing this, he often saw me, but paid, as I have said, no heed.

I, on the other hand, listened as intently and turned round as often as he.

It seemed to me that I heard a familiar noise in the distance, but I could not be sure how near we might be to some bizarre railway line or extraordinary factory, which might produce such sounds. Then, too, it sometimes seemed to me that shadows appeared at the ends of streets which bisected those pavements along which Uncle Constant rattled. Yet too I was never certain ordinary objects might not somehow have cast these shadows, and besides they were always fleeting.

Meanwhile other people and things moved all round us in the normal manner. My uncle occasionally barged into them, so oblivious was he of anything but the persecuting pursuit.

He never returned from his expeditions by the same route he had set out on, but always via a roundabout circuit. For presumably he was afraid, if the machine of torment was somewhere behind him, he might otherwise meet it head-on.

Uncle's outings were mundane and sketchy. Sorties upon shops of food and chemists' emporiums, and once a journey to a well known and reputable bank. On this last foray, he emerged from the august portals amid cries and clangs, and squirreled down the steps, clutching at his left leg and muttering: "They're near." He was obviously in pain, and intercepting his terrified glance, I too looked back along the street.

The vista was thronged with people, and on the road were several carriages. It was apparent that no vehicle could pass unseen, if it were really there. As I gazed, it seemed to me that there was indeed something moving slowly and ponderously under the archway that opened the street. A faint greenish beam was struck from the place that might only be the morning sun upon some harness or other metallic item. My uncle distracted me with a hoarse scream. I turned and saw he had dropped to his knees. A bank-note fell from his hand, and I ran over, stopping the money before someone should snatch it, and next trying to assist him.

"Uncle — "

"Let me go, wretch!" screeched Uncle Constant, hitting me so violently in the chest that I too was flung on the ground. Before I could right myself he was up and hobbling, moaning away.

I then decided that, rather than rush after him in the usual fashion, I would wait at the roadside to see if any unusual carriage came past. I was encouraged in this idea by a repetition of the unlikely noise I had heard before — the **chug** and **whoop** of a mad engine, whistle or hooter. Then again, the street was noisy itself and I could not quite be sure.

I waited at the kerb for twenty minutes, by which time all the approaching traffic had gone by and my uncle was completely out of sight.

Irritated, I then stalked back up the road, and found an intersection. Staring down one of the opposing boulevards, I had the impression that something was trundling away there. Before I could go after it, a band of religious choristers enveloped me, and I was forced to give them cash before I could escape. By then, naturally, any hint of what might have been a strange vehicle, or only an optical-illusion generated by sympathy and hope for the unnatural, had vanished.

I returned to my uncle's house in a bad mood, and he was already indoors, the portcullis down and all signs of life concealed.

After this jaunt he did not venture out again, though I waited for many weeks.

Unfortunately my own life was becoming complicated. I was supposed to be at work upon a new volume of tasteful obliqueness, and had neglected it sadly. Various creditors were restless, and I was already receiving fewer social invitations. My publisher advised me that, unless I took up my employment, the public would forget me, and I feared I would therefore no longer have the money to support my feckless parents, who were just then in the process of buying whole suites of unsuitable furniture, busts of Roman generals, and a black parrot.

Regretfully, I left my post at the low wall opposite to my uncle's house. It was a fine evening, the west still flushed with dusk, and a lone light burned in an upper window. And far off without a doubt at this moment, I heard it in the stillness, **chug chug chug** and then its **whoop** on a high weird note. It was circling at a distance, like a beast of prey, the campfire of that solitary lamp.

But I could no longer stay.

I went to my home, and my novel, so much more real than uncle's predicament.

4: The Machine

IT WAS on the afternoon that I delivered the finished manuscript of *The Fateful Kiss of Night* to my publishers that the last act of Uncle Constant's tragedy was played before me, and I was pulled irresistibly into it.

A beautiful afternoon of early summer, it had drawn the idle and the pleasure-seekers into the park. As I walked along beside the river the swans glided past like pillows with white necks, and the nurse-maids wheeled their bonneted toy babies up and down in perambulators. Young men pensively reflected in the glassy water, maidens sat reading under the statues, hoping the young men were secretly watching them, which, usually, they were not.

About two hundred yards off, over the wall of the park

and its line of tall trees, an ominous sound came and went, and I had glanced that way in a consternation I did not at first fathom. But although an apparatus was out there, it was only a steam engine, resurfacing the roadway with pitch. With a sense of relief or disappointment, I returned my eyes to the picture-postcard scene of the park.

Across the flower-beds lay a lawn, at the centre of which was a coloured bandstand. Here the bandsmen were going at full blast, and on the lawn couples bumpily danced a polka.

The warm day lay limpid on the park with all its safe and proper comings and goings, a postcard view, as I say, into which an unsuitable figure abruptly burst: Uncle Constant.

Of those assembled, I was not the least startled.

How he had come there was beyond ascertaining, he seemed merely to erupt into being. And my premonition of the steam-roller was appropriate. Uncle was as usual in headlong flight. Indeed, he was in the most abject condition I had yet beheld, and through his wheezing, he faintly screamed.

As people hastened from his way, a few turned their heads anxiously to see what it was he fled from, what it was he saw as his head craned at a painful angle over one shoulder. But having turned, they shrugged and one or two made good-mannered gestures relating to insanity; while three pompous gentlemen began to shout for the police.

I also turned, more from habit than from the hope of finding anything.

And so I saw, at last, coming across the wholesome green grass on which little children played and young ladies walked with their parasols, the moving engine of my uncle's terror.

It was unmistakable. It was tall as the second storey of a fashionable house, and it glided smoothly forward on great black runners. Its look was of a monstrous bathchair, but one which bristled like a porcupine. Pipes and nozzles protruded from it, ornamental and deadly: One glance assured me that each must be a variety of gun. And even as I stared one indeed gave off a puff of dull viridian smoke followed by a quick white flash. And over the merry noise of the park I heard my uncle howl with pain. I did not look to see if he had fallen. My eyes were fastened to the machine of his persecution.

Aloft, on a sort of balcony above the horseless, rolling carriage-front, were packed about ten persons. Perhaps they were men, they appeared to be, and yet . . . and yet there was something palpably wrong about them which my study unpleasingly revealed. Their dark overcoats were moulded to their bodies in the same manner that wings mould to the back of a black beetle. Their black moustaches quivered and seemed to move of their own will. And their eyes had been goggled over with curious dark green glasses that were faceted in many tiny winking panes.

Above them, and behind, a funnel rose from the top of the machine. Even as I glared at it, one of the riders touched its side with a gloved hand on which, perhaps, there were two or three extra fingers. The funnel responded with a dim glow and a gout of steam burst from the crown. Over the horrible thundering rattle and chug of the vehicle's progress shrieked a deafening **Whoop! Whoop!**

Frantically, I at last gazed about, to see if the bystanders were forced to put their bands over their ears.

But, just as they did not appear to see the machine, so they apparently could not hear it.

Even so, even so. As it trundled its inexorable and menacing way forward over the emerald grass, the children gambolled from its path, the girls increased their pace and swept aside. As if at a whim. Yes, as it advanced, the crowd parted before it, but not one of them paid it the slightest overt attention. Not one — save I. And my Uncle Constant.

He had certainly collapsed, but soon struggled up again. And now he limped and tottered on, striving to escape across the park. How desperate he looked. His face was white and blind with fear. He did not think, it was evident, he could on this occasion get to safety.

The machine went by me. It passed within three feet. I too must have taken some instinctive steps aside.

A furnace heat came from the thing, and the terrible chugging was accompanied by showers of cold green sparks from its runners.

Uncle limped over the flower-beds and rambled out on to the dancing sward. Couples bumped into him and waved him aside. He skirted the bandstand and went painfully on towards the wall.

The machine did not, or could not, improve its speed. Yet its unavoidable quality was somehow augmented by its very slowness, as in a dream.

It ploughed in among the dancers, who bounced and swung from its way, not looking at it, not hearing or seeing it. Unlike my uncle, seeming to have to move in a straight line, it came directly at the bandstand, and there, peculiar protuberances, like the rubbery legs of some enormous fly, poured out and raised the runners, and so walked the whole contraption up into the midst of the band, the top of the machine only narrowly missing knocking off the roof.

The musicians were forced to scramble to the perimeters, juggling their instruments.

And yet — even in this extremity — not one man regarded the invader, and not one lost the beat of their foolish dance.

And then the horror had marched on, and over, and was down on the lawn again, and all the band resettled, banging and tooting the jolly tune without a break.

A fierce ray flashed.

I saw my uncle sprawl headfirst.

Instantly he had pushed himself up, but now he could not rise from his knees. He began to crawl towards the wall of the park.

For a moment I stood at a loss. And then some primal spirit took hold of me.

I raced.

I sprinted over the lawn, scattering and possibly felling the polkists left and right. I tore past the machine itself, and felt again its awful heat, and smelled its metals and its odour of a chemical swamp, and of some location inexplicable.

Even past my Uncle Constant I sprang, and reaching the wall, I bolted through the gate.

Outside, the steam-roller majestically moved, and its motion was very like that other one, that wallow of the machine. I flung myself upon the steam engine and wasted no time in hauling myself up its side. The driver was startled as I barged in beside him. I thrust some coins into his palm and cast him out, and he plummeted angrily on to the pitchy road, shouting.

I turned the steam engine with difficulty but with determination, and drove it back through the gates.

My uncle was crawling steadfastly on, but thank God he had the sense to pull himself from my road. I cranked my colossus onward, until I beheld the persecution machine exactly in my path.

It did not veer, perhaps it could not. No expression crossed the faces — if such they were — of its malefic crew. Only the moustaches wrinkled and the goggles glittered, and from the stack of the funnel went up another gout of white and another fiendish whistle.

I sent the steam-roller headlong. With a grinding of gears and a furious hissing, it pounded forward into battle.

Until I could see every beaded decoration on the nozzles of the ray guns, I held to my post. Then I jumped away. I landed in a rhododendron bush. And at that moment the two leviathans came together.

There was an explosion like the Trump of Doom. And then a tumult only like that of some apocalyptic train crash.

A light like an incendiary burst, and out of it huge pieces of things were hurled into the air and dashed all about, boiling and gushing, and black metal rods, wheels, plates, cogs, screws, all types of mechanical and peculiar debris smashed down over the park.

Not a single cry or scream attended this.

But looking up from my bush, I saw the monstrous crew of the machine also, hurtling through space, and they were broken in a way human creatures do not break. Black blood or slime rained all around. It smelled medicinal and acid.

Presently the hurricane ceased, and a great stillness should have settled, but did not, for the park had gone on at its music and its chat uninterrupted.

I stared. Swans swam peacefully among black irregular objects in the river. Young ladies, blood-splattered, danced brightly with their bloodied gentlemen between rivets and black smoking shafts stuck down in the earth like flaming bones. Craters had appeared. And these the dancers carelessly circled. While the band played on, despite the green-goggled heads which had fallen on the bandstand roof, the instruments streaked with blood and coiled with what were, conceivably, alien entrails.

Of the machine nothing but a sort of heaving slag remained. There was little either of the noble steam-roller.

I went to my uncle and helped him up.

"It is over," I said.

"Who are you?" he demanded.

Outside the wall, the driver of the steam engine had left off his complaints. He sat smoking at the roadside, as if that was his only purpose, and touched his cap to me.

I assisted my uncle to his house.

ANTONIUS BEQUEATHED

SILVESTA was late for the funeral. She wore a black costume, long black hair, and pale violet gloves.

The old chateau lay in a forest and was not quite simple to reach. A private plane had deposited Silvesta at the forest's edge. From here she had had to continue on foot along a winding and in spots rather overgrown track. The forest was nearly black, dense with pine and larch and hung with ivy. Sometimes the faces of wolves might peer out at Silvesta, or a hare bound away. Birds sang in the trees and frogs croaked at hidden pools. Otherwise Silvesta saw no life for two hours, until she reached the gates of the chateau, an impressive building of stone, with round turreted towers and galleries of windows.

An elderly servant admitted Silvesta and led her up into a wide hall on the second floor. Here the other mourners were assembled. The priest had already addressed them, and they had begun to follow him out of the room. Silvesta joined the end of the procession. She knew nobody there. Everyone wore black and a stern expression, but none were in tears. The corpse, which was that of an aunt of Silvesta's she had never met, was borne on a bier draped in purple, by four tall young men in black top-hats, and wearing masks, of an owl, a fox, a locust and a crocodile.

The party went up many flights of stone stairs, with griffons carved on the bannisters, and eventually emerged on to the broad flat roof of a tower. Here the chateau dead had been buried for years.

All around were long granite vases, some six feet high or more, from the top of which spilled varieties of prolific flowers. In the centre of each flower bush might generally be discerned a brown human skull in different stages of decay.

The priest took up his station by a flowerless vase five and a half feet in height. As he spoke the words of the service, two gardeners shovelled some rich black soil into the empty vase. Then the four top-hatted, masked young men drew Silvesta's dead aunt from her bier, and lifting her high in her lace frock, let her down slowly into the jar until only her head showed above the rim. The gardeners quickly filled in the vase with soil, and packed it tightly around the dead woman's neck until even the pearls in which she had been buried had disappeared.

The priest concluded his words and folded his hands. A hunchback appeared and went to the vase. From a bag he took some white seeds, like grains of rice, and climbing up a small step-ladder, put them carefully into the mouth of the dead aunt. The chief mourner, a gaunt woman with beautiful false teeth, tipped the hunchback a little bouquet of notes.

Everyone went to the dead aunt, and sprinkled about her head some fertilizer from a crystal scoop. Most had to ascend the step-ladder to do so, and the more decrepit ones had to be assisted up and down, making feeble anxious sounds.

When this ceremony was over, the mourners moved below again into the house. A light rain had begun to fall on the forest. Silvesta paused to look at the vase of a more recent death, whose head had not yet completely rotted. From its greenish dough a myrtle had started to grow strongly. This was perhaps the remains of her uncle, who, the previous year while out shooting, had been killed by pigeons.

In the hall of the chateau the funeral guests were given cakes and wine, and then the will was read by the chief mourner.

Silvesta paid little attention to the will. She had no expectations of it. Instead she gazed at the stained glass pictures in the tops of the windows, which showed scenes of violence and murder from the Bible.

"And to my niece, Silvesta," said the chief mourner suddenly, with a snap of her beautiful teeth, "for her special care and protection, I leave Antonius."

All the other mourners raised their heads and stared at Silvesta.

Silvesta said: "What's that?"

"It is being brought," said the chief mourner.

Just then the door opened and in came two of the servants, propelling a large silver cage on wheels. As the cage rumbled nearer, it was possible to see inside an armchair, in which sat a very ancient, slender, white and almost transparent old man.

The servants opened the door of the cage and the ancient old man got up from his chair and came out. He stood beside Silvesta.

"This," said the chief mourner, "is Antonius. He is now yours."

"But what am I to do with him?" exclaimed Silvesta. None of them answered, and so she turned to the old man himself. "What am I to do with you? Surely you belong here?"

"I am yours," said the ancient man in a voice like a thin shaving of steel.

"This is ridiculous," said Silvesta. "I don't accept you."

"It was your aunt's dying wish," said the chief mourner.

Silvesta smoothed her gloves, and left the room. She descended the chateau and let herself out of the door. As she walked towards the gates, in the fine rain, she was aware of a narrow white shadow at her heels. The ancient man was following her.

Silvesta re-entered the forest. The canopy of the trees was so thick no rain fell through, and very little light. The ancient man glimmered behind her. Silvesta turned.

"It's a long walk. You'd better go back."

"I am yours," said the ancient man, "Silver Star."

Silvesta quickened her pace. Surely he could not keep up with her for two hours?

But the ancient man, Antonius, did so.

Now and then, the wolves looked out of the pines, but Silvesta barely saw them, she was so disturbed. She hurried until finally she was running, but Antonius trotted after her; his ankles might have rested on springs.

At last she came to the edge of the forest and saw her plane waiting on the meadow.

"You must go back now," said Silvesta firmly.

"I am yours. I shall go with you."

"There's no room," said Silvesta.

She walked to the plane and got in, and the ancient man climbed in after her. She tried to push him out but he was both resilient and adamant and somehow he had arrived in the seat behind her.

Presently the plane took off with Silvesta and Antonius aboard, and flew back to the city.

SILVESTA lived in a marble block overlooking the river. She was a designer of unusual clockwork animals, whose creations were very popular. Even the Mayor was often seen with a furry orange flamingo with two heads which Silvesta had designed for him.

The apartment had a studio, a bedroom, a garden room, a bathroom and a kitchen. It was full of plants, masks, weapons, statues, small trees, architectural finds, books, jigsaws, games, dolls, and furniture. Now there was also Antonius.

Antonius sat down in Silvesta's peacock chair and switched on the television. He dialled the sound up very loud. Once the television had been put on like this, it was never off, except for a few brief moments when Silvesta turned it off. Then Antonius would turn it on again.

Antonius did not sleep, so the television was also on all night.

Because he had no teeth, Antonius did not eat anything solid. He would therefore go to the kitchen and put everything he could find into the blender, whole oranges, cashew nuts, cold chicken, zucchini. He made these gruels several times a day, and often during the night.

Occasionally he would go about and inspect Silvesta's rooms. He would take down swords and spears and leave them lying in a tree, or the bath; or books, which he hid in cupboards. He put a doll into the washing-machine and started it.

When Silvesta left the apartment, Antonius would follow her. Sometimes she would rush across busy intersections, but somehow he always kept up. She could not lose him in the most crowded store.

He spent two hours every morning in the bathroom and two hours every evening.

He wore Silvesta's clothes, without asking her. They fitted but did not suit him, and he spilt orange and cashew gruel on them.

"I want you to go!" shouted Silvesta.

"I am yours," said Antonius.

One morning, after her normal sleepless night, Silvesta went out, and as always Antonius followed her.

She led him to the centre of a savage park where half-wild tigers were allowed to roam, and most visitors stayed in their cars.

"Do you like this tree, Antonius? I hope you do."

And so saying, Silvesta handcuffed Antonius to a low bough.

Then she went for the day to the sea.

That evening, when she returned, two florid kind people were waiting at her apartment door with Antonius.

"We found him for you in the park," they said, beaming. "How worried you must have been."

"He was handcuffed to a tree," added the florid man. "The things these old fellows do!" And he winked at Antonius, who was wearing Silvesta's golden skirt and four-inch heels.

"One of those naughty tigers was licking his feet," put in the florid woman. "I gave it a Choco-Bite."

AFTER A MONTH, Silvesta brought some of her acquaintances to the apartment and showed them Antonius.

"What a wonderful old man," they said.

They told Silvesta how exquisite Antonius was, added things to his gruel, turned the television up even louder for him, and soon went away.

Silvesta did not sleep and could not work. In her studio she could hear the television even over the blasting music she played, and the sounds of the blender breaking again on a meat bone. In the city shops Antonius came after her like a ghost. In the elevator mirrors she saw his white image, behind her left shoulder.

Exhaustedly she conducted him to an antique tea party, and two lovely cobwebby old women took a fancy to Antonius. But as they presently informed her, "He says he belongs to you."

Silvesta packed a bag by stealth. She left her possessions and her apartment, evaded Antonius, and flew to another city. On the third day a police escort howled into the street beneath her hotel, and next Antonius was brought up to her room.

"Here you are," they said. "How worried you must have been."

IN THE second month, Silvesta remembered something. She went to a firm of specialists who twelve days later delivered an amazing cage. It had a remarkable bathroom cubicle that required no maintenance, and in the open area was a comfortable armchair. It was quite difficult to get Antonius into the cage, but the burly men managed it, glaring at Silvesta afterwards and mutely accepting her large tip. Through the bars Silvesta slipped tiny earphones into Antonius' ears, and then turned on the television picture for him.

A blessed silence filled the apartment.

Silvesta worked in her studio all day on a blue feathered buffalo that sang Strauss. In the evening she made Antonius a gruel of roses, onions and Mozzarella cheese - one of his favourites.

Antonius did not eat the gruel. He sat staring at the silent television that only he could hear, and large silver tears slipped down his white pure ancient face.

"Why?" said Silvesta. "What more do you want? Do you want to drive me mad?"

That night in the silence she could not sleep. At dawn she let Antonius from his cage. He went at once to the apartment bathroom where he remained two hours. Then he came out, splattered the kitchen with avocado and halibut, turned up the television to gargantuan pitch, and concealed a Samurai sword in the arbutus.

ANTONIUS followed Silvesta to a dark glass building in the lower area of the city.

Seated on one side of a desk, with Antonius standing at her left shoulder, she detailed what had occurred.

When she had finished, she signed a paper, and a vast volume of notes changed hands.

Then two gigantic men came in. They wore snow white and looked impossibly wholesome. They lifted Antonius between them, and carried him away. He did not protest.

Silvesta said, "But he'll be well treated? Loud television, and his gruels . . . "

"Of course."

When Silvesta emerged from the building of dark glass, she went up in a helicopter to a high place. She sat there for hours surrounded by cedars and syringa.

When she got back to her apartment, she was tense and wary, but no one was waiting. No one came.

Some days passed, and some nights. The silence was profound. It grew and blossomed. Silvesta had a firm of professional cleaners in to see to the kitchen. When they had gone every trace of Antonius was obliterated. A last crossbow surfaced from the humidifier. All was calm.

Silvesta had dreams of a white figure riding after her on the back of the blue buffalo. She drank heavily for a month, until she no longer saw Antonius behind her shoulder in the mirrors of elevators.

After that she made the Mayor a yellow lemur with

three tails, the earth turned, and Silvesta re-became herself. She donated Antonius' cage to a famous aviary.

SOME NEW apartments had gone up in the middle of the river. In the topmost of one of these, the party was to be held. Silvesta, in a long white gown, joined some of the guests, who were gazing down from the balcony at a brown jade slice of river lapping the base of the building eighty feet below.

One of the guests had a striped parrot on his shoulder which was a design of Silvesta's. The parrot went through its tricks, and the guests questioned Silvesta about her work and her success. She was a celebrity, and they treated her with astonishment and great respect, so a transparent wall seemed to form all about her, isolating her from everyone.

It was the mode to drink a mauve wine, that tasted like cold iron, and Silvesta did not drain her goblet.

Presently she was persuaded to an ornamental table in the middle of the expensively bare and bony apartment.

On the table was a pot out of which a pretty miniature tree was growing. The tree bore fruit the shape of tiny lemons and the colour of pomegranate hearts. In a dish lay a heap of the fruit already plucked. The hosts invited the guests to sample it.

"This is my aunt," said the hostess, pointing at the small fruiting thing. "It's the latest method. They shrink the cadaver and pop it in a pot. Then they plant one of these little trees. A lovely memorial. And the dearly departed can always be with you."

She petted the tree and went on to confide she made a jam from the fruit, and leading them to an enormous fish tank peopled with fat black finny ovals, she demonstrated the feeding of the jam to the fish. The fish plainly relished it.

"They're carnivorous," said the hostess. "I suppose the jam . . . "

Some of the guests did not seem pleased that they had chewed and swallowed fruits nourished on an aunt's corpse.

But Silvesta sank into a reverie, remembering all those years ago, when she had attended the burial of her own aunt in the vase. As she was doing this, the other bright guests leaving her alone inside her walls of transparency, Silvesta passed before a tall skeletal mirror. She stopped in surprise. In the mirror was a very old woman in a long white dress and long white hair, and wrinkled ashen skin. It was Silvesta. Seventy years had gone by since the funeral at the chateau. How quickly and playfully they had gone, changing her one iota at a time, and now suddenly here she was. Silvesta studied herself with interest. At her back a few of the guests spoke of her complacently, knowing her as well as an heirloom. She was extremely deaf now and could not hear what they said.

Silvesta turned from the mirror and moved towards the door of the apartment. The host and hostess regarded her exit benignly, for an old and eccentric celebrity was permitted to behave as she wished.

Out on the street, Silvesta summoned a helicopter. She noticed how streamlined and shiny it was, an unfamiliar model. The helicopter rose into the peachbloom sky, and bore her away to the building of dark glass which, over seventy years, had added further angular terraces to its heights.

She was driven by a strange compunction, perhaps of guilt or sorrow, she did not know.

When she had reached the inner chambers of the building and explained her case, she had to wait more than an hour while computers sorted through the institution's records. Finally a man with a beaded scalp entered the room and opened a file before her which Silvesta could no longer read. He read aloud to her solicitously.

"No," said Silvesta, "you've made a mistake. I've only come for the remains. He was an old man then. It's been seventy years."

"Yes, yes," said the beaded man, soothingly. "But you see, we have it here. A room with a bath and television. Gruels ten times a day. Money has been extracted automatically from your account."

Silvesta had made so much money she had not missed these payments, evidently.

"If it's true," said Silvesta.

"But it is."

"Then I should like to see him at once."

"Someone shall take you to his apartment."

Silvesta said that she would prefer that the unbelievably elderly person be brought to meet her here.

The beaded man set off to see to this, and another half hour went by. Silvesta sat still on a couch, watching a moving news mosaic on the wall about countries she had never heard of. Then an ancient man, pale as ice, was guided into the room.

Silvesta stood up. She was utterly astounded. He had not changed as she had done. He was just the same.

She went towards him hesitantly.

"Antonius?" she asked, in her reedy voice.

"I am yours," said Antonius, "Silver Star."

Silvesta took him in her arms.

SINCE SHE no longer slept, Silvesta and Antonius would sit up all night, watching television with the sound very loud. Sometimes they played games, and now and then one of them would take something from its place in the nine roomed apartment, and hide it somewhere for the other to find. Although Silvesta had kept all her teeth through the wonders of modern dentistry, they were very fragile, and she was happy to eat the exciting gruels she or Antonius prepared in the unbreakable blender. For two or three hours in the morning and the evening, they companionably bathed together in the bathroom. They had no secrets from each other. They talked and talked, about everything. He never called her Silvesta, but always Silver Star.

Quite often they went out, and wandered the city hand in hand. In the park they fed the tigers; these beasts were now quite tame, although they occasionally attacked cars. As Silvesta and Antonius rose together in the elevators of stores, Silvesta would point to Antonius in the mirror. "There you are."

Antonius smiled.

One day they visited a display of mechanical washers, wearing each other's clothes, and put a bag of oranges into the works. Juice and pulp sprayed the audience. Silvesta and Antonius hurried away before they were caught.

In secret, Silvesta left Antonius in her will to the daughter of the Mayor. Then she hid the will in a lacquer box, and went to watch Antonius watching television.

ONE FOR SORROW

With thanks to Gary Cooper and John Kaiine

1st FEATHER

Daisy saw the dress the way you see a light come on in a darkened window — sudden, surprising, to be expected.

She had been in the new flat a week, and was dutifully exploring the area, finding the supermarket and the green-grocers, the library and the off-license, then branching out into the back lanes of curio shops and antique dealers. Here she found a rewarding shop which sold china masks, and finally Vanities. Vanities sold clothes, not the kind for normal wear, but what you wanted as a little girl when you were dressing up. Creations of silk and satin, crushed velvet and lace, beads and sequins, buttons, hooks and eyes.

Daisy quickly located a pair of purple shoes that might have been made for her. As she was paying for them, she saw the dress.

It hung in a row of other dresses in incredible colours and shapes, and some careless hand or side had dislodged it, so it had, in a way, stepped out from among the rest. It was black and white, the thinnest silk, and marked just a little, just a little tarnished, by old age.

Daisy left her shoes and went to the dress slowly.

She could see at a glance there was no way on earth she could ever have squeezed into it, for although she was slim, the dress had been fashioned for a figure that was a wand. And it was fragile, too; to force oneself upon or into it would be to rend.

A long tight white underskirt fell to an invisible ankle, and over that a waisted tunic of black, cut in a gracefully jagged way, dropped to a vanished knee. A V-neck, with a tiny glimpse of white there too, and three-quarter-length sleeves, with white slashes, somehow described the absent body of the nymph for whom it had been formed. It was a magpie dress. And sure enough, above the right breast of the bodice flew a tiny embroidered magpie.

"It's an absolute curse," the fat woman said from the counter.

"I'm sorry?"

"That dress. The black and white. I'll swear it moves about. Half the time it's on the floor, or else it gets over into the hats."

"It's — beautiful," said Daisy, although she was not sure that beauty was quite the word.

"Like to buy it? I'll tell you now, only an anorexic schoolgirl could squash into that," said the fat woman. "I measured the waist — eighteen inches. And an anorexic school-girl couldn't afford it. It's two hundred pounds."

"Neither can I," said Daisy.

Outside she put on the comfortable purple shoes, but after she had walked a hundred yards, they had begun to hurt after all.

DAISY THOUGHT the magpie dress was datable about 1912, which made it almost eighty years of age. Then again, it could have been a later copy.

She thought about the dress, actually, a lot; it was like someone she had met.

Who had worn it?

Daisy put aside her commissioned art-work, and

made a drawing of the dress, and then a drawing trying to put a woman *into* the dress. But it would not come out in the right way.

As she was going to sleep in the new south-facing position of her bed, she thought: *With that cheque coming, I could probably afford it.* She had been going to have a long weekend at the seaside, and if she made it just two nights, instead of three, she could buy the dress.

But why should she buy the dress?

On the edge of oblivion, she saw a magpie flying round her bedroom. Fascinating birds. She had never minded only seeing one, although it was supposed to be, was it not, unlucky? What did they say? *One for sorrow —*

There was something about the dress, but it was not sorrow.

THE NEXT AFTERNOON Daisy went back into Vanities.

"I bought a pair of shoes here yesterday, but they hurt a bit. I don't suppose you could recommend anything?"

"You should have tried them on," said the fat woman.

Daisy gave a mental shrug. She turned and went over to the dresses.

The magpie dress was not there.

"Oh — has someone bought it?"

"Bought what?"

"The black and white dress with the magpie."

"Oh *that*. No. Look, it's got up there."

Daisy looked where the woman pointed, and there the dress was, hanging up on a high rail, with its white tube of skirt depending and the black tunic fluttering a little, like feathers, in some random breeze.

"God knows how it got there," said the woman resentfully. "*I* didn't put it there."

"Does it have a history?" Daisy asked, still looking up. The breeze must be selective, for none of the other dresses were fluttering, but then the magpie dress was very thin.

"I expect so. You'd have had to ask Mrs Taylor, but she's retired."

"I can't then, can I," said Daisy.

"I don't know anything about it. I don't know anything about any of them. That's the only one causes trouble."

"Perhaps it flew up there," said Daisy.

But the woman only frowned.

MOST AFTERNOONS, Daisy would walk to the shops, to give her body a change of movement from standing up before the drawing-board or crouching over it on the table. The illustrations had hit an unseen rock. She was having trouble with them she had not anticipated. She brooded on them as she shopped. She did not turn down the lane towards Vanities but, on the fourth day, she went into the mask shop for a present for Agatha Soames. And when that was seen to, there was Vanities, and Daisy walked in.

The fat woman was not in evidence. Instead a young fat girl was sorting through a pile of hats with speckled veils.

The magpie dress lay crumpled on the floor.

Daisy had an urge to run to it and pick it up, to comfort it, poor helpless thing.

"You'll never get into that," said Young Fatty, with vicious pleasure.

"No, I'm sure I shouldn't."

"They was smaller then," said Young Fatty, with slight fear.

TWO CHEQUES came in next morning's post, one for some drawings Daisy had done for a magazine which had folded. They had honourably and amazingly paid her for her work, although unable to publish.

Daisy examined the cheque, cautiously. It was for three hundred pounds.

"What would I do with it?" she asked the flat, to which she talked off and on, getting it used to her. "Hang it on the wall . . . like a carpet? It's stupid. I don't collect old dresses."

At two thirty she went out and walked to Vanities where, with her BarclayCard, she bought the magpie dress.

"I tell you what," said Old Fatty "I think you've got a bargain. I think they underpriced this. Present, is it?"

"Yes," said Daisy "for my anorexic niece."

The dress hung from a picture nail in the wall of the bedroom. It seemed composed and calmed. Being black and white it went with everything and nothing. Daisy kept coming in from her work, to touch it, look at it.

One for sorrow, two for joy . . .

What made for joy, though? What made you happy? Well, to be able to work at what you were good at, and to get paid for it; to have a few good friends. Maybe, one day, to meet a man she could have more than just a fleeting relationship with, but then he would have to understand her, how she worked . . . And any way, she did not mean herself, not Daisy. "What made you joyful, Magpie Dress?"

And what brought you sorrow?

2nd FEATHER

DAISY WAS at a party and she was sure she should not have come. Perhaps she had not been invited. Everyone wore wonderful clothes, even the men, for their evening wear was dated and ornate, starched shirt-fronts, tiny embroideries ... And the women were like flowers from a show, hot-house lilacs and roses of fire.

Before she could look down nervously to see what she had put on herself for this auspicious fancy-dress occasion, Daisy's eyes were attracted by a flicker of something up in the air. A magpie was flying round the room, round the quaint gas-fitments with their golden glow. But no. It was not a magpie. It was a woman on a wide stair.

She stood there with her hand on the gilded banister, looking down. To Daisy, the artist, she was the most beautiful thing, apart from an animal, that Daisy had ever seen. Her face was exquisite, and just touched by rays of colour and the gold of the lamps. And her hair was like white gold, the utterly pure shade of nature, and coiled back from the perfect triangle of her face into a gleaming shell on her long neck. And from her hair rose a black and white feather and on her slender perfect body was the black and white dress.

I'll have to tell her I've got it, Daisy thought. But of course, the woman was wearing the dress. How odd.

The woman was descending the stair now, without hurry. Some of the guests had looked up, and seen her.

She greeted them coldly, indifferently, and their faces were false. A few good friends — no friends were here.

I care for nobody, no not I, if no one cares for me.

Surely they would, if she let them. She was so lovely — but then, beauty frightened a lot of people, a threat to a man, a slap to a woman.

Daisy could not hear what any of them were saying and she realized she was dreaming, and now she wanted to wake up before the Magpie — for she was the Magpie — came to her. Because what could Daisy do, confronted by this dream creature? Would she have to explain herself? How could she, when there was no sound-track?

The woman moved nearer, through the crowd. Her eyes were dark. Her beauty was almost painful. She had the strangest look — as if she anticipated nothing, ever. As if she were old and dry and blind.

No wonder they hated her. To meet those gorgeous eyes and see nothing in them, nothing at all.

Daisy woke.

In the half-lit dark of the city night, she saw a little, enough to register the dress had fallen off its nail, leaving the hanger on the wall.

The dress lay on the bed, with its magpie sleeves wing-spread as if to fly.

"No, I don't want you to do this," said Daisy. "Get off." And wildly she kicked with her feet through the duvet, and the dress slid away on to the floor.

"Sorry," said Daisy, "but the carpet's quite soft. Don't spook me. We have to be nice if we're going to live together."

The following morning, one of Daisy's posters leapt off the living room wall with a flapping electric noise, making her jump, so she splashed paint where she had not meant it to go.

She thought nothing much of this, however, for she was no handy-woman, and even hanging up posters was sometimes outside her range of skills.

Then she found the bathroom light was on. And later, the fire in the living room had switched on too, making the room very hot.

"Great," said Daisy.

She went and looked at the dress, and it lay there on its hanger, silent, still.

"I'm doing it," said Daisy. "Dotty Daisy."

Something went crash in the kitchen. She ran to see, and found a saucepan had come off the stacked washing-up and landed on the work surface across the room.

"Don't panic," said Daisy. She moved back into the bedroom and took hold of the tunic of the dress firmly. "Listen, lady, if this goes on you go *out*. Maybe you're used to that, if you are what I dreamed you were. But I won't play games. I mean it."

The rest of the afternoon passed peacefully. No lights or fires, nothing falling.

Daisy finished work for the day. She had not been shopping, working through, with salad in the fridge for supper. She opened a bottle of white wine, and went cautiously to look at the dress.

"You've been good. Don't think I don't appreciate it."

If I'd met her, she'd have hated me like she did everyone else. But then she didn't hate them, she just — didn't care.

Daisy sat on the floor before the open balcony window, looking out over geraniums and avocados to the long street, the big trees and on and off traffic.

What would it be like — not to have no one to love, but to love no one? *No one. Nothing.*

The wine had gone to her head and when she heard the smash, Daisy only got up gravely and went to look. In the bedroom a china cat her dead mother had given her was in four pieces on the carpet up against the wall.

"You bitch," Daisy said to the dress. And she threw the last of the wine in her glass across the front of it.

It swallowed the pale fluid. The mark was barely visible. How many times had they struck at the Magpie? Not physically, for it had seemed she was a lady, a society woman, protected, and yet certainly the blows had come in some schematic form, for she would incite them.

"I loved my mother. Fine, you didn't love yours."

Daisy pulled the Magpie off its hook, rolled it up — it was so slender it went to the thinnest, most flimsy coil — and put it into the built-in wardrobe under a box of shoes.

She slept with the light on. But nothing moved. There were no dreams.

"OH THIS is just wonderful," Agatha cried. And she bore the white beaked mask before her like an offering. "What's in the other bag?"

"Chocolates."

"Evil, wicked weasel."

"And she's brought wine," said Tony.

"Also this." Daisy handed Tony the fourth bag. "I'm sorry, but I know you're brilliant at fixing things."

"It's Lettuce," he said. "Oh, poor old Lettuce. Did you drop her?"

"No. I've got a poltergeist and it threw her at the wall."

As they sat in the large room full of books and plants and statues of Egyptian gods, Daisy told them of the Magpie, and its deeds.

"It couldn't just be a coincidence?" asked Agatha. "The flat settling, or something."

"What, and turning on the fire?" said Tony. "No, she's got a nasty there all right. I think, love, you'll have to take the damn dress back to the shop."

"But how can she?" cried Agatha. "She's dreamed about the woman who wore it."

"Does that mean she owes her something?"

"She was so beautiful," said Daisy, "and so — awful."

"You've heard the expression," said Tony, "bored to death? It can happen. Sounds as if it did, to her." He drank some more wine, and then said, "I don't know if I ought to tell you. But you're getting there anyway."

"Tell me what?"

"You've never heard of the Magpie Fashion?"

"No," said Daisy. The hair rose sharply on her scalp and made her shiver. "Tell me now."

"About 1910, 1911. There was a vogue for black-and-white dresses for women, sometimes with feathers or feather effects. And little black hats with a feather sticking straight up. And magpie brooches. It was actually to do with the start of the cinema — everything in black and white."

"Why not pandas then," demanded Agatha, "or cats?"

"Magpies can fly. It was the element of flying in black and white."

Daisy mused. "I see. In the dream, she was the only one wearing a dress like that."

"Fashions come and go," said Agatha.

"That fashion didn't just go," said Tony. He looked uneasy and refilled their glasses and his own.

"Well?" said Agatha.

"Well," Tony said, "that particular fashion was *advised* to a stop."

"Advised — what do you mean?"

"The police advised that women, especially young, blonde women, should give it up."

There was a silence.

Daisy felt strangeness. She asked, "Why?"

"You've heard of Jack the Ripper," said Tony. "Have you heard of the Magpie Hunter?"

"Oh, you're making this up," said Agatha, with some pride.

Tony shook his head. "No. In the summer of 1912, there was a guy who used to go around a certain area of London, slashing to bits blonde women in magpie dresses."

"I feel weird," said Daisy.

"Tony!"

"No," said Daisy, "tell me some more."

"Not a lot to tell. He did it. Murdered about eight girls. Unlike the Ripper's, his victims were from all walks of life. Shop-assistants, house-maids, a couple of so-called ladies straying out on their own. And then the murders stopped. I can't remember if they caught him. I think — no, I just can't recall."

"But you do think she — I mean, the Magpie — ?" Daisy took a gulp of wine.

"She was blonde all right. And you said — bored to death."

They sat in silence again, looking at nothing.

Then Agatha got up.

"I'm going to inappropriately baste the chicken."

When she had left the room, Tony said, "Sorry. I didn't mean to make it worse."

"You haven't. But what do I do?"

"Take the dress back."

"Will that be enough? Maybe they won't accept it."

"Just dump it in between a couple of others when they're not looking."

"But what does it mean?"

"I don't know," said Tony. "But there is one thing."

"Yes?"

"She can't have been wearing it — I mean, not that particular dress. Not if he did get her. He used a knife, you see, and — sorry — just slashed. They, and their dresses, were in ribbons."

Daisy felt inured now. She sat demurely and said, "How odd."

Agatha returned with another bottle.

It HAD obviously been a relief to go out. Coming back at two in the morning, pleasantly tiddly and nicely tired, Daisy knew a slight sensation of fear.

The driver of the hired car watched her to her door, then drove off; and Daisy let herself into the sleeping house.

When she opened the door of her home, and switched on the light, she had only the violent first impression that she had entered the wrong flat. Then she know that she had not.

The worst thing had happened. Burglars had got in. The foulest type of burglar. They had thrown her ornaments and plants about the room — even thrown over her drawing-board and squirted coloured paint up the wall.

And then she realized it was not burglars.

For, no longer rolled up in the wardrobe, but on the carpet, neatly spread out with its wings unfolded, lay the Magpie Dress, the one quiet seemly object in the ruined space.

Daisy ran to the bathroom and lost Agatha's excellent dinner.

3rd FEATHER

When she was a child, Daisy could remember, it had usually been very quiet in libraries, but now there were constant comings and goings, soft and not so soft conversations, the buzz of electronic gadgets. Nevertheless she sat there doggedly at the long table, from ten in the morning until four thirty, and read the book they had found for her. She went out once and bought a sandwich, and ate it on the bench on the forecourt. All the time, the dress stayed coiled in her bag.

She had not slept the night before and her eyes were gritty. But even so, she read all the book. *The Magpie Killings* it was called.

At five in the morning, when she had finished as much of the cleaning up as she could manage, Daisy had spoken to the dress.

"I'm going to presume you want something. It isn't just spite. I'm giving you that chance."

The dress had lain quiescent where she had thrown it. It had not moved and it caused no further damage. It let her roll it up again and push it down in the bag, and take it out to the library.

At first they had said they had nothing on the subject Daisy wanted. And then someone had discovered the old book in their reserve stock. "I'm afraid all the plates are missing. Dreadful vandalism."

She was too stunned to care about the plates. She just wanted to know some facts.

Basically, the book was a list of the murderer's eight victims. There was a chapter on each one, how and why she had been in the notorious Faithways area, which the author, with inappropriate wit, had quickly re-christened the Black Whitechapel of the Magpie Ripper.

Of the murderer himself there was no proper information. He had been variously sighted and randomly described, sometimes as tall, dark, and gliding; and sometimes as stocky, squat, and creeping. He was alternatively a shadow, a ghost, a preying tiger, a lurching toad. Those who claimed to have caught glimpses never concurred. And so perhaps none of them had ever spotted the true murderer. What had become of him too was as much a mystery as his identity. As with Saucy Jack, the slayings had abruptly come to an end. The reason for his massacre was equally or more obscure. The author did not put forward any theories. Indeed, he smugly asserted that he had resisted them in the face of lack of evidence.

His concern was with the victims.

Daisy read the chapters with a slight sickness and a dim apprehension. The eight lives were very different, only similarly tragic because of their inevitable plunge on to the Magpie Hunter's knife — for, in each case, it really did seem as if they had been drawn to him, had almost sought him out. But was this one the owner of the Magpie Dress — or this one? It was impossible, horribly and frustratingly impossible, to tell.

And of course the plates could have — might have — answered the question at once. For evidently, judging by the table at the beginning of the book, there was a picture, although now and then only a sketch, of each of the dead women. Plus certain other drawings and photographs, labelled:

THE FATAL ALLEY;
A WEDDING AT ALL SAINTS CHURCH,
FAITHWAYS;
TWILIGHT IN FAITHWAYS;

and so on. The missing frontispiece bore the note:

A GLAMOROUS EXAMPLE OF A FASHION
WHICH KILLED.

AT FOUR THIRTY when Daisy had completed the book and her pocket mirror told her her eyes were inflamed, she felt dissatisfied and uncomfortably anxious. She seemed to have learnt nothing, or nothing that might reflect on the enigma of the violent and evil dress. And conversely, Daisy had been swimming in blood, the blood of eight blonde girls, slashed from throat to groin, silk and muslin, cotton and voile, skin and arteries; bone.

"Excuse me." A plump and pretty and blonde young woman stood, almost perversely, at Daisy's side.

"Oh, are you closing? Sorry."

"No, not for another two hours, worse luck. But look. The van came over, and I was able to get hold of another copy of your book. This one's got all the plates."

Daisy felt a wave of nausea. The last thing she wanted now was to see — to see the whole forms of those women hacked to ribbons in the alleys and squares, in the very church porch, of charmingly named Faithways.

But the assistant had been diligent and kind, and it would be rotten and rude not to respond.

"Oh, thank you. That was good of you. I'll — just take that one then."

And so Daisy checked out and put the second copy of *The Magpie Killings* into her bag with the Magpie Dress, and went back to her flat.

THE ACRYLIC MARK would not leave the wall unless she repainted. The red splotch on the curtain was never going to go either. Like a splash, of course, of blood.

Daisy tried to drink a glass of wine, could not; a cup of tea, could not; looked at her provisions of smoked fish and new potatoes with sadness. They were not going to be eaten.

Eventually she sat down, next to her bag, and withdrew the book.

Meticulously she turned to the first picture, the frontispiece. It was a dense black and white photograph; and it drained the vitality from her heart, which began to beat in slow loud strokes.

For the frontispiece — **A GLAMOROUS EXAMPLE OF A FASHION WHICH KILLED** — showed a slender, exquisitely beautiful girl on a stairway. Her hair was coiled shell-like on her neck and a feather rose from it. She wore the Magpie Dress Daisy had bought from Vanities. And she was the girl from Daisy's dream.

"All right," Daisy said aloud. "All right. I do believe it. Just — give me a minute."

Then she read the rest of the caption, under the photograph:

Margaret Shawn, a society hostess of the era, and said to be one of the most beautiful women of her day, dressed in an elegant version of the so-called Magpie Fashion, even to a feather in her hair. Margaret Shawn, although she defied police advice against such garments, was not one of the murderer's victims.

Daisy spread the dress out on her bed. She addressed it.

"Let's try; I'll trust you. But no tricks, Margaret Shawn. Or I'll burn you. And if that lets your demon out, then I'll find a priest. I'll stop you. Understand?"

Daisy rolled the Magpie up and put it under her pillow.

Then she drank some very hot tea with a little gin in it and swallowed two herbal sleeping tablets.

Would they work, against this sort of stress?

Let's hope so, Margaret Shawn.

Or Margaret Shawn might prove unhelpful. Margaret Shawn might pick up the bed and throw it through the window, and Daisy with it.

But no. That was not the way for Margaret Shawn to get what she wanted, whatever the hell that was.

Margaret . . . it meant the same as Daisy, did it not . . . Pearl.

The room floated, and Daisy felt the dress stir under her neck, like a snake. But it was too late now—

SHE WAS WEARING pale green tonight, *eau de nil:* Nile Water.

The man across the table from her, across the candles and the pyramid of fruit, the crystal and the wine, looked at her, could not take his eyes off her.

"Maggie, can we . . . It's been a long time."

"If you like."

"No, no, I'm sorry, I shouldn't have said anything."

He had been asking permission to make love to her, that was clear, and she had not refused, yet she had put him off. How could you make love to that beauty, any way, with those agates of eyes watching.

Then servants came in, the ubiquitous dummy creatures of the big houses, always there, eyes and ears, and suddenly Margaret Shawn had got up.

The male port had arrived. Was that it?

Whatever it was, she was making some gracious, uncaring, flinty excuse, and leaving the room.

Up a stair, gas-lamps, a tapestry hanging, and smart pictures of long, long people with long, long dogs. Now a bedroom. Hers.

Margaret Shawn was sitting before her mirror in a lacy

flounced gown, and one of the maids was brushing over and over that undone stream of lemon-gold hair.

"Tell me about it," said Margaret Shawn.

"Oh Madam — I can't. The Master said — "

"Never mind what the Master said. He knows I see the newspapers. He knows everyone is talking of it. I want to hear."

"But Madam. It's horrible."

"Yes it is. Horrible and fascinating."

"They say he does it because of the black and white dresses."

"I know. Lady Pane told me. But someone saw him, didn't they?"

"Oh, Madam."

"I shall be angry," said Margaret Shawn.

The maid flinched. And Daisy knew, as she had known about the refusal to have sex, that Margaret Shawn did not punish physically, but through the psyche.

"It was — it was Liza, Madam. Liza Meadows."

"You know her?"

"Yes, Madam. Sometimes on my afternoon she and I — well, she thinks she saw him. I mean, the murderer."

"Tell me," said Margaret Shawn. "No. Stop brushing my hair. That's enough."

And she got up, and walked to the long window, and there she stood looking down on to some interruptions of great trees, and beyond a square that had a garden.

The maid spoke. She said her friend, Liza Meadows, had had to go over to Faithways, to see her aunt. Unlike Red Riding Hood, Liza had not strayed from the path, but even so, in the onset of darkness, she had beheld before her a tallish figure swathed in the coming of night.

"He was dressed like a gentleman," said Margaret's maid, "only he hadn't a hat on his head."

This was strange to Liza, and made her check. And then she realized that she had put on her only good dress and jacket, which gave the effect, in twilight, of black and white. But she thought to herself, *Why should it be me?* And she went on gamely.

There was a street lamp which had been lit, and under it, he was.

"She said he was like a prince, Madam. I mean, from a fairy tale."

Liza, and Margaret's maid, did not have the words for it, yet it grew like a flower, out of the compost of dull sentences.

He was beautiful. So beautiful that when he looked at you — you were trapped. His hair was blonde, too, like the hair of the victims. His eyes a pale sere blue that gleamed. He seemed to hold Liza by a rope of fire, and she was drawn towards him now helplessly. And then she was under the lamp also, and he must have seen — her clothes were chocolate and pale green. Not black and white at all. And suddenly, as if the light itself went out, he turned his flame from her. And he was gone.

"Liza felt faint, Madam. She had to lean on a wall."

"Has she been to the police?"

"Oh, no, Madam. She had no business being there. Her Missus had warned her to keep away."

Margaret Shawn stood looking out on the busy square. A few autos came and went, like handsome insects. People walked. There too the gas-lamps had been lighted.

"It's all right, you can go," said Margaret Shawn, and her maid slunk out.

Margaret Shawn held the velvet drapes in both her hands as if she clutched at something, drowning. Yet her face was calm. Only her lips slightly parted. And her eyes rapt, wide.

Her husband looked at her like that, when he asked her to sleep with him.

But she wanted the murderer. She wanted the murderer of women. She wanted death. *That* death. The phallic knife, the orgasmic scream —

It was in every line of her immaculate, frigid body. Blonde Virgo. For whom the magpie is a special bird . . .

And she asked the maid for news, the way the schoolgirl asks for stories, anecdotes, about the boy she has a crush on.

Out there, out there he is.

And Margaret Shawn let her curtains fall and turned to stare at her bedroom. She wanted nothing, disliked everything. Lusting for one thing only. Hair and eyes, the shadow, the hand and the knife.

I want to wake up.

Daisy shifted and half felt her flat about her and then she was down again, in the dark, with beautiful Margaret.

It was another place. A long street which Daisy knew at once, from the plates in the book that she had forced herself to see. Linden Avenue. Tall houses in the dark, and between, the greenish cat's eye glow of gas lights. And the turning — the alley. The Fatal Alley.

And Margaret Shawn walked into it.

She wore her black and white dress. No feather in her hair, just the pristine coiling. And she moved like a swan, the swan in the evening — over the lake.

Her face was avid, like the face of a madonna which works miracles if you go to it with pain and blood and tears.

Margaret Shawn walked through the alley, and back again.

It was a summer night. And nothing stirred.

How often had she come? Did she arrive by cab, perhaps, making the excuse to her ineffectual husband that she visited some non-existent friend, for friends she did not have. Only one potential friend — Him.

Margaret Shawn walked exquisitely along the alley again, and so across the avenue, and the square, where a great church brooded. Were there no police? She must have eluded them, or else the watch had flagged and she had taken advantage of that.

Death and the Maiden. She had gone out to find him. But he did not come to her. Coitus interruptus. Yes, her face was like that now, the lips a little slack, disappointed, a thin line between the brows.

How terrible. She had dressed for him, bathed and scented herself. And he had stood her up.

A blot appeared on the pavement. The lamps sizzled. Rain had fallen. Overhead, a rumble of thunder. Daisy heard as she had heard the conversation in the bedroom.

How often had she come here, Margaret Shawn, searching in vain, refused by death. In heat and in rain, fire and water. Jilted.

THE PHONE was ringing.

Daisy woke. It was ten o'clock.

"Yes?"

She felt hung-over, which did not come from a single gin in tea and two herbal tablets. But she had been dreaming. What — ?

"It's me."

Tony.

"Tony?"

"Are you okay? You sound odd."

"Overslept."

"Damn. Sorry to wake you. Only — "

"Yes?"

"I wondered if everything was all right? I mean, the dress."

"No. And yes. I suppose so. I suppose it has something to say. Can I call you back in five minutes?"

"No," he said, "call you in ten."

Daisy stumbled to the bathroom, relieved herself, cleaned her teeth and splashed water on her face. She came out and put on the kettle for Assam tea.

While it was brewing, Tony rang back.

"Sorry about that," said Daisy; I have a contact with Margaret Shawn."

"My God," he said, "she's in the book. Was it hers?"

"The dress — definitely."

"The thing is," Tony said, "I got intrigued. You know Martin over at Streatham? Well, I phoned him up and he had a book in the shop —"

"Not *The Magpie Killings*," said Daisy. "I've read it."

"No, this is older. Very small. About eighty pages. But you see, I sent it off to you. And now Agatha says I shouldn't have. Are you going to be okay?"

"Oh yes," said Daisy firmly, pouring and sipping the Assam, clenching her toes. Under the pillow she could see the edge of black and white. "I'm going to be fine."

"It'll probably arrive in your second post."

"Thanks, it was kind of you."

"Maybe you shouldn't read it."

"I think I'll have to."

"Look, if you need us — " he said.

"I know where you are."

THE BOOK CAME with the second post. It was a slender volume, black cover, white lettering. Its title was: *Sorrow*. Nothing more. Inside, on the title page, small lettering added: *Some speculations on the Magpie Murders.*

And under that was printed part of the old rhyme, not quite as Daisy had remembered. *One's sorrow, two's mirth.*

Daisy made toast she did not want and ate portions of it — not the crusts, *My hair won't curl* — and drank more tea. Then she sat down, in her nightshirt, to read *Sorrow*.

It was a strange book. Somehow intensely personal, as if the writer, whose name she kept forgetting, and which did not really matter, had become obsessed with the events at Faithways, and driven his obsession on into the realms of dream, and so the quasi-supernatural. In parts it touched poetry, and in others the prose was blunt and mundane. It mentioned the victims, not as individuals, like the other book, but as a sort of entity. Only to Margaret Shawn did it devote an individual section:

For Margaret Shawn, society hostess and celebrated beauty was in fact also one of the Hunter's victims.

Testimony was quoted from Margaret's maid, Alice Dimpson, from her diary, and illiterate letters she had penned to friends. How 'Madam' had become fascinated by the murderer, and spoke of him constantly in private, such as when Dimpson was dressing her or doing her hair. 'It was as thow she had a lova,' wrote Dimpson, 'a fance man.' Dimpson indeed found her mistress's interest prurient, without knowing quite how or why. Then, when her mistress began to be absent from the house, saying she had gone to dine alone with Lady Pane-Rosythe, Dimpson realized that Margaret Shawn went to walk the alleys and streets of Faithways, in her black and white dress. 'Masta puts up wiv it,' wrote Dimpson, pragmatically. She believed he thought his wife was seeing another man. Dimpson herself was terrified by now. She reckoned Margaret would be 'sliesed up.' She did not dare to speak.

Faithways, said the author, whose name Daisy kept mislaying, was a corruption of the old Featherways, or Fetherwies. Featherways Lane had run on down to the river, and once there had been both a nunnery and a house of monks situated along its length. These religious buildings had been founded after the visitation of the Black Death.

The summer was erratic, and one night when Margaret Shawn was out walking, a massive storm took place, with torrential rain. Margaret returned about midnight, soaked through.

From this outing, apparently, she contracted a chest cold which swiftly turned to pneumonia.

Alice Dimpson believed Margaret Shawn had gone out courting the Magpie Murderer; instead she met Death in another form. A week later she succumbed.

"Not this way," the author of the book reported Margaret Shawn's dying words to be. "A straw death."

That was what the Vikings had feared, the book said, the 'straw' death — death in bed, as opposed to violent death in battle which would carry the warrior to Valhalla.

But Margaret Shawn had died through the Magpie Hunter as surely as if he had slashed her in bits. She too was his victim, the ninth. His choicest and most lovely, although he had never met her.

IT WAS THREE in the afternoon. Daisy went and made coffee instead of tea. She returned to the book with a rabid reluctance.

The dress had not moved. Nothing had. A weird stillness enclosed the flat, into which the noise of traffic came from far away, as if through water.

Faithways, Fetherwies, was a haunted area. Halfway

along it, in the fifteenth century, said the book's author, had been a statue of the Virgin. One night a priest from the monastery was found cut to pieces nearby, among the trees at the Lane's edge . . . He had been used to hear the confessions of the nuns.

Magpies, said the author, like nuns and monks, in black and white. Magpies, sacred to the Virgin, who had conquered the demon realm of darkness and the moon.

"No," said Daisy, "that's enough."

She shut the book on the last chapter, which was called 'The Murderer Vanishes.'

She went and had a bath. She felt exhausted. She ate cheese on toast and an apple.

The stillness had persisted. It was twilight now. The day had gone. Why had this book, so much smaller than the other, taken so long to read?

She was confused, too. Images of girls from 1912 in black and white and mediaeval nuns in black habits . . .

Finally she read the concluding chapter, propped up like an invalid in bed. The words blurred, came and went.

He did not keep his appointment with Margaret Shawn because he had had to escape. Apparently the police had sussed the murderer, and he, getting word of it, fled. He ran from London, out into the rolling orchards and fields of rural Kent.

And so he came to a once notorious inn, which happened to be named The Magpie.

This must be pure invention, Daisy thought.

Yes, certainly, because —

At the inn, he was recognized. And in the night, the village people stormed his room and took him out. They took him to an old gallows across the square, and there they hanged him by the neck until dead.

And this was hushed up, remaining only as a rumour and boast.

The Magpie Inn had always, it seemed, vaunted a window which overlooked the gallows. The rich and curious had once paid to take it and watch the hangings of highwaymen. That night the room was empty. They were all down in the square.

They buried his body in an unmarked grave. There was no proof.

But, put down in black and white —

The phone rang.

"Sod it. I woke you again,"

"Hello Tony. I got the book. It's very peculiar."

"Martin says the writer was a known laudanum addict, who wrote under the influence. Most of it's — make-believe."

"What about the inn?" said Daisy.

"Oh that exists, I checked a Kent guide. A place called Asham."

"Sounds Indian." Daisy closed her eyes. Christ knew what she would dream now.

"Look, I'll call you again in the morning. Agatha's been giving me hell."

"It's all right," said Daisy. "Where's Asham?"

"You can get there from Charing Cross. Off the Dartford Loop somewhere. Should have told you."

"Isn't laudanum too late for 1912 . . . whenever."

"You mean the book? 1913. Apparently not. I'll call you at eleven."

Daisy said, "Got to go to sleep now. Night. Love to Agatha."

She depressed the cradle, and then left the phone off the hook.

Daisy touched the edge of the dress under the banked-up pillows.

"Be gentle. Don't kill me. Or I can't."

She did not recall putting out the light.

5th FEATHER

IN THE WALLED GARDEN, the nun was standing with her arm up-raised.

The walls were high, but clad by roses. Roses like fat pink cabbages with red hearts. There was a small pool, and fish glinted there. Beyond, other higher walls. Grey, yet touched by sunlight.

In the sun, the nun's skin was young, and white as crystal. Despite the black garments and the pallid wimple, she was beautiful. And in her pale lifted fingers was a gob of raw and bloody meat.

Someone came through an arched doorway. Another nun. This one incredibly wrinkled, brown and warty. She turned to the beauty and tugged at her shoulder.

And the beauty turned her arrogant white perfect face.

Then they spoke.

Daisy could not understand a word. Well, maybe one word in twenty.

It's like Chaucer.

Just vision then, reading of faces, not lips. The young one was proud and disdainful, and the ugly one harassed and bustling; jealous.

Then there was the flap of wings and the beautiful one turned all her attention up into the air, as if at the approach of an angel. And Daisy knew she was saying, *Look! You see.*

The magpie dropped down. It was heavy and solid, black nun-mantle over white, and the wicked beak of a crow, and glowing sideways eyes. It landed on the white arm, where, Daisy now saw, there were already scorings from a hundred such landings.

It took the meat ferociously yet daintily from the girl's grip, and ate, standing there on her slender arm.

The old jealous one had drawn back muttering. She had even made a sort of sign that must be some version of the Cross.

With mouth sewn tight, she waited.

The beautiful one drew something up from under her habit. It was a precious stone, greenish, maybe a beryl. She jinked it under the magpie's beak. She was saying, teasingly, 'Do you want it? Bright, pretty — ' And the magpie seized the jewel and, green drop and shreds of bloody flesh dripping from the dagger of its beak, it flapped away. And the girl called after it, some name which meant a faithless lover.

The old one muttered. She told the girl — Daisy understood as if sub-titles were being printed in her brain — that the young one's brother was coming. And the young one said she did not care to see him. And then she told the old one to go away.

The daughters of the rich had sometimes been allowed to queen it in the nunneries. They must dress as nuns, but otherwise what they did was very much their own province.

And Beauty was of this order. Even to her jewels.

Now her dark eyes rested on the sky where the magpie had gone. And she smiled.

She was not innocent.

Daisy saw the magpie, like a dot in heaven, wink out.

"No, it's getting muddled." Daisy lay in bed, talking to herself or the dress. "We had 1912. But what's this now?"

The book, *Sorrow,* lay on the floor.

What had the laudanum addict said? Margaret Shawn's broken 'appointment' with the killer?

Did Margaret Shawn look like the beautiful, dark-eyed nun?

"All right," said Daisy. "All right."

I'm not being rational.

She washed her hair and dressed, and when Tony phoned her at eleven o'clock, she was already sorting things out for her journey.

"I've got to go to Birmingham. It's a real nuisance. But they insist on seeing me, and they're paying expenses."

Tony sounded relieved.

"Well, it will give you a break . . . "

"Oh that. I think it's fading out."

When Tony rang off, she phoned British Rail. And then she packed a small bag and put the rolled-up Magpie Dress in at the top. And stuffed *Sorrow* down one side.

"Sorry about this," she said to the flat. "Take care."

She felt wild and light, perhaps the way the successful anorexic feels before the pain begins.

THE TRAIN would take forty-five minutes. The long carriage was empty but for an elderly woman three or four seats further down. The windows were so thick with dirt the landscape outside was distanced, and though notices prohibited smoking, the space reeked of smoke. But perhaps it was only the pollution of the city.

London drew back. Old defamed tower blocks lined the horizon.

Daisy shut her eyes.

I'M NOT ASLEEP.

Yes, but I was awake in the other dreams too. A fly on the wall.

It was a kind of walkway, with arches, and the beautiful nun was there, standing quite still. She was looking down.

In the stone yard below, a fat woman, also a nun, and with a golden crucifix on her ample bosom, was walking about with a priest.

He was tonsured, and Daisy felt a distaste for this. She sensed that Beauty did too. For the rest of his hair was thick and blond, shining in the summer light.

The important fat nun and the priest were speaking rapidly, and now and then a phrase of strongly accented Latin drifted up.

This time, Daisy did not take in any of the words, rather she seemed privy to the unspoken phrases of the beautiful nun's body. In her white throat the pulse, beating. And her slender hands grasping the stone of the arch.

Then she called. It was very respectful, addressed to the Mother Superior or whatever she was, but both of them looked up, the fat woman and the blond man.

The beautiful nun bobbed a sort of curtsy. She was trembling all over with suppressed laughter, and with something else.

The fat woman was disapproving yet restrained. Obviously, the beautiful nun came of a powerful family, which had granted a large beneficence to this house.

And the priest . . . He looked only arrogant, proud in the flawlessness of his vocation. If he saw Beauty, he did not show it. He might have been glancing at the stone.

He seemed about thirty-eight years of age, and so

probably was in his late twenties, for Daisy imagined that Mediaeval maturity was evidenced early. In the same way Beauty, who looked twenty-five, was more likely about sixteen.

The priest was painfully handsome. Frighteningly so. And as he turned from the nun on the walk without acknowledgement, Daisy knew the heat of fire, the deep knocking of the excited heart, and the tingling awareness of its own loveliness which suffused the young girl's body.

"Have to get out here," said the station worker, sneering in at Daisy. "Unless you want to go back to Charing Cross."

Daisy got off the train, tumbled off, between two worlds.

SHE STOOD on the platform. Everything was grey. She had expected open fields and green hills, flowers and trees, but Asham was not like that.

She wanted him.

Oh yes, Beauty had wanted the priest all right. Daisy could recall those wonderful, awful feelings too well. They stopped you eating and sleeping, and working. But what happened if you were a nun sworn to chastity and he was at the cold-heat of religious devotion, given to his God, with no room for anything else?

Daisy walked out of the station.

It was a kind of village, but one which had sprawled and overbuilt and become a town. The rolling orchards of 1912 were only now the concrete suburbs of the nineties.

Wake up.

Daisy shook herself, actually and physically.

Above in the station foyer she bought herself a diet coke, the taste of her own time.

On the forecourt were three cars labelled as taxis.

"Do you know the — pub, The Magpie?"

"No. Try Jack."

She tried the second car. Jack said he had heard of The Magpie, but it was in Sidcup.

"No, it's at Asham. It's famous. They used to hang highwaymen on the square outside."

She expected him to look at her as if she was mad — maybe she was — but instead he shook his head. "That's in London."

Daisy took out the book, *Sorrow,* from her bag. She showed Jack the description of the inn.

By now the third one had got out of his car and come over. The first man had no interest and was reading a paper.

"That's the Old Mag you want," said the third man. "Blowed if I know where it is though."

Daisy drew in a deep breath.

"Would you be prepared to drive round Asham and help me find it? Whatever it costs, of course."

"Well," said the third driver, "I'll give it a go."

THEY GAVE it a go.

They drove through grey flat Asham, and finally they found the rolling fields after all, but they were cindery, and the trees looked scorched as London trees.

Besides, reaching the outer environs, the driver turned back. "It ain't out here. It's in the centre somewhere."

Back through Asham, up and down.

This pub and that.

The driver got out and asked at the Red Horse.

"We'll try up by the railway crossing."

They did so, to no avail.

Daisy felt contrite and determined. Any minute he

might get sick of it and ask her to get out. But in fact the driver now seemed as questing as she. He only asked her if she was still all right to pay.

They found the Old Mag about four o'clock. The sky was heavy with summer overcast, and in a narrow street of dress shops and cafés, a timbered front appeared bulging out, and a sign — of a magpie in flight.

"Oh thank you," said Daisy, as if he had delivered her baby in the cab or rescued her cat from a tree or fed her when she was starving.

"I'm afraid it's twenty-two quid."

She gave him twenty-five and he drove off happy, pleased with victory and money.

The pub was shut. A board told her it would not open until six.

Daisy went into one of the cafés across the street.

She was disconcerted there was no square. As she sat there over her hot ham croissant and Spanish salad, she told herself the square must have been built on.

She drank a lot of tea, and when the café filled up at five-thirty, she removed herself for a nervous walk along the street, being careful not to wander too far from the elusive pub.

In this way she found that The Magpie backed onto a concrete apron, packed with tiny shiny Japanese cars. This was what the square had become.

At six sharp she returned to the pub door. She was the first customer.

6th FEATHER

"YOU SAY you're writing a book?" The woman was blowsy and aggressive.

"That's right."

"About the Magpie Inn."

"About the Magpie Murderer."

"Well — I don't know nothing about that. And George don't. We've been here six years, mind."

"It was really the room I was interested in."

"Well, as I say, we don't let rooms."

Daisy, on her second white wine, felt a deep hot desperation. And as the drink took hold, felt too the stupidity of her plight.

For she was in over her head. She did not know what she did. To bring the Magpie Dress to the Magpie Inn had seemed logical and sensible, actually consequent. But the dress lay limp, just a crumpled up bit of black and white silk, fragile enough to tear in two. As indeed had been its owner.

But what had Margaret Shawn, who courted death and died of the wrong brand, to do with the black and white nun and the arrogant priest?

Yes, thought Daisy, *I do know.*

An appointment. A meeting not kept.

"But would you show me the room?"

"I should think not," said the woman nastily, and then softened her voice a touch. "All our old junk up there, and stuff from the pub. Spiders, God knows what."

"What is all this?" asked George, coming up.

George was also blowsy, but genial. He liked a tipple and accepted Daisy's offer of a drink, as his wife had not.

After they had talked a while George said, "We could let her see the room, Rita. No harm."

"I don't think — " said Rita.

"Come on," said George to Daisy. He gave her another wine she had not asked for and waited for her to pay. Then he took her out the back, through a brown hall and up some floral stairs that creaked.

The landing was uneven.

"This is it, I reckon."

It was very low, the room, but the beams were long gone.

It was also, as promised, full of lumber, boxes and crates, a stag's head, skeins of cobwebs, and a window filthier than on the train. Which overlooked the concrete and the cars.

"The square was out there," said George. "I remember old Mick — he had the place before us — he used to say they had hangings there. People used to pay to have the room and watch, in private. Funny things people get up to."

"I'll pay," said Daisy straight out, "to have the room tonight."

"What?"

"I know you think I'm crazy, but it would help my book."

"But — where'd you sleep?"

"That doesn't matter."

"God help us," said George. "Here, I don't think I can let you do that—"

"Fifty pounds," said Daisy. "In cash."

"Oh now look — "

"Seventy," said Daisy. "That's it."

Her mouth, despite the wine, was dry. She felt like a bad actor in a bad TV crime play.

George was a worse actor. He bumbled away to himself. Then he said, "Rita won't like it. And I'll tell you now, she won't do you breakfast."

"I don't want bloody breakfast," Daisy shouted, astonishing herself, "or a bloody bed. I want to sit in this horrible room for the night and I'm offering you seventy pounds to do it. *Yes?*"

"Just hold on —"

"Yes or no."

George hung his head. "It's your funeral."

"In fact not."

When he had taken the money and gone out, Daisy leaned on the wall the way Liza Meadows was supposed to have done after her brush with the murderer. Daisy too felt faint and weak. Then she drank off all the third white wine, and went to the bathroom she had glimpsed down the hall. Too bad if they did not want her to use it.

In the bathroom, which was puce, she found like a gift a hanger, and she took it because for seventy pounds a pee and some soap and water and a hanger seemed reasonable.

The dark was coming. It was nearly nine.

Down below noises came from the pub.

Daisy took out the Magpie Dress and smoothed it. She put it on to the hanger, and then hung the hanger on the window-frame. The dress faced out to the concrete apron, and the arrival of evening.

"Here we are," said Daisy. She sat down against one of the crates and began to cry.

After a few minutes, the pain left her.

She thought, *In pieces, but not broken.*

At ten she went down and bought a bottle off George, who stared at her guiltily, and some sandwiches from the bar which Rita did not want her to have, but what could she do, Daisy was the ultimate paying customer.

Then Daisy went back up to the room with the junk in it and the view of the cars.

She did not know what was the anniversary of the possible mooted hanging of the Magpie Hunter. But even if she had, would it have been useful? The Earth shifted constantly, and time zones subtly altered. Greenwich Mean

Time, daylight saving, leap years — all these would make havoc of exactitude. And if it would happen it would happen.

"Cheers," said Daisy to the Magpie Dress, and drank from the uncorked bottle.

7th and LAST FEATHER

SEVEN'S *for Heav'n and eight's for Hell,*
And nine's for the Deil, his ain sel.

THE NOISES in the pub went on until midnight, because Rita or George obviously had friends in, drinking after hours. Then Rita and George came to bed, and there were tooth-brushings and lavatory flushings, and a final door slammed. Daisy heard Rita say, "— Might be anyone." But no one came to the closed door of the junk room. No one came to disturb Daisy and the Magpie Dress. Daisy had drunk most of the bottle and long ago eaten the sandwiches, which had been, oddly, very nice.

The dress hung in the window, faintly glared on by the street lights of Asham as by the lamps of the capital. It looked thin and flightless.

Daisy thought, *I wish Agatha and Tony were here.*

Then she fell asleep. She was not surprised by what she found there.

ALTHOUGH the chamber of confession was not as Daisy would have guessed it to be. No, it was just a small room, lacking windows, with a crucifix on the wall, and a candle burning.

He stood there, the handsome priest. And he was beautiful. Yes, you would have to be insane not to want to possess him, or else, not a lover of men.

And she was, the girl. She had loved men before. She was stirred by their bodies. The gorgeous hardness, of muscle, of penis. Their hair and eyes that were like angels'.

And this one, this one —

The young nun spoke as she knelt there. And Daisy, hearing the words, knew them now not like sub-titles, but as if a parallel translation occurred within her inner ear.

"*Mea culpa.* I have sinned."

And he said nothing, only waited.

"I have sinned," said Beauty, her white face bowed, "because all I can think of is you. Not the Christ. You."

And then she stood up, and she looked at him. Her black eyes burned, but his eyes were blue and sere, cold as glaciers. He said nothing.

"Let me," she said, "let me touch you." And she crept to him and put her hand on his chest. "You have a heart," she said, "I feel it beating. Let me — oh, let me— " and she put her other hand on his face and tried to draw him down. But the handsome face of the blond priest would not allow it. Like a mask, it floated over her. He said, "You will damn yourself. You are giving yourself to the Devil."

"No," she said. "Only to you."

And then she slid her other hand from his heart and put it over his groin.

He moved then, away from her.

He had the face of a king confronted by the most abject and filthy suppliant.

"No," he said. "Hell has got into you. Kneel down."

"I die," she said, "I *burn* — "

"You will burn in Hell. On your knees."

And she lay on her face then, and she wept. She said, "I love you."

Then he lifted her and struck her across the cheek so

that she fell once more. She lay on the ground again, weeping, and she pulled up her habit and her shift, black and white, and showed him the mound of her sex, which was covered with pure blonde hair, as on his own head.

"You are *here*," she said.

"And you are a demon," he said.

She sat up slowly. She was much paler than white. She whimpered. "Others," she said, "led me astray."

Then she confessed to him. How her brother had seduced her. How she had lain with grooms and soldiers. She said the Devil had come to her. She said she wanted to die. And all the while she wept, and her body, although covered up now, glowed like the flame on the shivering candle.

He listened like an icon. And when she was done he told her he must seek guidance. And then she was afraid, afraid in the midst of lust and love and agony. And she begged him not to betray her, he must not, the seal of the confessional protected her. Only he could save her from the dark.

No, he said. She was beyond him now.

Daisy went with her down a winding stair and up to a cell, in the shadow. Alone, the beautiful nun wrote a letter to her brother. Her tears fell on it like blazing acid not yet invented. The letter told how she had been forced to betray their fraternal secret. *Kill him*, the letter said.

And then Daisy saw the old rough track, Fetherwies, by night, no moon, the hard cold points of stars, and the priest walking there in the dark from which the beautiful nun had asked him to save her.

Near the statue of the Virgin, blanched and dry as a bone, the assassins came to him. There were seven of them but an unseen eighth — her brother — and an unseen ninth — herself.

"Do not forgive me, Father, for I have not yet sinned — "

They stabbed and slashed with their blades, and he was cut in pieces, and broken.

His blood made a river under the trees.

When the dawn began to come, an angel did fall from Heaven.

It was the magpie.

It stooped above the carrion of the pale priest, it alighted on his breast. But then it only stared at him, stared and did not plunder. And eventually it lifted up into the gilding sky and flew away.

K ARMA. They had lived then, died then, and were reborn . . . She owed him her death, for his, since she had caused his death. And she had loved him. Had he gone looking for her, too, through the alleys and streets of Faithways in 1912? With a knife. Eight times he killed. And then he missed her, though she had gone to meet him. She had caught her death, had died — but wrongly, without his kiss. Margaret Shawn, the frigid nun, and her priest of the knife. *Lovers. Magpies.*

Daisy looked at the window of the junk room. Beyond the dress, there was no light. It was wholly dark, and dim, as if a fog had come and there had also been a power-cut. The room was abysmal.

She got up slowly. And walked to the window.

Outside was — nothing. Nothing at all.

Daisy was giddy. She backed away and sat down on a crate.

She put her hands together, held her own hand.

And then she heard them in the square that was no

longer there. The crowd shouting as it pulled him along to the gallows. He had died twice. She heard the lurch and grind of wood. Then silence.

The silence was so thick.

I can't bear it.

But she must.

And then she felt the stirring through the air. Up out of time and night. A touch came on the window like the brush of a wing. And the dress quivered.

A slit shot through the window — and through the dress. Once — twice — again, again. Daisy felt the power of the air and of the dark. She fell sidelong on the floor, still holding her hand.

The knife — invisible — sliced through the dress over and over, over and over again. And in the air, soundless, the high orgasmic scream. Penetration, perfection, payment.

Then it was gone.

It was gone.

Daisy looked.

The glass was cut in shards, none of which had fallen out, like a pattern of strange frost.

And the dress was all in ribbons. Black and white. White and black.

"At last," Daisy said. She put her head into her comforting arms. Peace and quiet. And as the street lamp light of twentieth-century cities came back into the window behind the shreds of the slashed and murdered dress, she said again, softly, "At last."

LaVergne, TN USA
19 December 2009
167539LV00005B/15/P